AS FAR AS YOU CAN GO BEFORE YOU HAVE TO COME BACK

A NOVEL

ALLE C. HALL

Black Rose Writing | Texas

ISBN: 978-1-68513-147-0
PUBLISHED BY BLACK ROSE WRITING
www.blackrosewriting.com

Printed in the United States of America
Suggested Retail Price (SRP) $21.95

As Far As You Can Go Before You Have to Come Back is printed in font Georgia.

*As a planet-friendly publisher, Black Rose Writing does its best to eliminate unnecessary waste to reduce paper usage and energy costs, while never compromising the reading experience. As a result, the final word count vs. page count may not meet common expectations.

The following chapters originally appeared as short pieces in the following journals. Many thanks to their editors, who were willing to publish difficult material and whose input I greatly value.

The chapter, "Onions in the Tea Garden" originally appeared online as a short story in *Another Chicago Magazine* (February, 2022).
The chapter, "Land, Vault, Land" is an adaptation of the short story, "American Mary," which originally appeared online in *New World Writing Quarterly* (March, 2022).
The chapter, "Crashing" originally appeared as flash nonfiction by the same title in two issues of *The Lascaux Review*: No. 8 (December 2021) and earlier, online (November 25, 2020).
The chapter, "Good Girls Don't Get Stoned" appeared online as a short story in *This Great Society* (June 2011). It was reprinted online in *Fresh Ink* (October, 2021).
The chapter, "The Great Ultimate" originally appeared online as a short story in *The Evergreen Review* (Winter 2019).
Parts of the chapters, "I Was Watching Myself from Beside Myself" and "I Wanted Ten" originally appeared in online the short story, "I Wanted Ten" in *Blue Lake Review* (October 2018).
The chapter, "Let Me Feel for You" originally appeared online as a short story in *Tupelo Quarterly* (June 14, 2018).

Praise for
AS FAR AS YOU CAN GO
BEFORE YOU HAVE TO COME BACK

"As I read Hall's remarkable novel, I kept hearing the book's title as a question: how far can you go before you have to come back? *Before* can be anything. Before trauma. Before love. Before letting go."

—Sue William Silverman, author of
***How to Survive Death and Other Inconveniences*, winner**
of The 2021 Clara Johnson Award for Women's Literature

"Captures perfectly the scene created by troubled western young people wandering Asia in the pre-internet era. Her protagonist Carlie is a canny survivor, a vulnerable soul, and a fascinating character to watch as she stumbles towards healing. In urgent prose, this compelling story takes its place alongside backpacker classics such as *The Beach, Losing Gemma*, and *My Life in Men*."

—Zoe Zolbrod, author of *Currency*

"An inspirational journey of an emotionally-wounded nomad who comes of age to become a memorable heroine."

—Dan Lawton, author of *The Green House*

"Alle C. Hall has created part fever dream and part epic journey of survival, recovery and awakening: a world with characters who search for the truth about themselves and the people who have hurt them."

—Ronit Plank, *When She Comes Back*

To Donna Bevan Lee: Not only did you save my life, you showed me how to live it. Thank you.

To all Leasons, Ullmanns, and Meyers: your care, your acceptance, and your love have meant the world to me. Thank you, family.

To my beloved, Cliff: so much to rejoice! None of it could have come to fruition without you. You remain the best thing that ever happened to me.

And to my sons: you are the best thing that ever happened to us. Each of you is my whole heart.

AS FAR
AS YOU
CAN GO
BEFORE YOU
HAVE TO
COME BACK

4/16/23

to Mary Ellen Kearc~
Congrats on your
retirement!

Alla Hall

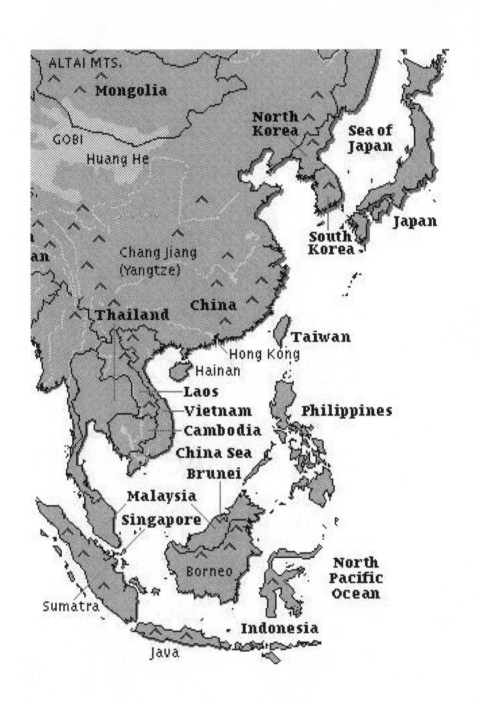

I Was Watching Myself from Beside Myself

I was watching myself from beside myself. I saw myself crouched in the dim light of our hall stairs. I was eavesdropping on my father and Lyle, one of my father's best friends. My father and Lyle whispered about my older sister, Patrice. I heard Lyle say, "Patrice has gotten mighty curvy all of a sudden," and it wasn't a compliment. My fingers dug as far as they could go into the blue parts of the Persian-style runner that carpeted our hall stairs.

My father agreed about Patrice in a voice as plush as the runner. He used the carpet voice only with Lyle and their other buddy, Ted. When I heard that voice, I left for the ceiling. Didn't press against it; I was as empty as light, looking down at myself on the stairs. Same Catholic uniform as all the girls wore, but I knew what was coming. For three years, my father and his friends had left me home to take care of Little Matt while they took Patrice to Lyle's cabin in the mountains. The next time they went, they left Patrice at home to take care of Little.

I Wanted Ten

My family was in Rome. For the past six months, wherever I was—Saint Christopher's Academy, city bus to Saint Chris's or home—I was also in that dim light on those hall stairs. Right now, I was in Rome, leaning against the railing of what Mom's Fodor's called "a classic pedestrian bridge," Ponte Sant'Angelo: a series of arches over a river, expansive greenery on one side, white tents down by the water on the other. The river was the Tiber, I knew from that morning's peek into Fodor's, bullet points on hotel paper tucked into the pages, Mom's Hallmark script. That first time they took me, Lyle's cabin emerged brown and boring from beside the dirt road in the forest, far from the tree-lined highway and the boarded-up windows of the failed logging town. It was evening. I watched from beside myself while Lyle, Ted, and my father played pool and drank St. Pauli Girl. My father and Lyle bellowed, "You never forget your first girl," and each time they sang it out, Ted observed them as if he were a lizard watching the stupidest people he'd ever seen. On the bridge I touched the railing—hot; in the forest, the room smelled more like sweat than it did like beer. Each time he set up, my father said, "Rack 'em!" and each time he was more gregarious than the last. Ted removed his wedding ring. He said, "Looks like we are out of beer," and my father, with the forward-thrusting gesture of a long-ago king leading troops into battle—from the bridge, I could see Castle Sant'Angelo—my father put his pool cue into the holder on the wall.

I was on the Ponte Sant'Angelo Bridge, built in 134 A.D. by Emperor Publius Aelius Hadrianus—I was at the cabin and absorbed into the water below the bridge, an ethereal green in the Italian afternoon maybe twenty-five feet down, not far enough to do anything but hurt. I could always aim for the rocks.

Ponte Sant'Angelo had lots of statues of angels built onto the railings. There were street vendors, goods laid out on blankets, sightseeing throngs and artists doing that Italian thing where they painted the scenery or sketched tourists. Where was Mom in her pretty, cherry-patterned dress? Where was Little Matt? And Patrice? Each time Patrice came home from a cabin weekend—I never asked, she never told—but each time Patrice came home, she looked swollen. How did I come to be alone on Ponte Sant'Angelo? Then I remembered.

I'd stopped.

The four of us were crossing the bridge over the Tiber, and the person that was me stopped. My mother's dress became a balloon when you let go of the string, and I was thirteen and alone. For the past six months, I waited for it and then waited for it to be over. Even stopped going to ballet. Couldn't imagine wearing a leotard and tights. The Sisters at Saint Chris's expressed concern. Since kindergarten I'd been quiet but inquisitive. Now, they said, I simply sat. There were conferences. My mother talked the whole time, and my father sat there and looked concerned. I sat there.

At the bridge's side, the sun beat down and the wind—the top railing was thick stone, flat-topped, would be easy to stand on. However, it was higher than my head. The sun beat down. The wind brushed my face. The metal rods connecting the top to the bottom railings didn't leave enough space to slip through, making impossible what happened every few weeks at the cabin, my legs were dancer-agile. They worked hard when I wanted them to. I could use those legs to climb to the flat top and sail. It would hurt, but after, nothing. No more numbness. Numbness offered survival. The price was my life. I could give life up, oh yes.

But I didn't want to.

I wanted to be here for Italian summers.

I wanted to take the summer sun inside me and grow tomatoes with it.

I was not going to die.

I was going to get out.

The pat on my shoulder came with too much caring in it to startle me. One of the artists was holding out a piece of paper with a friendly lift to his mouth, his brows. He couldn't hide the concern in the eyes beneath them.

I took his sketch. A girl, hand on the flat-topped railing of Ponte Sant'Angelo Bridge, castle visible. He'd really captured the desolate curve to her spine.

I must have stood with the picture for a long time because the artist was gone, replaced by Mom, who was screaming. Before she clutched me, it registered that she'd smeared her lipstick. Her cherry red lipstick. Her smudge of lips moved weirdly fast, issuing disjointed noises, like a movie rewinding. "Why?" she asked over and over. Like I was keeping the answer from her. For six months.

Mom took my hand. Our usual procession had Mom barely bothering to call over a shoulder for me to keep up. She would hold Little by one hand and Patrice by the other. Little was only eight, her baby, and with Patrice so curvy at fifteen, the Italian men were always whistling. With my hand in my mother's, maybe I was the beautiful one.

Patrice pinched my upper arm with the confidence that comes from Wonder Woman hair and eyes that, even with too much make-up, looked like she woke up that hot. She said, "You just wanted attention."

Kind of not, really. It had never occurred to me that I could not be there the way the good girl always was.

Back home in Seattle. Stealth personified, I scoured newspapers for stories of runaways. Generally, the kid made it as far as Portland, occasionally to San Francisco, but her parents had the police on their side; they had the newspapers and the TV blasting her picture all over the place. Nobody ever asked why she ran away. Those idiots gave her right back to the parents she ran away from. Unless she was dead.

I switched to books about runaways. In my favorite, a brother and sister hid in the Metropolitan Museum in New York City. Little and me, it wouldn't work. Little was too soft. That book, those kids had no reason to run away. The girl said so right in the beginning. She just wanted to mix it up. So lucky and she didn't even know it.

In another book I loved, someone poisoned the rich grandpa. No big surprise: the murderer turned out to be his will's primary beneficiary. (I went to the dictionary for "primary beneficiary.") The primary beneficiary was a kid. When it all came out in the last chapter, everyone wondered why a girl would murder her grandfather. I had my theories. Plus, she wanted the money.

Who were my parents' primary beneficiaries?

There were assets. I looked up that word, too, assets. My father was in real estate. He swung big deals that tapped their available capital, which included a lot of Mom's inheritance or salary, which they always fought about before she always let him have it. After each fight, he poured her a glass of rosé and brought out the pictures of our most recent vacation. Italy. Greece. Spain. By the time my mother finished her second glass, her face was tucked into his neck, seemingly forgetting that she spent half of each trip tearing her hair out because "those people" didn't speak English well enough.

They would never find me in a foreign country.

I had no money.

I didn't know anybody.

I only spoke English.

I could do it.

I had to.

It was the end of summer. I was back at ballet three times a week, working to get my arabesque to where it used to be. I welcomed the pain, was gratified to feel the sweat of a deceptively delicate girl. When school started, my friends didn't seem to be my friends anymore. I didn't make new ones. Girls always asked, "What's your dad do?" I knew they meant his job, but still.

Little entered fourth grade, and we all went to his school carnival. I threw a ring and won a goldfish. Less than two inches long, she—I decided it was she—looked dead in her plastic Baggie when we stopped at the pet store for a fishbowl. When we got her into her new glass home, she revived slowly. First her tail, then her head, then what remained in the middle. So spunky.

After three months, Spunky died. The guy at the pet store assured me that I didn't kill her. Carnival goldfish never last, he said. I got another, named her Spunky II, and brought her home with tips for keeping her alive longer. When that Spunky died, I brought in Spunky III. Pretty soon, my father brought new fish home on an as-needed basis. They were all "Spunky." Every morning and every night, I dropped a pinch of orange-brown flakes, smelled like spoiled shrimp, into Spunky's round residence on our kitchen counter and watched her kiss the food bits into her mouth. Goldfish don't swim the way sharks do, with that slow ripple through their body. A goldfish's tail is the only part that moves. Flippy flip-flip. A sunset's glowing colors, Spunky looked so safe in there. She peered, unnoticed, as grownups double-checked plane tickets. Maybe Spunky told me that traveler's checks left traceable numbers, so don't use them. Spunky saw how parents operated one way for daytime and another for night. Spunky understood that nighttime didn't exist. What also didn't exist, a movie happening to someone else, was when they took me to Lyle's cabin. About twice a month, or whenever my mother was out of town for work. And every other night, my father came into my room.

When you sensed danger, you left for the ceiling. That's when you found yourself looking down on yourself, thinking, *Look what's happening to me.* When it wasn't so scary, you moved only to the side. The first time it happened in my room, I was reading in bed when there was a noise from the hall then the sound of him paused in my doorway.

"Still up, Jen?"

When it wasn't so scary, you moved only to the side. When you sensed danger, you left for the ceiling. That's when you found yourself looking down on yourself, *Look at what is happening to me.* His naked rump pumping. *Look what's happening.* When you thought you were going to die, you were gone.

"I love you," he gasped, faster, faster. Then his dick was in my mouth and then more sour than anything. I was gone.

After, his face pressed into my neck. "I love you so much, Jenny-Jen-Jen. That's why I do it."

He sounded only as old as Little. I spent the night vomiting. Several times, my mother paced by the bathroom door. I could tell it was her from the mouse-like tread saying, "If I save you, there goes my life." There was no way out.

Ballet wasn't out-out, but it was afternoons of classes and weekend rehearsals for *The Nutcracker*, sweat growing cold on our bodies in the cavernous space of the stage as we moved from light cue to light cue. I lived that emptiness, the girl who always remembered the combination but never got the solo. I used to care. Right now, my concern was bumps, all of a sudden taken up residence on my chest.

Girls my age, thirteen, whispered about periods. Shouldn't I get mine?

Ballet girls weren't curvy. If I got curvy, the cabin, my father, it would stop. But—ballet. Ballet and Spunky and Little, that was what I had. That was all I had. I would not allow curvy.

Mom was thin. She put her fork down after every bite, chewed, took at least one sip of wine. I tried the same with water. The bumps stayed small. Was it a victory? There remained the cabin, my father in my room at night.

January. The casserole hit the table, *thunk*. Patrice was on a first date with some guy she'd met at an Iron Maiden concert. Skeeter. He'd honked and she went running. "Don't wait up." I wanted to be sixteen and run.

At the table, Mom poured herself a drink. The hard stuff. Usually, it was rosé, two glasses before dinner, two after. She became someone to stay away from. After *thunk*, she poured the hard stuff, then poured one for my father, then ignored her food the way my father did his drink.

She said, "Ted is dead."

I thought I might laugh, until Mom's silent draining of her shot glass made clear that she was serious. Ted had been driving home from skiing. There was a terrible snowstorm, and an eighteen-wheeler ran them off the road, them being Ted and not his wife. The next morning, I got my first period. For weeks, over steaming casseroles—for us, as Mom un-quit smoking rather than eat much—my mother kept us up to date. Ted's brother produced a letter dated after Ted's will naming him, the brother, the beneficiary. Ted's wife contested it. Mom wouldn't say how much of the estate's value ran down the lawyer drain. She did say she would never let the same happen to us.

It turned April. At the same dining room table, my father and mother sat me down. "Matt's too young to discuss this."

My mother didn't mention Patrice. No one had, not for two weeks. The day before my thirteenth birthday, Patrice found out she was pregnant and ran off with Skeeter. No one called the police or the newspapers. Mom kept Patrice's room in faultless order. Without being told, Little and I knew to remain similarly circumspect—around our parents. Nights in a row, Little came into my room, into my bed. He cried for both of us.

On the April afternoon my parents sat me down, Mom announced that, if Ted had co-signed his now-broke widow's name to his bank accounts, she would have their money. My parents were going to give me that kind of access.

To money.

"To specific accounts." My mother grazed my father with a look. "And we won't have another word about it."

We signed forms, lots of forms. The size of the numbers was a gut punch. I said, "No bank's gonna let a kid take out that kind of money."

Mom said, "*Going to,* not *gonna.* It will never happen, Jen. This is a precaution against an emergency."

And I became able to withdraw any amount of money from four different accounts. Legally.

If you booked a plane flight and had no credit card, you had to pay with cash within twenty-four hours. Got that covered. Ish.

And go—where? To fly overseas, you had to show a passport.

Had one. Said Jennifer Brewer in bold, bold type. My parents sent out an APB, anyone could find—I was not going to get out.

I was gonna get out. As far back as only January, I'd had nothing. It was May. I was fourteen and had access to as much money as I was brave enough to take. A whole afternoon of yelling between Mom and my father over a bounced check— "Seven thousand dollars?"—told me that ducking out with a large chunk of cash would never come off.

My father kept a wad of bills in his pockets. Several hundred, sometimes a thousand dollars at a time. I bet he loved to feel the money, even though Mom called it ticky-tacky that he ran drink tabs for clients then pulled out the wad to cover them. The wad left his pocket only at night when he put it on his bedside table. It was remarkably easy to swipe a twenty every so often—he could blow that on lunch—and hard not to do it too often. He might notice if I did it too often so I kept it to forty or sixty dollars a month. I sequestered my stash in the ol' standby, a hollowed-out book. I approached sixteen proudly, $540 tucked throughout my bookshelf.

It was June. My father told me that, over the summer, I would work at his office, where the walls were butter yellow and the carpeting forest green. The furniture was heavy. His theory was that good furniture and at least one filing cabinet for each year he'd been in business were important impressions to create for people who wanted to trust you.

I spent my time in the back room, filing. Granted access to the murky world of his finances, I paid particular attention to the four bank accounts with my name on them. As a real estate investor and developer, my father could bounce thousands between accounts for a day or a week, most of it the monthly payments from his rental units. That money didn't get the to-the-penny accounting he had to give properties in escrow. I practiced my father's signature. I worked my way up to sorting the afternoon mail and running errands—first coffee and sandwiches, then FedEx drops, and finally, bank deposits. My goal was to handle cash transfers.

Nutcracker again. Thunk, Mom told us Dead-Ted's estate was settled. By some act of God, Lyle moved to Maine. He sold the cabin, so it all went on at home now. I was surprised to find myself sad about Patrice being gone. More, she could be caring for Little when my father was in my room. One evening, not long after I turned sixteen, I went into the kitchen to feed Spunky. My mother was making dinner. She was halfway through a glass of rosé. I hoped her first. The phone rang. Picking it up, I heard highway sounds. I heard quick, shallow breaths.

I said, "Patrice?"

Mom swirled, knocking her wine to the floor. She snatched the receiver and started shrieking. Little ran up from the TV den. I dragged him to my room and threw together some pillows. We held each other and rocked as Mom's voice found its way through the closed door and around the fingers we'd stuffed into our ears.

"It's been two years, and you expect money?"

The screeching ended. Dinner-making sounds began again. My father came home. We were called to eat. Spattered rosé and broken glass had vanished. Mom had a fresh one; probably counted it as her first. No mention of my sister—where she was, what made her desperate enough to call. I'm not ending up on some highway. How much money did she need? I had $780.

And the ability to forge my father's signature.

After ferreting out his Social Security number, I used his signature to assist in the setting up of a business account in both our names at a bank he knew nothing about. The interest was pitiful, but the minimum opening deposit was only a hundred bucks. I wrote a twenty-five dollar check on one of his accounts, a sum my father might easily think, if he bothered to think, that he forgot to record. The twenty-five dollars showed up at my secret bank. No bombs detonated.

I was at work, sorting mail, when I spotted the logo of my secret bank right there on an envelope. The monthly statement.

I should have been ready for this. I slipped the envelope under my blazer and took a break. Running to the pay phone down the street, my feet pounded out, "Wednesday, thank God," pounded out with the emphasis on the first syllable, "Tuesday, Thursday, Friday, ballet." No notion what I would have said, confronted with a statement in both our names; no idea what I was going to say to the bank. When the bank lady answered, I asked if I could arrange to pick up my statement.

The lady said, "We are not allowed to hold them."

It could not happen like this.

"However, we could send the statement to a P.O. box."

In my most grown-up voice, which is on the deep side, for a kid, I said, "We were considering that," and a month later, tried it again. This time, one hundred dollars. I blew it, writing that first check. My father would never write himself a check for only twenty-five bucks.

The hundred bucks cleared. I wrote one check each month for that amount, making sure to bounce between accounts. Every three months, I drained my secret account of all but the hundred-dollar minimum and kept snitching those twenties. My fingers were in his wallet one morning as he showered. Mom was supposed to have left for work. Behind me, I heard, "What are you doing?"

I snapped around. How did she—

Mom's eyes darted to their bed. I felt an untrammeled joy I did not want or understand. With two quick steps, she crossed the room and smacked my face. The shrieking began. From the bathroom, my father called out. I ran. All day at Saint Chris's, my knees bounced and my head went, I am so stupid I am so stupid I should have grabbed the money I could just take off I am sixteen I am so stupid.

After school, I did what good girls do: went to work.

The office appeared to be its buttered-walled self. The secretary handed me the mail. I sorted it, chanting my excuse to myself. I'm a drug addict. I stole to support my habit. That happened to Tisha, a really rich girl at Saint Chris's. They stuck her in rehab. I could handle rehab. Just don't find my money.

My father called me into his office. He passed a file folder across his desk and asked me to arrange a cash transfer. "You'll receive a raise for the increased responsibility."

How easy it was to imagine him stroking Mom's arms, lying in a voice like a warm wind at the beach. I returned to my desk and arranged my first cash transfer. My first legal cash transfer. At home, I packed an old duffel bag with clothes and some money and then stored the duffel in the garage, a precaution against an emergency. I still didn't know where I was going.

It was the Christmas before I turned seventeen. A new girl at ballet, Cecile, invited me to a party her parents were throwing. I'd never been to a party. Cecile's older brother, Jeff, was visiting from Japan, where he taught English. He looked like he should smell like sunscreen. Catching me staring, Jeff came to me through the crowd of adults. He smelled like soap. He told me that he respected the discipline my slimness represented, did I want to sneak out?

No one had ever asked.

We tiptoed into our coats and to the back patio, just the two of us, where Jeff talked about Jeff and the strong yen. My concept of Japan was limited to smooth, green hills and kimono ladies. Jeff bragged about saving ten grand in only ten months and then bumming around Southeast Asia. He stepped toward me with stories of jungle adventures and sunny beaches.

I was still pasted to Jeff's ten grand. In ten months. "Could I teach English?"

"As long as you have a college degree."

Jeff was in my face. As if he were the pinball and I the bumper, I asked, "What if I don't?"

"Marry someone with a visa."

A dot gathered in the centers of Jeff's eyes, drilled mine as he told me about the Lonely Planet guidebooks, "travel survival kits" that detailed cheap travel. When Mom took me to the after-Christmas sales, I ditched her for a bookstore. A map showed Japan as, like, half way around the world. Go much farther and you're coming back. I'd stay in Japan.

That night, I read *South-East Asia on a Shoestring*. Despite its cheery, yellow-and-green cover, the view it offered was less entrancing than Jeff's. There were horrible diseases and thieves. The "Getting There" section swamped me. I would never get out. I heard, "Still up, Jen?"

I slid the book under my pillow. He was used to this. So was I. He settled heavily onto the bed. "How 'bout a good-night kiss?"

Far away, there was the tiniest speck of light, barely a dot against a black background. Behind the background, I saw velvet glued to cardboard, which was the stand holding the background up. Everything was so fake. I was about to leave for real when I went to that speck of light. It said: Stay. It's in your blood, too. You have to get out.

In the morning, I covered my Lonely Planet with brown paper and determination and read it at school every day during lunch. Southeast Asia was unbelievably cheap. In Indonesia, you could get by on less than five dollars a day. I mocked up a budget: a thousand bucks for a flight, a couple thousand to live on until I turned eighteen, and a couple more to set me up in Japan until I found a job teaching English. Five grand.

My current stash weighed in at just under three.

At this rate, it would be two more years before I could get out.

I put my elbows on the table, lips buried into clenched fists. All around me, kids got to throw food, flirt, or prep for that afternoon's algebra test. Meanwhile, I could still taste him.

I was going to steal a big chunk of money.

If five grand would work, eight to ten would be more comfortable.

I wanted ten. That bastard owed me at least that much.

March. I turned seventeen. First thing that morning, Little Matt gave me an adorable treasure chest for Spunky's bowl. Standing at the kitchen counter, we edged it into the water and then fed the Spunkster, laughing as she gobbled the stinky shrimp flakes. Mom squealed like a ballet girl who got Clara in *Nutcracker*. She wanted in on the action. My father said, "Let them have their fun." Mom stuck her hand in anyway, spilling the smelly stuff all over. The kitchen went silent. Little slunk to the TV den, leaving the mess on the counter and the cabinet door hanging open.

After a moment, my mother announced that she had to work late that night. My father avoided my eyes.

It was a movie happening to someone else.

I cleaned up the fish food. I'd run during a vacation, or school would call when I turned up absent. By summer, I should have $3,540, plus another grand from wages and birthday presents in the college savings account that everyone knew about.

Five thousand, four hundred and sixty dollars short.

Five thousand, four hundred and sixty dollars.

Okay, so that was a lot of money. So what? I regularly transferred thousands for him. Also, I needed a new name.

The summer before senior year, my mother scheduled us for whitewater river rafting in Idaho, an eleven-day trip with a long day's drive on either end that conflicted marvelously with my rehearsals for *Cinderella*. I faked unwillingness to give up my parts—rodent, broom, partygoer—and arranged to stay with that ballet girl, Cecile. She appeared to have as few friends as I did. The difference was she wanted them.

Thirteen days. Including a stopover in Seoul, the flight to Hong Kong ran fifteen hours. I would slate two days for Hong Kong, to arrange a safe-deposit box for the money and to buy a ticket to Manila, Bangkok, Jakarta, whichever was cheapest, where one misleadingly insubstantial girl was easily lost. Not long after they hit the rapids, I'd be deep in the Southeast Asian jungles. Fuck me then, pal.

It was the day before they left. A call in a professional girl voice confirmed availability on the next day's flight to San Francisco. You had to show ID for international flights but not domestic. I hung up, called back, and in my regular voice, used the name Leah Rowan to reserve a one-way ticket, to be paid at the airport. Later, if a detective checked passenger lists from the Seattle-Tacoma airport, they wouldn't find one Jennifer Brewer. Three hours after landing in San Francisco, Jennifer Brewer would fly to Hong Kong on a different airline.

Any random person might recognize a photo of me.

Dark glasses. A hat.

From wherever I flew after Hong Kong—Indonesia was five dollars a day—I would go overland by train or bus. Even if they tracked me down, they couldn't prosecute. I was not an adult.

It was the longest day of my life, and it continued. Ballet thought I was at work; work thought the same about ballet; I borrowed Mom's car. The number I had in mind was $450. I was testing how much a kid could ask for without bringing in the FBI. Dressed in a newly pressed Evan-Picone jacket and culottes, I made the withdrawals in person from two of my father's accounts, transferring identical sums from two others into my secret account. Twenty minutes later, I withdrew every penny and bought a sturdy backpack.

New total: $6,337.

I stared at the pile of cash in my hands.

I could run right now.

No.

I wanted to hurt him.

Them.

It was the night before. I called Cecile from a pay phone. "Mom wore me down. I'm going on this dumb trip."

"No way! Madame will totally recast your parts!"

"Then you'll probably get broom. Make sure to tell Madame I'll be gone for two weeks." That should take care of any calls from the studio tomorrow morning, *Why aren't you at rehearsal?*

Cecile made one last attempt to keep me from ballet disgrace. "Madame will keep this in mind. She won't give you anything good in *Nutcracker*."

I was on the verge of never seeing anybody, not Little, not Spunky, ever again, and Cecile was worried about dancing some lollipop in *Nutcracker*. I suppose I hung up because I was pacing the meager footage of the phone booth. What if the banks won't give me the money? That's why four different banks. What if I got caught? I slammed my palm flat against the glass wall. I was getting out. That night, I endured him by putting my mind on an airplane. It was the last time. I was already out. I just had to get there. In the morning, I hovered near the phone as they loaded the car, though it was way too early for a call, checking on me.

My family drove off just after seven. Zooming as well, only to my room, I stuffed my new backpack with a list from The Lonely Planet: underwear, swimsuit, jeans, shorts, three t-shirts, a sweatshirt for cold nights, sneakers, plus a lightweight jacket. In addition: toothbrush, toothpaste, soap, razor. On the plane, I'd wear sandals and a nice dress. The Lonely Planet said to wear nice clothes, so you looked good for Customs. I carried my pack through the garage to the car so that no neighbors would see me. Finally, I drove to the first bank.

"*Merde,*" I chanted in French, the way ballet girls have for centuries, for good luck. Merde meant, "shit."

It was nine a.m. sharp. The bank was cool and relatively busy. Having watched it for three years, I knew that they usually had a small rush right when they opened. That's what I wanted. In the movies, when the bad guy was about to be bad, he acted like he knew it all and had no time to waste. I tried this routine with a teller whose rounded face reminded me so much of Little's that I had to dig my fingers into the counter as if it were the blue carpet runner on our hall stairs.

"Hundreds will be fine."

"Miss, you should really take this as a cashier's check."

"Sorry, no, can't wait."

Nine-twenty a.m. From a pay phone, I transferred one grand each from the second and third banks into my secret account and was on my way downtown to bank number four, a bigger bank, one I figured wouldn't raise a pulse over fifteen hundred dollars.

Before heading to my secret bank, I stopped at the Westin Hotel on Fifth Avenue. My backpack needed to be downtown, so no neighbors would see it. I would grab it right before catching the airport shuttle.

At the Westin, I asked the concierge, "Can I leave my backpack while I see Pike Place Market? I checked out, but my flight doesn't leave until afternoon."

"Certainly. Room number?"

I'd watched how many checkouts, and hadn't thought of this?

Rage slammed through me like a bull I'd seen in the Basque country years ago. This little merde-head with his merde-y scrap of a mustache was not coming between me and getting out.

I said, "No. It's not like that. You're wrong."

Taking advantage of his confusion, I grabbed my backpack and stalked out. Courage deserted me on the corner of Fifth and Stewart. I needed water. A Burger King.

Entering the French-fried air, I saw the dining area opened into a bus station. Well, then. I rented a big locker for the backpack. It was 10:45 a.m. Later than I wanted. Time for the final secret bank.

The morning rush was over. The lunch one hadn't begun. After looking at my withdrawal slip, the slope-shouldered coward of a teller asked me to her supervisor's office. I tried to be casual though I was certain they were leading me into a room full of FBI agents. The supervisor-lady examined my request. Her nametag said Shelly. She wore a brooch. It was in the shape of a long-legged bird fighting a snake, which was almost weird enough to distract me.

Shelly brought me back by saying, "This is unusual." Almost imperceptibly, she glanced at the signature on my withdrawal slip. "Jennifer."

My excuse had been ready for months. Pronoun specifically chosen. "We do this all the time. Shelly."

"We are not accustomed to giving this amount in cash to someone your age."

"Look at the ledger. I transfer larger sums on a regular basis.

For my father. He went whitewater rafting. Left this morning. This came up last night, okay? He told me to handle it."

The more I talked, the more suspicious she looked. "We do this all the time," I repeated, and finally, just shut up.

"Your account showed similar activity yesterday—"

"That's what I mean."

"—but for a much smaller amount."

Another pause, me-driven.

Shelly said, "Can we please have this go by wire transfer?"

"That is not what he wants."

"Can I at least have you take a cashier's check?"

"It has to be cash."

"Why?"

"Truly, I couldn't say."

I had to smile to myself at the sincere way I delivered that one. Shelly took it at face value. I got my money and got home.

Twelve-twenty p.m. Late. Wearing my favorite cobalt blue Ralph Lauren dress that I thought made me look taller, grown-up, I stopped one last time at Spunky's bowl, armed with a timed release food tablet. My fat little fish stared as if she knew.

Little would do the feedings. He had to.

Mess of fish food on the counter. Cabinet door left open.

My hands ran down the familiar coolness of Spunky's round home. I glanced at the clock. There were those who sank and those who swam. I was barely dogpaddling.

Little would feed her. I took the bus downtown, collected my backpack, pulled out dark glasses and a big white hat, and caught the airport shuttle. In the hour before takeoff, I squinched into my seat, pulling the hat again and again around my ears and then buying a flat box of red licorice to chew through so that I could concentrate on not screaming. I was the first one in my boarding group on the plane. A fog-related delay in San Francisco forced a three-hour wait at the gate. My family was halfway across Washington State and moving farther east every second. They had no reason to be suspicious for two weeks. Or maybe they just wouldn't care. Patrice left. Patrice nicknamed Matt, "Little" when he was a newborn. "Because he's little," she'd said, seven years old.

I sobbed. Two kids across the aisle stared. I rushed to the bathroom, locked myself in a stall, and flushed and flushed so that no one heard me cry. People probably wondered about bulimia. Ballet girls did that all the time.

In the austere metal stall, my reflection. I tipped back my hat to see my face. My eyes and my chin. Strong and sure. I washed up and returned to the boarding area, whispering "Merde" to calm myself like I did when we waited in the wings. No one ever noticed the girl who didn't have the solo. Within minutes, they called my flight. I held my breath until lift-off. The last thought I had before passing out was: I did it. I got out.

American Mary

TEN BUNKS LINED the gray walls of the cheapest hostel in Hong Kong. Clutching *Southeast Asia on a Shoestring* to my chest, I peered into the dorm room at Chungking Mansions. Seven bunks each held a guy or a pile of gear. Five of the guys looked like maybe they were from South Asia. Two were white. All were mostly eyeballs.

Next to me, the proprietor chewed the inside of his cheek. Hoping I didn't appear too seventeen-and-a-half, I said, "I'd prefer the girls' room."

"Toilet is share. Ha!" Chew. "You have it?"

Taking my silence for "Yes," the proprietor bowed slightly and left. Alone, I had to face all those eyes. With a liar's stride, I crossed to an empty bottom bunk and stowed my backpack. A thin white guy slid off his top bed, his skin rusted from acne scars and the sun. Right away, two things happened. The Asians rolled onto their backs and the second white man rose from his bottom bunk, a linebacker. He could have been thirty and shaving his head or fifty and bald for real. All pleasant and German-accented, he was Franz. Then the bony one, "May I ask your name, *ma belle*?" Jean from France.

I hadn't counted on meeting people. No way I was going to give up "Jen Brewer." Not even "Jen." I couldn't use the Leah Rowan name; whoever could be following me might check.

Mary! American Mary should stereotype around with Strong German Franz and ma belle French Jean.

They asked where I was from—I said only "America"—what the flight cost, how long would I be in Hong Kong. With a shoelace of a grin fastened to his oblong face, Jean said, "Do you have plans now?"

For two years, my first twenty-four hours in Hong Kong had been scheduled: change money, get a haircut, buy a ticket. Indonesia, five bucks a day.

"Take a ferry with us, Mary. We cross Victoria Harbor."

Jean's hand came so close to brushing mine that I sensed air moving. If I could have felt anything, it would have been terror at how easily Jean maneuvered me to the hall. I knew the day was muggy because a soggy heat pressed into my skin, yet I was as sweat-drying-cold as if I were in the wings, merde.

Franz was our caboose to the smoke-filled corridors, lined with man after man, Black, Brown, white, sitting, crouching, leaning against the wall. All of them eyeballs until they took in Jean, at which point, they went back to smoking or playing cards or reading their own Lonely Planet. The tight ambiance made apparent the "survival" part of "travel survival kit."

On the sidewalk, the heat brought me to the present with the whap of a wet towel. I said, "I have to change money."

French Jean said, "The Hong Kong side is better for changing money than here. Take the ferry with us."

Jean led us to the street. As we stepped into a crosswalk, a motorcycle nearly mowed us down. The next car was a champagne-colored Rolls Royce. The gloved hand of the driver waved us on. Arriving at the ferry terminal without dying, the three of us climbed to the upper deck of the Star Ferry. A breeze spoke of rain. We bobbed across the harbor like a Tater Tot in hot oil. The only other white person on board was a tall man in a suit. Everyone else was slick-looking dudes in pricey sunglasses, old ladies toting bags and parcels, and young women dressed like fashion models dressed like secretaries. They posed for pictures. French Jean wanted me to, with him. I struggled with "No"—couldn't; a girl was flipping her hair the way my sister used to.

Patrice was pregnant when she ran. Yet here I was, Star Ferry.

I said, "No," to Jean and returned to rubber-necking huge cargo vessels and tiny brown boats with outsized orange sails.

As rain clouds started to gather, we disembarked within view of the glassy, modern skyscrapers of the Hong Kong side. Jean convinced me to meet up with them at sunset, on the southwest corner of the street near Chungking Mansions. Having said, "No," I felt confident enough to say, "'K." We parted—them for something called Victoria Peak and me for the first bank with English signs in the window, relieved by the air conditioning, prepared to lie. Meticulous perjury about a dead grandma's wish that I travel before college never saw daylight. The polite lady teller had excellent English but zero need to know why a kid would need a safe-deposit box for eight thousand dollars—all but the two thousand I would spend over the next six months, five to ten dollars a day. The lady teller rented it to me with so little fuss that I was nervous only when she photocopied my passport.

After changing thirty bucks into Hong Kong currency, I returned to the sweaty street to trot downhill toward the Star Ferry terminal. Everyone in the crush of people had a purpose, buying plastic shoes, household goods, vegetables, and dead things—whole fish, the organs of a large animal, a cow? A goose minus its head was split to display its glistening innards. The long neck flopped.

The clouds cracked open. Rain came down, bounced ankle-high when it hit the hot street. The new rain against the oily pavement smelled like freedom.

Against the tangerine sunset, I could see the heat-whapping southeast corner near Chungking. French Jean and Franz waited with another traveler-lean guy. Franz ran a baseball mitt of a hand over his scalp as Jean introduced Pete, who surveyed me, his brows drawn toward his aquiline nose in evident frustration.

French Jean said, "Mary's a Yank, too."

Pete said, "I know a place. Beer's cheap."

Franz said, "I go to the station. My cousin comes in."

I said, "I'll walk you as far as Chungking." Ignoring Jean's disappointment and Pete's relief—who ate the peanut butter out of his Reese's?—I followed Franz past bright shops blasting chilly air into the hot evening.

"—blokes, they chew your ear, where did you go, what did you do. Then to the fag jokes. No one thinks I'm gay, but I die. The *schwein*, Pete, all he waited for—excuse me to say, Mary. To go to the brothel."

"Those guys suck."

Whoever said that sounded a lot like me. I was proud of her.

We pulled up to Chungking. Softly, Franz punched my shoulder. "You're a mate, Mary."

His casual warmth caught me. For all its fire, Hong Kong offered precious little warmth.

The dark halls of Chungking were still lined with smoking men. I missed having the bulwark of Franz as I made my all-alone way to our dorm, empty except for one man, fast asleep. I stirred several times during the night, frightened by one guy or another climbing into his bed. When the Whoremongers of Hong Kong returned, rank with alcohol, I faked sleep. The next time I woke, Jean lay on the opposite bunk, snoring. Gross. The time after that, he was also awake, concentrating on me. I sensed that as a teen, he'd picked his acne.

Pure bewilderment. German chatting. I must have fallen asleep again. Jean was gone. Franz introduced me to a guy who had to be his cousin: same shape of the head but with curls, same open, cheerful face. Jorn had barely an accent when he said, "What's on your agenda today, Mary?"

"Buying a cheap ticket."

His eyes flashed, a harbor in the sun. "Where are you going?"

"Somewhere cheap."

"Good on you. Dragon Travel. Say you don't care where you go, or when. They'll offer the deals, like a free stopover or open-ended for a year. Be bored. Under no circumstance do you believe when they say the fare increases tomorrow. Bollocks."

Dragon Travel was located at the top of many hot and hotter stairs. I went through Jorn's prescribed rigamarole with Guao, a man in red polyester slacks. One-way to Bali would set me back only $100 US and was in Indonesia—although it didn't leave for whole 'nother day. Jakarta was also in Indonesia, albeit $375. Bangkok was $120, but Thailand was closer to ten bucks a day. Not to mention that I was going to have to show identification. I already did, yesterday, when I rented the safe-deposit box, but this time, my passport number was going to be attached to a destination. This was terrible, even though I'd known it was coming. I gripped *Southeast Asian on a Shoestring*, yearning for the competence declared by its green and yellow cover.

"Manila leaves soon. Tomorrow morning," Guao said.

For the millionth time in the two past two years, I flipped to the start of the Philippines' section of my only friend, The Lonely Planet. The island with Manila on it, Luzon, had a single international airport. Here I was, two days into my escape and I was only just buying a ticket. Maybe because I was so upset, nice-guy Guao offered $350 for a return to Hong Kong with stopovers in Manila and Bali. I bought it, and then was stumbling through the punishing heat to a crosswalk. A tall man there looked like the white guy on the ferry, yesterday. Following me.

I scurried along a deliberately circuitous route to Chungking, my freak-out increased by the men in the halls, the immovable air, my narrow top bunk. Curling into a ball, my knuckles in my mouth, I rocked as if I were me holding Little. Someone, nudging. Again, I was disorientated until things registered:

ticket, tall man. Once more, I had fallen asleep. Whoever was waggling me did so again.

It was Franz. "Come for a meal, Mary."

I retreated with a raw whimper. Behind Franz's soccer ball of a head, Jorn's ringlets bobbed like bait. "Got the Hong Kong belly?" They'd bring me a cup of tea, that'd set me right, and through the door they bounded. They were so free.

My clock read 5:53 p.m. Fourteen hours until I left for Manila, another city where I knew no one, where gazing-gazing men would probably hold up the walls of low-end hotels. How I wished a cup of tea could set me right.

When you sensed danger, you moved beside yourself.

French Jean was paused in the doorway. My father did that. Jean approached my bunk. We were alone in the room. He was thin but looked as if he had wiry strength. He leaned his elbows onto my mattress.

"*C'est difficile*, Mary, to travel alone. A beautiful woman."

My sister was the beautiful one. I was skinny. Or too fat. I could never tell.

"Come to China with me."

I hovered in a space where I didn't want anything to do with Jean yet did—at least it wouldn't be the Philippines, alone. I certainly couldn't say or do anything.

Jean slouched out. The now-empty door made me feel like I should have done that differently. Why didn't they assign us who to like the way they did airplane seats? I napped fitfully until it was time to leave. When I reached for my backpack, I saw on the floor near it a Styrofoam cup of used-to-be hot tea.

The street, not yet insane but already active. I felt skinless. Searching for the tall man, I spotted no one white. I skipped breakfast and found an open salon, where I said one last good-bye to my hair, to Jen Brewer. The lady chopped, snipped, bleached, and rinsed. My hair was now a creamy blonde, a good four inches shorter than it used to be, which had been the perfect length to twist into a bun.

No more buns. I was a traveler now. I looked at least twenty.

And far prettier than I thought possible, though nowhere near beautiful. French Jean was a big faker. I climbed aboard the red double-decker bus to the airport, counting the days I'd been gone. Matched the number of steps to the farebox: three. They didn't even know I'd left. At the airport, I was drawn to a large fish tank of teapot-sized goldfish with frondy tails. I ran my hand down the glass. It wouldn't let me in.

Good Girls Don't Get Stoned

DAAN MEANS "ROAD" in Filipino. Of course, I didn't speak Filipino. I learned *daan* from the guy who checked me into the hostel. There was a big *daan* just outside the dorm window. The trucks up and down it panicked me, but I was more terrified to go out. I'd hunkered upon arrival. Safer to wait out the time in the bottom shelf of one of the eight metal bunk beds lining the walls, chewing sticky Filipino caramels, small lumps that I couldn't resist buying at the airport. Big lumps occupied most of the room's other bunks. I couldn't see them too well in the dawn non-light, but they smelled male. I fell in and out of sleep—the side of the bridge, my parents' mussed bed; Mom slapping me—until three Australian girls invaded the room, a brown-eyed frenzy of tanned cleavage called Cathy, Cassie, and Katherine, "just off" the overnight bus from the north. The rice terraces were "good fun" and "the local product" easily obtainable. They knew in a second that I'd never smoked hash, so I accepted when one of them—Cathy?—offered a "coffin nail." They cackled as I gagged my way through my first puff of Cathy's cigarette.

"Bet she's cherry, too," she said. One of the other girls called me "mate" and asked me along for a beer. It was maybe ten a.m.

The streets of the shoestring traveler area, the Ermita, were wide and sweaty, the buildings lining them two-storied and flat-roofed. The restaurant was pineapple yellow to go with the pineapple pancakes the girls ordered—I was liking skipping breakfast, so asked Cathy for my own cigarette—and the music was too loud and all from a couple years ago, that "We Are The World" one, then "Would I Lie To You," sung without irony by the only other girls here, Filipinas wearing tight tops and teensy skirts. After eating, my new mates ordered a pint each. I asked for a Diet Coke. They went googly-eyed.

I said, "What?"

Cathy called me a no-hopper, whatever that meant. Didn't sound good. After breakfast, without asking, the girls led me onto a city bus, and we spent two days doing everything listed in our guidebooks: cool old fort, cathedrals, Chinatown, the smell of roasted ducks hanging by their headless necks. Being around the girls drained my panic until the night. In a bar. Two nights in a bar. Men in the bar. Panic. The first night, the girls made a great show of examining the menu. The American guys at the next table bought our dinner and drinks. I ignored the first and tried the second. Beer tasted the way wet, moldy bread smelled. Happily, after five minutes of increasingly enthusiastic sips on an empty stomach, I was able to let go of not being able to take part in American rants about the crappy way Cory Aquino ran the country. Hookers bobbed around the bar like the plastic birds in the baby pool at Little's school fair, waiting to be snatched up, flipped over, and checked for the prize. The men who were going to buy them and fuck them needed to be smashed like white, wooden chairs into the cement wall.

The American buying me beer ordered me another. Later that night, some subset of the girls poured me into my bunk. No nightmares, at least. In the morning, my head thumped like the trucks banging past our window. My anxiety returned, and my stomach was in upheaval.

Cassie and Katherine advised me to get to the technicolor yawn and be done with it. I asked about Cathy. Either Katherine or Cassy went all sniggery. Either Cassie or Katherine said, "We'll meet up at breakky."

As if by magic, Cathy strolled into the restaurant eight minutes after I'd bummed my first smoke. Her account of the night was excruciating in its detail, told with proud indifference. How could she eat pancakes, talking about the smooth feeling of his nob against the roof of her mouth? That night, I threw all the distain I could muster at the Brits who offered to buy us dinner and beer. One had some local product, which he called a spleef. The girls eagerly partook. Right in the bar. The Brits did not miss the effect that smoking hash had on all those curves gyrating to "Dancing Queen."

Dear Little, began a letter to my brother that shocked me by starting in my head. *Good girls don't get stoned.*

Don't get stoned, don't spend the night. When I cold-shouldered the guy wanting to buy me another beer, Cathy demanded to know if I really was a virgin.

I drained my pint. "Fuck off."

The goal, Little, was to deliver the phrase with the girls' nasty nonchalance, but you know I've never said it out loud, and I gave it too much gas. When I tried to bum a cig, Cathy told me to get stuffed and buy some for her, for once.

I stalked to the cash register. I didn't even know what kind she liked. I asked for two packs of the only brand I recognized, Camels, then returned to our table and slid one across the grainy wood. Cathy grinned. "Cheers, mate." It was settled. The next morning, I snuck out while she slept. The other two weren't back.

The sky was purple, the wide street practically deserted. The air was the coolest I'd felt since landing in Hong Kong. The thing about being with jerks was at least you were with somebody. By the time I'd walked to the bus station, I was still alone, just around more people. The morning was brighter but still misty. Next to a two-story building of bullied cement stretched a parking lot packed with large, colorful buses: blue on top, yellow below; yellow on top, green below. I pulled out my Camels. *Dear*

Little. Smoking is still harsh on my throat, but I am beginning to love the way the cellophane crinkles when you unwrap a pack, the way you whap the pack against the heel of your palm to settle the tobacco. The way it gives you something to do when you have no idea what to do. I couldn't work the match.

A lighter snapped close to my ear. The guy attached to it looked like most of the traveler guys in the bars: thin with dirty-blond hair, though a lot of them were tall, and he was more my size. Also, he was not drunk. His smile was as hesitant as the Manila morning when he said, "Me thumb's burning."

I took the light, marveling at his steady hands. We were standing in the same cold. I said, "Where d'ya buy a ticket, then?" Sounded like one of the girls.

The guy used his cigarette to point to the cement building. Moving off, I was glad to shed him, wished I weren't alone, imagined how the girls would swear when they found me gone.

I hauled out the ol' travel survival kit, quickly reading about Northern Luzon, the area the girls had just come from. First stop, city of Baguio. The bus, blue on top, red on bottom, smelled like gasoline and corn and was about half-full, mostly with men in worn-out-but-neat-as-new short-sleeved button-down shirts, straw hats, and tense faces. I couldn't fathom why all of them were so edgy. The few moms looked tired, traveling with a passel of kids, live fowl, or both. I was the only white person until the lighter guy climbed aboard. Sitting across from me and one seat back, his head ticked to the side as he gave me his guarded smile. Those were some blue eyes.

He leaned over to present me with a coffin nail. My shoulders declined for me. From the way he tapped his fist once against the back of my seat, I had the French Jean feeling: I should have done that differently.

In time, the bus sputtered to a start. Picking a painstaking path through the increasingly crowded streets, we took almost an hour to clear the congestion that was Manila. The sun decided, yes, she would shine a bit today. The light was soft but crisp, and there was a golden, moist feeling in the air. The highway took us past dense fields of wide-leafed bushes, smudgy blue hills in the distance, with an occasional brown hut at the side of the road. It started to sprinkle. I smoked more, relishing the almost-vanilla sharpness and, at long last, relaxing into the ragged plastic of the seat.

Find me now, pal.

Eventually, my pack went empty. Even more eventually, the lighter guy leaned over, another head tick to go with what might be his final offer of a cigarette. His name was Bob. He was English. I was mellow from my cigs but aware that the last smoke was indeed my last, and so I shrugged yes. In the two hours spent winding up the rainy road to Baguio, everything reminded Bob of India. "You think this trip is long? Calcutta to Varanasi, there weren't no seats left, see, so we hung off the back. Eleven hours." Tick. Something tickled inside my stomach. "But that was nothing compared to the trip to Goa. Now that . . ." *So pleasant,* I thought toward Little, smoking yet another of Bob's while he talked, *to put off considering all I would need to accomplish when the highway ended.* Only as we approached Baguio did Bob say he was twenty-three. I said I was twenty.

"Oy, you got a name?"

I took an infinite drag. Time to become who I planned to be. "Carlie Adams."

That cautious, compelling grin. "Carlie Adams." His voice bounced along with the bus. "Nice name."

That is why I chose it.

The bus slowly closed in on Baguio's main terminal, passing neon pizza parlors and yuppie-looking restaurants. I barely saw them—not because they weren't what I imagined I would find in a mountain city north of Manila. I wasn't really seeing the cobblestone streets and horse-drawn carriages, either. The highway was ending.

Things were blurry, the only reality the damp, black pavement of the parking lot, hard against my feet. Bob slung his pack over his shoulder. His spine slumped into the same question mark I saw on his face.

"Hear of any good guesthouses, Miss Carlie Adams?"

My new name in his mouth was too much pleasure to admit to. Nose to my Lonely Planet, I spearheaded the finding of an alleged cheapie. The street was cobblestone and quiet, but the place had no dorms. The proprietor displayed the only available room. Modest but spotless, single beds resting along opposite walls of creamy blue.

Bob ticked his head. Guess whether to share was my decision.

The thing about having your own room was that any creepazoid could break in. At least Bob seemed kind of something. We could go find another hotel where maybe they only had one room and maybe it only had one bed; in the meantime, maybe we'd lose this room. Anyway, short of murder, nothing could take place that had not already taken place.

That thing happened again, where someone who sounded a lot like me did my talking for me, "Do you want to share it? It'll be cheaper."

The puddles that were Bob's eyes darkened at their center. "I don't mind."

Quickly, me, "Let's grab a beer."

We wandered until we came across what Bob decided was the right bar. He ignored the hookers, acknowledged the travelers, and ordered two pints. I asked if he studied Filipino. His shoulders spread with the confidence of his India-talking. "Not Filipino. They speak Tagalog, here."

As we drank, I watched Bob's mouth on his cigarette, some Filipino brand, wondering what that mouth felt like, then pushed the thought back, angry at myself. I reached for my glass, for the ragged plastic respite from the bus. Eventually, Bob ground out his cigarette and tucked the butt into his pack. It was time to return to the guesthouse. As we walked back, the dark, cloudy sky reached through my very nice buzz, trying to lift me away. In our room, Bob folded into his bed, apparently blasé that, over in mine, a once-again-curious girl was noting the way the weak electric light turned his dirty-blond hair to gold. We'd split the bill. I liked that.

"Have you ever gone with a hooker?"

Bob was back to tentative. "Once. Most blokes do. To see what it'd be like, yeah?"

"And what did you think it would be like?"

Bob tapped twice against the wall. The second tap sounded harder than the first. The darkened dots in his eyes moved to my mouth. I pulled as close to the wall as I could and stayed frozen until he turned his back to me. Slowly, then, I was able to relax— and woke gasping into the pitch black.

Across the room, a lethargic rustle. I bit back a wail. From the darkness, more movement—oh, God. No.

A recognizable click. In the perplexed light from his Bic, Bob monitored the situation. He lit a smoke, passed it. My hands shook as I took it. "Sorry." Couldn't look at him. I wanted someone to hold me, but safely. He would do.

For three days, we roamed the windy, wet city. All touch appeared accidental, elbows bumping as we perused the central market, knuckles brushing if we reached for the same star fruit or wooden carving, the knuckles on him that rapped tabletops in bars shutting down at nine p.m. sharp. There was a government curfew, enforced by soldiers in the streets. I was drunk by nine p.m. sharp. If you were not drunk by nine p.m. sharp, you would wake gasping and the cute guy across the room would think you were insane.

On day four, we moved to the town of Bontoc. Pulling out of the bus station, Bob ripped through his day pack for his smokes.

I didn't wake him, last night; I'd made sure. Maybe he was mad because he hadn't gotten anywhere with me. Maybe he didn't want to.

We arrived in Bontoc as dark settled, dodging raindrops as we rode the flow of white travelers to the Happiness Hotel. Rooms, thirty pesos per person. Bob said, "Pricey."

I drooped into the only place to sit, the hard mattress. Normally, it was great, the way Bob found the cheapest way to accomplish anything. I'd spent only two or three dollars a day rather than five. But it was not worth toting my stuff through the downpour to save a nickel a night. "Can't we stay here?"

Bob hovered inside the door. This bed was a double.

In popped the fellow who'd led the white wave from the bus. This time, he was peddling something he called Purple. Local product, I bet.

The first head tick in about a day. "Purple don't grow here."

"Okay. Is Baguio Gold. More cheap, good for smoke all day."

After some negotiation, Bob peeled a bill off his wad as if it were a scab. I didn't want this double bed.

The door closed. Bob was in my face with his most expressive smile to date, demonstrating how to cut the not-Purple, the real local product, Baguio Gold, into a cigarette to make a wacky backy. He grinned with the up-and-down of the phrase. Twice I inhaled deeply, hoping to pass out. Instead, I discovered more quiet bliss than I knew existed. At first, the tips of my fingers tingled, but after one more hit, even that went away. We lay on the bed, contemplating the plink-plunk of the rain as Bob smoked a little more. He stroked my arm. When I didn't stop him, he started on my back. Our bodies fit together so tenderly. The warmth didn't run away when he kissed me. Even his tongue was nice—not pokey or spitty, just soft. Nice. Then nicer. I had never been kissed this way. I lost track of everything except his lips and tongue running from my mouth to my throat until his hands forged a path up my shirt.

"Unh," I said into his mouth. "Not ye . . . I can't . . ." I couldn't complete a sentence.

"Crikey."

I wanted to know what he meant. Not the word. What was under the word. Strong sunshine pulled me from sleep. The serene angle of the light said late morning. Bob was right next to me on the bed, holding an ashtray and grinding out a cigarette, trying to act like he hadn't been watching me. I wondered if he was planning to kiss me anytime soon.

"Did I totally pass out?"

Bob slipped the butt into its pack. "Sleeper-creeper."

I must have look confused because he offered a dawdling smile. "The skunk can do that, if you're not used to it."

"Guess I'll have to practice."

Bob brought out the spleef. Still harsh, but worth it. I heard my voice saying how soft and safe it made everything. Was I talking to Little? Bob rapped his knuckles low against the headboard like he was dealing with a mental case. As if changing the subject, he kissed me, kissed me for a long time before trying anything else, for such a long time that when his hands finally slipped under my shirt, I ached for them. I started to hear several low moans timed exactly to his gentle squeezes. Hey, that was me. Bob crushed me to his chest. I couldn't take a breath. His tongue made me feel like I had oatmeal stuck all through my mouth. His hands were prodding. Lot of things prodding. It hurt.

"Hurry up."

He froze mid-thrust, then obliged, sliding silently off me when he was done in a way that said he'd be gone with the first dry dawn. I wanted to slam my own fist into the headboard. That would drive him away for sure, so I curved the front of my naked torso against his bare back. Slowly, his breathing leveled off. I had no idea how I dozed off but must have because I gasped myself from sleep. Blood had been spurting, up to my neck.

"Crikey Moses," Bob said, rolling away from me. I slid

alongside him with the synchronization of the girls in that famous quartet from *Swan Lake*. I wanted to enjoy it. Even so, it hurt, him inside me. I bet it wouldn't if I were still stoned. At least he reached for me again, when the sun came up. Hopefully, that meant he didn't think I was a bad lay.

Bob spent the week verifying this. Or not. Moving from Bontoc to the next town, smaller town, Sagada, he head-ticked enough that I wasn't so worried he would leave, which would result in me, alone, in the mountains of the Philippines. He sure seemed more into getting high, though.

"Where's the backy?" Bob said one night, rooting through the grey, stinky mound in the ashtray.

"You finished it this afternoon, right before . . ." It did hurt less when I was stoned. "Are you mad at me?"

I sounded like some desperate, clingy girl. *Little, I made Mom mad once, so mad that she hit me. For the instant between doing what made her so mad and dealing with her reaction, I had power. To make her feel that much. About me.* I wanted to shriek at Bob, "Are you my boyfriend?" I almost did, the next morning, on the next bus to the next town. We went by miles of rice terraces, an unbelievable shade, Lime Jell-O green, cut into the steep hills like steps for gods. The white people ooohed and aaahed. I wanted to shriek, "Or are we just screwing?"

Wouldn't matter if I did, if I hit, strangled him. He wouldn't care. I almost didn't. As long as he didn't leave.

Next town: Banaue, population sixty-two or something. We found a two-dollar room and blazed it. After he came, we hiked up and through mist to the rice terraces. We had paused for a cigarette in one of the three-walled huts that dotted the trail when out of the surreal green came about ten men in ragged, sort-of uniforms. There was no way to know if they were army or revolutionaries—or real—except that, unequivocally, they did carry rifles.

"Get behind me."

Abruptly and completely not high, Bob stepped out of the hut and tossed the lead guy his pack of smokes. With only the briefest glance at me, the squad mooched through the foliage.

Someone sat next to me on the plank bench. Bob. He rested his fingertips lightly on my knee. Who taught him to be so kind?

I said, "Fuck."

His head ticked, but slowly. I slapped his hand off me.

"Did that just fucking happen? Fuck." Screw *short of murder*. As long as you have a pussy, worse can always happen. "I'm really just seventeen."

His face was impassive. "I sussed as much."

"You know, fuck you."

Bob banged the fatty side of his fist into the wooden wall. I grabbed my day pack and stormed down the very path the soldiers had taken. Let them rape me. Then Bob would be sorry. Tragically, I reached the village unharmed. I got to the restaurant across from our guesthouse before bursting into tears. Fumbling for my cigarettes, I realized that I'd left them on that plank bench. Oooh, they had banana bread. I had a piece, then another that I shouldn't have, blistering for nearly an hour, wanting Bob to come find me, to apologize. Waiting for the sweet, patient fellow I thought I had met on that first bus ride from Manila. I asked for more banana bread. The terror of being alone was creeping over me when along came two Swedes from the bus to Banaue. Their skin was suntanned into caramel. They bought me a beer. The table boasted a fair number of empties by the time the one with the longer hair asked where was that guy I'd been hanging out with. Bob was an asshole for not appreciating me. Single girls along the Lonely Planet Trail were about as rare as hot running water. I said that whole thing aloud. The Swedes bought me dinner. Fried noodles. I ate them.

When curfew sent us back to our hotels, Bob was not in the common area. It was not possible that Whitney Houston's "How Will I Know?" was playing from someone's room. Bob was not in the toilet; he was not in our room. It was nine-thirty. On our bed, I wrapped my arms around my bent knees and rocked. From the direction we'd hiked earlier came a sound I had not heard: gunfire. At six past ten by my travel alarm clock, there was a rap on our door. I knew instantly that it was Bob's knuckles and that he was okay. When he called, very naturally, "Hello," I waited. *Little, I wanted to hear him use my name. He hadn't said it, not once, since the day we met, when he said it was a nice name. Probably didn't remember it.*

"Carlie, open up."

I flew to the door and pulled him roughly into our tender fit. We disentangled self-consciously. I asked, "Where were you?"

"The restaurant next door. I missed getting back for curfew and had to wait until the soldiers cleared out."

His blue-eyed bravado was easy to decipher. He drew me to him. This time, it was a long, slow kiss. Very movie-like. When we did it, it barely hurt. Even his smell told me he needed me, too. After, Bob lit a cig. He exhaled thoughtfully as he passed it, saying, "I shouldn't smoke so much."

I ran a finger along his jaw line. Second to his neck, it was the part his body I liked best. "You want me to finish it?"

"No. I mean the skunk. I know it makes me . . ." He closed his eyes, hands locked behind his head. "I'd given it up, right before I met you."

It was definitely the kind of thing they said in movies. The boyfriend-ness of it pulled me close to him. "My name's not . . . it's Jen. I changed it. I ran away. My father . . . oh, Jesus." I looked to Bob, certain my confession would drive him away.

He was asleep.

I woke to more rain. In me, a similar gray uncertainty. Bob wasn't acting like he had heard, last night, wasn't acting like anything. Just smoked, looked out the window at the flank of damp gray, said, "Bloody mizzle."

He fell asleep, last night.

Right when I was telling him.

Bob tucked the last of his cig into his pack. God, I hated it when he did that.

"Why do you always do that? Save your butts like that."

The way he rapped his knuckles made me wonder if he was planning to punch out another wall. At least it'd be a response.

His answer was clinical. "I'm trying not to smoke so much."

"You said hash."

"Why do you care?"

"I really don't know, Bob."

Now he'd leave. I wanted to burrow into our bed, to curl and rock. That would make Bob want some, so I said, "Let's go back to Manila."

He tapped his pack against the table. As an old man, Bob would be thinner, leathery, with careful, selfish movements. When he finally said, "I don't mind," I could easily have shaken him, demanding to know if he ever went so far as to want anything. At least my father told me he loved me, after.

Leaving the cool mountains, Little, for the heat of the flatlands, I couldn't believe that I'd wanted to be out of the rain. Surprise of the year, Bob stayed distant. Manila was visible on the horizon when he laid it on me. "I'm skint."

I was not completely sure that meant broke. Bob tore through his day pack for his "Whichever's cheapest" shitty-tasting smokes. "I . . . er . . . didn't change pounds to pesos before we got to Banaue."

Today was Saturday. Banks closed early and didn't reopen until Monday.

I shouldn't have to give him money.

Bob lit his last cigarette, suspiciously silent.

I said, "You do have more traveler's checks, don't you?"

He blew smoke out the window. For the rest of the hot journey, it was as if there was a rat trap between us.

Manila. The flat-roofed buildings and packed streets threw

me right into the mood I was in when I fled the Australian girls. Bob looked about seven stops past furious. I pulled out a business card from those Swedes. "We will be staying at the Palace Pension on Jorge C. Bocobo Street."

"You don't know where Jorge fucking coconut Street is."

Two muscled Aussies lumbered up. Apparently, they knew Bob, although I could tell they didn't remember his name. He was quick with theirs: Nigel and Rudy. Rudy stared at me with a stupid look on his fat features while Nigel, his shorn head bobbing on his stalwart neck, invited us to meet them later, "You remember the place, ey, mate?" I waved down a cab and climbed in with a look at Bob that I hoped said, "In, dickhead."

The coconut pension turned out to be blessedly cool, a red tile roof with substantial white walls and bricks under our feet that clanked like pottery against a table when we walked over them. Bob whistled.

"My treat," was all I said as we entered our thick-walled room. Bob considered me, making me wonder what else I'd done wrong until he asked for money. I said, "I figured I'd pay for stuff until you got some wired in."

Bob's head tick came with the slow smile I hadn't seen since our first days together. "Those Aussies, Carlie, they'll want cash."

"You said we weren't gonna smoke—"

"How much did I buy for you in Sagada? In blinking Banaue?"

"If you'd been more careful with your own money—"

Bob grabbed my shoulders and shook. He was wiry and strong. He threw me onto the bed, nearly cracking my head against the clean white wall. Standing over me, his face went neutral. "Give me the dosh."

I reached into my fanny pack, fumbled for whatever bills. He snatched them and took off. I tried to stop trembling. Mom hit me, but my father never did, not really, just to make me still. Bob deliberately used force to hurt, used it the way he used the name Carlie—twice when he learned it, once when he wanted me to open the door, and now, when he wanted money. Wanted, wanted, wanted; the only reason he tolerated me.

Because I let him. Blackness. Far away, near the edge of it, was a speck of white light. I went to that dot and understood that the thing to do was move. I sat up straight.

"No." I said it out loud. Grabbed my stuff, marched to front desk, told the desk clerk that I was checking out, that I wanted a refund. He tried to persuade me this was highly irregular.

"I do not care."

On the sidewalk, the clerk rushed to me with Bob's backpack. The gentleman left this in the room, he said.

"Put it in the street."

My ticket went to Bali. Next flight, three a.m. I was on it.

Land, Vault, Land

Bali. Hotter than anything. Baggage claim, outside. Dude my father's age, good suit, gleaming hair. He lifted my backpack from the rotate-y thing. Said things: " . . . George," " ... going to Kuta Beach?" "Come with me to Kuta ... " No discussion. I said, "No." I said that out loud; here? Or at the coconut pensi—no; here. Yet when his fingers found my arm, I couldn't even feel terror. He slid his palm to my elbow, bent it gently, my father's age, piloting us toward the taxis. I thought, I'm no outboard motor. I had said, "No." Said it out loud. A lady, probably ten years older than me, stepped in from nowhere. A cigarette dangling from her lips, she said, French accent, "Quit this punter," whatever that meant, and reached for one of the thick straps hanging off my pack, which the punter was carrying. She took it back. She was tall, but it was not her height that gave her power because, except for the arm muscles, she was shoestring-traveler thin. She just took it back. I wanted to be someone who just took shit back.

She passed me my backpack with no interference from the punter, though he all but hissed, "Lesbian."

"Child molester," she tossed over a well-shaped shoulder and strolled away with a shake of auburn hair: thick curls, runaway strands, shot through by a single, ribbon-wide section of gray. I all but skipped after—another girl! When I caught up, she offered me a smoke. The design on her cigarette case was intricate: red, gold, and orange beads amongst turquoise ones made glossy by the morning sun. It took me time to discern a fox's face amongst all the teal.

She held out a lighter. "I'm Lise. How do you call yourself?"

I let myself take a bottomless drag before speaking. To decide. "Mary."

"Mary. From America, *oui?*" She glanced where that creep had been, by the taxis. As if coming to a conclusion, she tossed her hair. "We together travel, American Mary."

She mentioned something called "Oo-bood." Who cared; she wasn't male. "What's a punter?"

"A sex buyer, my *petite* American." Lise picked a fleck of tar from her tongue to flick it with deliberation. "That one wants them young. Unless he stalks another as fresh-emerged from the egg as you."

It was as if her words bent my elbow. I remained unable to speak as she led me in changing money and then to the local buses. Lise chose the one designated "Ubud." Okay, then. As we waited, Lise twisted her gray streak around and around a finger. The poise of her chunky silver rings reached through the blur caused by the pressure of the bent elbow.

I supposed Lise thought I was staring at her streak of gray hair because she said, "I dye this."

"Why?"

"Young, pretty women have bad times to be taken seriously in the academic world."

Up pulled the bus. Climbing aboard made me feel normal: on the local to the next town. Walking the aisle, that magnificent shock of hair swayed toward two seats. Lise cozied into the in-front one. Sitting behind her, I hooked my hands over her seat back. "I mean, why only that little bit?"

The bus revved, a sound similar to the surprised relish that was Lise's laugh. As the driver guided us with care through big-city streets, she rotated so that she half-faced me; solely, I bet, to be able to stretch those legs into the aisle. But in doing so, she couldn't ignore me. That awesome cigarette case reappeared.

"You travel alone, American Mary?"

I nodded a too-willing *yes*. She lit up, all the while examining me as if I were a book she might check out. After a long drag and longer exhale, she said, "Never again talk to those type of men, oui? I have for us good a *losmen* in Ubud."

I didn't know if Lise was using French or—Balinese? Indonesian? I could have looked it up in my Lonely Planet, but she wore a flawlessly lived-in *sarong* with a trippy pineapple pattern in flame colors. My kelly-green shorts had a pink belt, for Christ's sake. Anyway, soon enough, the bus got onto a two-lane highway, where the engine made too much rump-a-bump for conversation. Outside my window, cityscape dwindled into storefronts and two-storied, gray-brown wooden buildings, then into green fields that painted themselves all the way to cadet-gray hills. Despite verdant proof of a second chance, a pressure lodged behind my eyes: Bob, the airport, the punter.

Road signs told us to expect Ubud. Two lanes became four, and the buildings squished together as they proliferated. Lise hopped us off the bus a five-minute walk from a wall painted aqua. Inside the main gate was a dream world of bamboo-roofed bungalows set among luxurious greenery and blossoms. I dallied on my terracotta porch. If this was a losmen, sign me up. Jumbo goldfish in a tear-shaped pond roiled over each other, kissy-kissy lips begging for food. The to-do coming over the wall—toot-toot, vroom, birds, and mom-like voices—finally discharged the Bob and airport anxiety.

A gecko skittered across the steps Lise was moseying up. She carried neither daypack nor travel survival kit. A cigarette served her fine. She handed me a fold of material that, when shaken, turned out to be a sarong, emerald-colored with the yellow outlines of flowers.

"Until we buy yours." Lise adjusted the supple fabric lower on my hips, wider than hers, but she complimented my waist. I didn't believe her, was able to relax only after she said, "We get together lunch, American Mary."

Lise's watering hole was done up tiki-style, with the same terracotta floors as my porch, geckos included, and a juke box near the door playing that new-ish, Wishing-well-kiss-and-tell song. The place was empty except for an older man behind the bar. As we took stools, he offered the lunch menu. Lise's shake of curls brought pink to grandfatherly cheeks that might not have flushed in quite some time. She said, "Two Bintang."

I said, "And for you?"

"I like this, American Mary. I like this." Once Lise found out I'd only been to the Philippines, she did most of the talking, twirl-twirl, Asian anthropology and the month she was taking off from her Ph. D. program. "To gather my brains. *Pbbff.*" The room half-filled with white guys: *bule*, Lise called them. Several sent over beers. She waved away the beers yet ordered us another round. Then something over my shoulder drew her attention like a razor. Two guys. They gave off remarkably similar vibes, buff and looking good in perfectly white t-shirts and tight jeans, their onyx hair done up like James Dean's.

Lise said, "So, now. Why I don't dye most of this hair."

All she had to do was cross those legs. The taller guy was cuter, if not by much. He introduced himself as Ketut. Lise said, "Balinese males have one of four names, which signifies birth order. Wayan, Ma-de, Nyoman, Ketut. Am I right, boys?"

I couldn't have tracked that information sober. I did get that Ketut was way better at English than his brother, Ma-de, who specialized in smoothing a lock of hair at the front that kept springing from its James Dean shellac. It'd spring, he'd smooth it and then flash movie-star teeth until it sprang again. Adorable. Nevertheless, Lise and Ketut got to gab, their voices like the birds serenading our losmen. I still didn't know which language was spoken in Bali. Why did she take Ketut rather than spring-and-smooth? More beer. She wanted the better-looking, that's why. We ordered lunch. Lise and I paid, even though the boys wolfed down most of it. She made sure we settled up at warp speed as the three of them joked about what could possibly be done to pass the time during the afternoon rain and—

Lise and Ketut, gone. When Ma-de said, "You beautiful hair," I was good and drunk, so pretty sure it wouldn't hurt.

We ran to my bungalow, fat drops splattering us. Inside, Ma-de stripped off his not-that-damp shirt. He took my hands to run them over his chest and abs.

When I didn't take over feeling him up, Ma-de removed my hands from his pecs and held them between his, our faces inches apart. Beer-wooziness overtook me and I leaned my forehead into his neck. I don't know how long we stayed that way. I grew to understand that we were on the bed, him stroking my cheek with the back of his hand and then kissing there, then my ear. Then really kissing me. Kiss and tell. It was okay. Good, even. My body pressed itself hard against him. He stopped kissing to cup my face, then rolled me onto my back with a cry. In that sound was my father. "Suck it, Jenny-Jen-Jen." I always did.

When it ended, Ma-de dozed behind me, his body curved to mine, his hands fitting over my boobs like they had been sculpted there. I wanted to like this pressure—I could, as long as I had a gecko to draw my focus across the ceiling, across the floor. Time rolled in and out. Ma-de got hard in his sleep. A steel rope, like a fishing-line for a great white shark, hooked between my eyes. It pulled me vertical. I had to escape the room or that cable would yank my head off. Out my window, the rain had stopped. No way Ma-de would take my things; anyway, who cared? I left without even snapping up my Lonely Planet.

The streets were rained clean. North of town, pavement became dirt road. Rice fields replaced buildings. The heat was starting to make me crave the metallic tinge of a cold Bintang when I came to a crossroad encircled by trees, branches thick with birds that looked like white flamingos, only smaller. It sounded like a kindergarten up there—I fucking sucked his cock. Why did I do that? Against the background of the setting sun, more pearly birds flew in from the fields. Goddamnit, he didn't even have to ask. The birds landed with a huge flapping of wings and then vaulted, individually or in groups, from tree to tree.

A motorcycle rolled carefully in front of me. The driver wore Ma-de jeans and t-shirt, his hair in the requisite style. He introduced himself as Lompok. Not one of Lise's four names. He followed on his bike when I started toward Ubud, agreeably inquiring where you from, where you go, where you husband. Having Lompok after me, unassuming, persistent, felt like hitting re-set. As if he could tell, he said, "I give lift to losmen," and my ability to say, "No," went the way of birds. Ma-de was at that losmen. In my bed. For all that, I couldn't make myself turn down the ride.

Lompok drove fast through the growing dusk. I had to cling to him, my boobs against his back the whole way. By the time we reached the aqua wall, I could barely say, "Uh," to a bar and a beer. Right then, my compatriots emerged from the gate. Lise and Ketut swung hands, pinkies locked.

"Mary! Where have you gone? Poor Ma-de!" Lise did not hesitate to face Lompok squarely. "Who is this?"

Lompok and Ma-de looked each other up and down. I tried to form a clever remark, one Lise could have gotten away with, but who was I kidding? I slunk toward the gate. At that, Lompok drew down his eyebrows and inched his motorcycle away. Lise shuttled the four of us in the opposite direction, her and Ketut in front of me and Ma-de, who did not take my hand.

Until he did. "Why you go? It not good?"

Lise called over her shoulder, "It sounded good."

"Jesus Christ!" I halted, so they halted. The cobbled street was not a busy one, open-doored storefronts where men crouched and smoked while women bustled this way and that, making things, buying things. I smelled coconut oil frying sweet meat. I hadn't been here a full day and already I'd blown some guy and almost been, whatever, kidnapped by an airport punter. I had to stop being so green behind the ears.

Ma-de was saying, "No, okay, okay," as Ketut chipped in, "He always loud."

"Pbbff." Lise's turquoise cigarette case materialized. Ketut got one, Ma-de got one. Not me.

Ma-de held out his to me. His independent-minded lock of hair sprung up as he asked his brother something. Ketut said, "Stay with me, and I never be mad ever."

Ma-de took both my hands. "Stay me, I ever be mad."

I smoothed his hair.

With a surprisingly high-pitched outcry, Lise linked her arm through mine. We led the parade to the bar. Three rounds, the right boy's arms around the right girl's shoulder became Lise's arm through mine as soon as the brothers went to pee. It felt stiffer than the previous time she interlaced us.

"I don't want to be hostile for less than only one day's acquaintance, Mary, but you don't shame me in that way again."

It was not possible, that I'd heard right. "Me shame you?"

Lise's mouth dropped open, like she hadn't imagined me capable of anything other than compliance: sarong! Beer! Sex! Certain of dismissal, I trashed my cigarette, my last.

She surprised me. "I'm sorry it was bad, Mary. Due to my affair gone sour, I travel now. The highest professor of my field."

"Did his wife find out?"

"Pbbff! We are French. *Non, non.*" Lise's cigarette case lay near the ashtray. She tapped the fox face, suddenly speaking quickly, as if relieved. "He obtained an undergraduate with no gray. Apparently, I am too pretty to take seriously without gray, yet with, he chooses six years younger than me. Pbbff! A Farsi little fatty."

She said it so blithely that I felt like the remark was my fault. At her wink, the bartender brought two more Bintang. I waited for her to suck down a healthy mouthful before saying, "I can't pay for them, Lise."

"My chick petite! You are destitute?"

"Not the beer." And I'd never ask Ma-de for 75 cents to cover his share of the room. "But, their food?"

"Given the difference in our economic statuses, how else can we spend time together?"

"It's whoring them out."

"Do not speak to me of whoring, Mary. I know of real whoring." Then, flustered, "My Ph. D. concerns the Asian sex trade with Westerners."

Lise used long arms to indicate a huge stomach. "Do you believe, Monsieur Fatty-liker, he tears down my dissertation with all my committee present. So he says, 'I hope you don't research too much this obvious thesis.' To such a point that they decide I no longer have the committee." A snap. "Out on the ass. Screw these white male pigs."

I liked the sound of that, *white male pigs*. Comforted by my silence or offering reassurance, Lise dropped an arm around my shoulder. Ketut and Ma-de chose this moment to return. Both looked surprised at the location of Lise's long limb. She sent Ketut a sidelong glance that lasted for the time it took her to remove her arm from me and let her hand slip under the table. Ketut gave a startle. Her cheek against his blushing one, she said, "His so-important specialty is the love rituals of the Ramayana enacted at Borobudur."

Again, French or Balinese? Indonesian? Ketut tossed his varnished hair with a, "Pbbff." Not a strand moved. The bill came. Lise covered the brothers. Right down to their cigarettes.

The next day, we met them for what Lise called "a jaunt," which meant taking scooters, boobs to back, up the long, curving street called Monkey Forest Road. It culminated at a temple of vine-crawled stone walls, columns, and shrines, its passageways overrun with small-scale, sassy primates. Ma-de asked Ketut something and then placed one pointer finger against each of his incisors. His lips bent and grimaced, saying, "Be careful, they bite." As if we'd never been together, I wondered what that mouth would feel like, against mine. Come gecko time, though, I blew him to get it over with.

The next morning, we went to a water shrine. "Gunung Kawi," Ma-de said, syllable by syllable, releasing an unanticipated heat into the lowest part of my pelvis. The four of us strolled down a long-ago water-carved quarry, where twenty-five-foot statues of Hindu deities were set into forty-foot insets. Jungle foliage hung lush over them. Through Ketut, Ma-de told me that Gunung Kawi was dedicated to Vishnu, God of Wisdom. I really liked the way Ma-de's overworking mouth made my body taut. Following Lise and Ketut out of the temple, I adopted a bit of Lise's saunter. Until gecko-time, when sensation fled. Later, drinking, drunk, I wishing-well-kissed-and-tell'd myself that our next outing would bring it back.

Day Three was a town that made flat, colorfully painted leather puppets, then another that offered silver. Ma-de taught me the numbers I needed to bargain for four chunky rings—five bucks. Still, I relied on geckos to get through the indifference that flooded me come the afternoon rain. Who knew why a Ph.D. would hang out with a seventeen-year-old, except that there was no her/Ketut without a me/Ma-de. If I kept it to a blowjob and a visit to my birds, there wasn't a round two. Not even at night. I made Ma-de match me beer for beer—300 calories each, but getting enough alcohol into him meant I didn't have to swing low until the next afternoon.

"It is good now?" Lise asked our fourth morning. We were seated on her terracotta porch. She was slid down in her chair, twirling away as she bit small, quick mouthfuls of out the Indonesian breakfast standard of buttered toast with chocolate sprinkles and licked the rim of her coffee with condensed milk. Mine was black, no toast, fiery pokers behind my eyes. Wasn't she ever hungover?

"He tells Ketut he loves your giving of head."

I should have stormed away. Like, permanently. Instead, I treated her to a plagiarized hair-toss. I still wasn't sure what I brought to the party, some stupid kid, but the more days stacked up and beer went down, the more she organized next rounds and daytrips, the more difficult it seemed to manage Bali without my walking Lonely Planet. She lectured through art museums and evenings dance performances—the stage an open-aired temple courtyard, mats for the *gamelan* musicians providing melodic, pulsating tings, plinks, and plunks. In *Oleg Tamulilingan,* Flower Attracts the Male Bumblebee, dancers in gold headdresses and shimmering yellow sarong gave the impression of skating rather than walking, their movements regal, subtle, overtly erotic. The flower drew in her big pollinator with bent knees held together, her shoulders off-center, her spine curved. Could she get away with just a blowjob? Would she at least be able to talk with him, after?

Lise saved her favorite show for her last night in Ubud: *Kecak.* As we entered the temple, she said, "They enact a famous ancient monkey fight from the Ramayana. Always there must be fifty but up to one hundred male dancers. Many beautiful, brown, bare chests."

She'd done it again, and again it was my fault. I let myself be drawn into the show. The performers, something like a hundred men, wore black-and-white checkered sarong with red sashes. They sat in concentric circles, at the dead center of which was a tree-shaped candleholder with flames lit along its branches. Like percussion and without stopping, the men chanted, "cak," moving their hands and arms, their torsos, even getting on their knees for certain combinations.

A couple entered the circle. "Sita and Rama," Lise whispered.

They were resplendent in gold-colored facemasks and crowns and gleaming turquoise sarong with gold belts. Next, the monkey character—again, Lise in undertones: "Hanuman"—entered to fight with a bad guy in a red robe, a name I couldn't process because the relentless "Cak-a-cak" was becoming a male ruckus that felt like coming-for-you; all interwoven with Lise practically drooling over one hundred bare chests. I couldn't do anything about my overwhelm until we met up with Ma-de and Ketut, when I downed half a Bintang in a gulp. I was more drunk than Lise by the time she dropped her arm around my shoulders. "Come, American Mary, we leave Ubud together, oui?"

When someone as hip as Lise asked you along, it was flattering. In the morning, she bid Ketut a breezy goodbye. I had no idea how to strap on her cheery balls, so I hoisted my backpack, and said, "Bye"—vexing myself as well as Ma-de. I didn't understand what else there was to do. Marry him?

A week of northbound buses. Lise replaced Ma-de and Ketut on our first afternoon. She assigned me a Wayan to her new Ma-de, and I was a white flamingo: land, vault, land. Twirl, twirl; curls everywhere, Lise made me known as "American Mary," which Wayan called me throughout. Our first time, I got way drunk and so couldn't stop the real sex. Most likely the reverse. Couldn't gecko-out, either; I kept thinking about having nothing but a "Bye" for Ma-de.

Wayan sweated and grunted on top of me. *Do not speak to me of whoring, Mary.* I pushed Wayan's chest. You were bounced from your program, bitch.

Wayan rolled off me, his chin jutting forward in indignation. I went down faster than I'd ever gone down, and everything reverted to normal: morning jaunt, Bintang lunch. Afternoon oral, walk. Soon, we'd get to "Bye." The guys lived on Bali. Bali was an island. Ocean was inevitable.

We left Bali by overnight ferry to Java, the subsequent island in the Indonesian archipelago. Allowed aboard as dusk hinted, I wanted to go directly to the bar. Lise, however, made me traipse the top deck, bow to stern. I had to hand it to her. In front of us stretched the Bali Straight and all around was wind and wind and wind, various gathering of deck chairs, and wind. Before we set sail, a crew of local boys clambered onto the railings. I said, "Christ, they're going to jump."

"You watch," Lise said. Turned out I was the only one not in the know because, within moments, everyone on the deck was at the railing, tossing loose change into the darkening sea. Shouting with the enjoyment of it, the kids leapt to catch the coins, swimming and then diving for the ones they missed, calling for us to throw more; that water sure was getting murky, though.

Lise said, "*Bule* incoming."

Indeed, three white guys, shaggy backpackers, were port-side and drawing closer. As soon as the hottest one asked Lise, "If you're here, who's running heaven, eh?" she found herself a deck chair, crossed her legs peevishly as she smoked, eventually to swan off. Tonight, she and I would share a cabin. There would be no sex, so I didn't mind flirting. As the Canadians vied to buy me a beer, I was usure if I was the coin, flung to be caught, or the child diving for gold in shadowy waters.

Clearly Lise was more vigilant about her goal because in the morning, she presented Budi, a Balinese man who, aside from his endearing John Lennon specs, was a dead-ringer for the original Ketut. Budi had a friend. Komang. He was perfect for me: good-natured and a tad shy. Not as good at English as Budi was. *Naturellement*. I could have slapped her.

"And not a Wayan, Made, Nyoman, or Ketut in sight."

Lise said, "Komang is the same as Nyoman."

The two of us lit up, not sharing cigs, not so much as a flame. In the pause, Budi set about explaining Bali's complex naming system. I cut him off with by turning to Lise, my hip jutted out.

"The four basic names are for boys as well as girls. Each kid usually has a nickname because, my God, not everyone can run around being 'Ma-de.' They can have a Hindu name, too, which can have its own nickname."

Lise blew an irascible stream of smoke. I couldn't resist saying, "I didn't spend every minute with Wayan on my knees."

It started slow, Lise's laugh. As Budi pushed his glasses up his nose, it blossomed full throttle, right across the Bali Straight. This time, let her be the outboard motor.

When we docked, I suggested a liquid breakfast. It didn't take that much to get us drunk. I was a bit high from taking her down a peg. She repeatedly called me, "my American *mignonne*" and dropped her arm around my shoulder, causing Budi once more to push his glasses up his nose and Komang to regard me with expectancy. Lise announced, "It means cutie. You are my little cutie!" She swooped in, a seagull, to kiss my cheek. Budi flushed. Komang's attention, however, intensified. After we tracked down the losmen Lise remembered and she asked for two bungalows, his face crinkled, defining displeasure. I went down on him so fast that I scarcely needed the geckos. That night, maybe I was super-smashed, but I could have sworn I caught sight of my father's luxurious dark hair in the crowd of a low-end bar.

Nah. My parents would never do anything so loving as to look for a second runaway daughter. The morning after Patrice left, all they did was go to work. What were they gonna do? Call the cops? And should they ever stumble onto my shoestring of Southeast Asia, they wouldn't recognize their Kelly-green Jenny-Jen-Jen in a sarong, her hair short in the back and chin-length in front.

Red.

Lise had asked if she could choose the style and color toward the beginning of our second week on Java, in the clear few hours between Budi and Komang's departure and the whoever would take their places as soon as the boozing began. In the beauty parlor, wearing a plastic drape that gave me a double chin, I acknowledged to my fat-faced self that she was right when, post-hairdo, she declared, "You now are chic and sexy, *alors.*" Shop windows and pools downstream from waterfalls tried to trick me into thinking it, too.

No. Patrice was that, alors. From Patrice's Wonder Woman hair fell something called curves. I was too fat, too skinny, still couldn't tell.

It was early evening. Lise and I appeared to be merely ambling. Her arm came toward me in the cunning way it did way back when she groped Ketut under the table. I felt that three-weeks-old weight behind my eyes. She was going to kiss me. A sparkling finale to this itinerant bacchanal.

Instead, we turned the corner. A scent—muted, pungent, well-known, unnamable—drew us to a neighborhood-seeming temple. I breathed in the only intimacy I understood: incense. We passed through stone gates and took our places with the old people, only old people, in front of a stone shrine laden with flowers and bowls of fruit, with long, marigold-colored candles, and figurines of women and gods. The elders made room for us as if every evening to this well of serenity came two redheads of the *bule* variety. The priest was heavyset with a curly black beard, swathed in a white wrap. He dipped long flower petals into silver vessels to sprinkle blessings over us, and shirtless old women passed incense without a blush about their saggy, naked boobs. They glowed with a what seemed to be their beatific norm. I could have kissed Lise for this gift.

After the ritual, the congregants disappeared without surrounding us with where are you from, where are you going, where are your husbands. Lise and I strolled in similar silence until we arrived at the bar she was looking for. Seated and drinking, she began, "Until 1597, when Dutch explorers arrived in Bali, the only Balinese women who wore shirts were sex workers. The Dutch, of course, thought the opposite." After our customary several rounds, I was certain I didn't say, "They raped those women." I only imagined Lise agreeing, "Pigs."

Hungover in the morning, I knew the truth: they raped them.

My only relief came from our nightly visits to the local temples that we sought out as we progressed toward central Java, where Lise promised to show me Borobudur, the largest Buddhist temple complex in the world. The intensely hot afternoon we arrived, stone statues of the Buddha three times Lise's height scattered across the first of what she told me were eight levels. The ground level clocked in at 401 by 401 feet. Each next-level-up decreased in size, and all were made of blueish-gray volcanic stone. I ran my hand along the scratchy bas-relief on the walls of the stairs to the second level, my veins pumping life in a way I'd never experienced. Although totally sober, I said, "I can't tell what's stone and what's not."

Lise's curls flew around with a surprising lack of sexual intent. She said to me, "My friend."

"My friend."

I reached to hold hands but dropped my arm before Lise could see. Even so, my loopy grin remained, up the third level, fourth, fifth. On the eighth sat a dome topped by a tower. We climbed as far up as people were permitted. No, definitely not; my hair was alluring, but I wasn't sexy. I just gave good head. Thank goodness for the three volcanoes rising above the dimming horizon, for all of Borobudur at sunset, mammoth pink and gold Lego pieces glowing the way I thought heaven would, when I was a kid.

"Hey, Lise. Do you believe in God?"

In my "hey," was a sound as blueish-gray as the stone. Lise peered into me the way she had the morning we left Ubud. I thought, She knows about my father.

All she said was, "I prefer the things people build to prove their belief."

"Then what's with the temple ceremonies?"

Lise brought out her beaded cigarette case. She did not open it. She stayed quiet for the time it would have taken to light up, inhale, and blow smoke. At last, she said, "In every holy place, I see the soothing of this pain in you I sense." Lise stroked her bedizened case. "It becomes right to ponder the karma of taking to bed another woman's husband."

Then she threw the case. Eight levels down.

Immediately after that, Lise winked the way she did at white guys when she had no intention beyond bumming a cig. On the way down, eight whole levels, I steamed like a volcano from our near miss at something real. That evening, on the overnight train to Java's capital, Jakarta, we were finishing our Bintang and fried noodles. I'd ordered the *mii goreng*, proud of even my grunty Bahasa, when Lise just had to, didn't she? She said, "Use *please* first. *Tolong mii goreng.*"

The train stopped at a station. Two white backpackers took seats at the far end of the car. I knew the drill: ignore them. If they came to us, toy with them; Lise allowed *bule* men that concession. I was poking at rather than eating my goddamn *tolong mii goreng* when, after the quickest look at the guys to establish eye-contact, Lise leaned in and flicked her tongue against my cheek. The bule all but hurtled to the seats across from us. Beer was three times as expensive on the train. They bought us several. When Lise led the more handsome to the platform between cars—how come she got to change the rules?—the need in his gait brought back my father's hurry to my bed.

One more week. Northern Java, Southern Malaysia. Temples, bule, beer, blowjob, bye. It really did get easier. The night before Lise flew home, she insisted that she treat me to my first whiskey. Macallan shots in a fancy place. They went down burning smooth. A third of a bottle disappeared—I was sure mostly into her, but heard myself begging, "No men tonight, 'k?"

"'K, my chick petite, all alone from now. How long goes your trip, after me?"

"Oh, I'll travel, survival kit. The Lonely Planet says people teach English."

"Oh, Mary. Mary, Mary. You are too young to teach, Mary. If you want to make money, sweet Mary, you do this."

Lise's slim arm floated to indicate a table across the room. Well-dressed white girls sat with Asian men. Lise told me that posh bars hired pretty bule to pour their drinks. No Pbbff. They even lent out clothes. Didn't give the impression of being entirely different than my M.O. of the last—how long? Except you didn't have to suck dick.

"Don't have to, right?" When did I start speaking out loud?

"Depends how much a lady wanted to earn. Enough to pay for a Ph.D?"

I know of real whoring. I sat with this new realization. In the end, I came to, "It never got easier. Do you know that? Never."

Lise cuddled me by the shoulders. That didn't stop her and that night's—but she'd promised—from tippling me into bed, just me and the upside-down geckos. I was scared they would fall off the ceiling. Lise once told me they had sticky feet. We hung on, me and the geckos. I could hear Lise and her guy through the wall. It'd never occurred to me to be drunk alone in my room instead of drunk with someone. I crawled off my bed so that I didn't have to listen.

"Mom!" I heard someone caw. "Mommy." My mother floated into the room, curled up with me on the terracotta floor. I stared at the ceiling, at times down from it. In the morning, Lise bequeathed me the Macallan and accompanied me to the transit terminal. We passed street stalls. The homey smell of frying eggs. I would eat those.

Right before Lise sent me up the steps to the bus, I readied to vault, no idea where I'd land. I wanted her to hug me. Instead, with a well-rehearsed dash of elegance, she said, "Stay pricelessly American, Mary." My head pounded with a combination of hangover, fury, and what was I going to do without her.

North

The bus Lise put me on was northbound. Near dusk, it left me in a no-horse village. No sights to see, no other travelers, A single, creaky hotel. If I'd snagged a guy like Lise always did for us, I wouldn't be alone while waiting for the proprietor.

Boom, four, five, six men formed a half-circle behind me. None even came to my shoulder, but that was a lot of men. One touched my boob.

I whacked his hand. Then the owner was there, saying something I couldn't understand, and all the guys laughed at the groper. I locked myself in the room I was given and paced until I simply had to drink. Lise's bottle drew down. It sure made easy images happen: smooth, green hills, sliding doors whooshing to the side. I overheard, "Oh, Little Matt, I ran out on you. Do they talk about me being gone?"

I said the last to the scruffy mirror above the sink. I hadn't seen my whole self naked in forever. I used to scrutinize myself in the ballet mirror to make sure nothing was getting fat, but I never really looked.

I pulled off the faded shorts and red shirt I was using as pajamas and would probably not change out of in the morning. Boobs were bigger than they used to ballet-be, but tummy flatter. Relief. Below that, I didn't want to know about. Guys in and out of my bed, never a last name. I picked up the phone. My home phone number flew out of my fingers. Wouldn't say anyth—just wanted—maybe Little would pick up.

The answering machine, Mom's outside-sales-rep voice as smooth as hair on a Ma-de Dean. "You've reached the Brew—"

—slam, receiver, my arm someone else's strong, white wing.

On the bed, I closed my eyes to the pulse of another long pull of Macallan. A couple of kimono ladies danced into the smooth green hills. They talked to me until dawn when I was outta that room so fast, outta that town, rage a churning lump in my stomach at the six who thought they could circle me, at Lise, at my—not my father. My mom? Didn't pursue the thought, just the bus from Kuala Lumpur north, crowded, seeming to carry nothing but staring men, staring. One white guy. He asked my name. Fuck, my head hurt. Soon as I turned eighteen, I'd make men stop.

However, when the white guy did that thing with the pack to make one cigarette pop up, the other men ceased ogling. I took his smoke, didn't think before answering, "Carlie." I hated sappy little follow-along American Mary.

The highway ended, Kuala Kangsar. Big, lonely city, so my wink made the guy suggest a beer. I requested whiskey. He ordered the local fire, called Mekong. He wasn't the brightest I'd ever come across, but never again would I let myself get stuck alone. Over the next spate of time, that occasionally meant N on the compass with fill-in-the-blank going on about the longest ride across the bumpiest road to find the most remote whatever. Northern Malaysia, southern Thailand, head. Smooth, green hills. Usually, after traveling together for a week—what week was it? I'd better start tracking; birthday was coming—whoever would want me to try hash. I stopped counting the number of times I became the speechy one. "Get caught with *banj* in this country, man, and it's prison for you."

You and anyone with you. Because we were arguing, I wouldn't have to suck him off. Five months proved that if I planned my vault for the a.m., he'd get drunk, get with a sex worker or someone as fresh from the egg as I used to be, and get over himself.

Six months. I was smoking through my afternoon walk, this time, along the canal in Chiang Mai, Thailand. In two hours, I was bus-bound for the Golden Triangle, where the northernmost part of Thailand squooshed into Burma and Laos. Sounded like what travel was supposed to be. Someone had told me there was a Coke machine.

And what-da-ya know: here, a Coke machine. I trashed my butt and bought a Diet. In eleven days, I would turn eighteen.

Ten feet downriver, a wooden houseboat. It thunked into the dock, came to life—ducks, kids, a mom with a genial wave. North of the Golden Triangle, Burma was open solely for day-visits. To the east, Laos was closed completely. Where could I go, after?

The smell of eggs frying. Magically, the mom crooked her finger, an invitation to come aboard. I ate those eggs.

Let Me Feel For You

Simon and I, and our best friends as of yesterday, the guitar-playing Israeli brother and sister, Nadav and Tallie, were in the line for the overnight train tickets, tip-top of Thailand south to Bangkok. Simon wanted to skip Bangkok, just transfer there straight to the train that would take us farther south, I patted through my pockets, no cigarettes, south to an island Simon talked about and the Israelis might go to, Koh Phangan—

I decided not to think about Simon's reasons for going to Koh Phangan. I wanted us to stay in Bangkok with the Israelis.

Simon tossed his Jesus hair to gesture me to the side. "The real dealing's meant to be on Pha—"

"Simon, do not mess with heroin. They hang you in this country for heroin." No wonder I liked to smoke. It burned.

Between our group and the dimly-lit ticket counter were a lean couple speaking German and a monk in a one-shouldered orange wrap. The monk looked like what my father would look like if my father were Thai and bald. I moved away from the monk. Nadav, with his eyes like chocolate cake, asked, "What's all your high-security whispers about?" and shook his pack so that out the top popped a single *siygaryah*—what these Israelis call a cigarette. My chin tilted as I took it, which Simon ignored because he was British, and British people are too British to call things out. He and I started hanging out on the bus to the Golden

Triangle. *Little Matt, Simon's a gentleman when he's not stoned and a prince when he is*—which was mostly. Sometimes I kidded myself that traveling with him if he were on heroin wouldn't be so bad. It was supposed to put you in a lovely mood, after the puking, the heroin. Except they killed you if they caught you with it. You and anyone with you.

It was our turn at the ticket window. Tallie gave Simon and me the once-over and didn't ask, just got four single-sleepers. Later, shelved and clacking south, I hung upside down, my bunk into hers. No hair dangled. Mine was back to Hong Kong creamy blonde, but the forever heat and humidity had made me shear it off almost completely. Butt up, head down, I nudged aside Tallie's guitar as I asked her how she knew she didn't need to ask.

"Oh, Carlie. Carlie, Carlie. I have screwed around so much more than you." Then she said, "Don't make the toy of Nadav. He hurts easily." In the morning, Tallie chose for all of us to spend some time in Bangkok. She knew dick about me and screwing.

How did that happen, Matt? It is already our fifth day in Bangkok. At the drippy end of the afternoon rain, I stood around, pat-pat, pocket-pocket, under an awning leaking less and less water onto the corners of narrow Chakrapong Road and wide Khao San Road. *Chakrapong Chakrapong, let me feel for you* strutted through my head on the high heels of a nicotine attack. No backpackers to bum from on the notoriously traveler-y street, and I'd left my smokes at the guesthouse, Happy Birthday to me. Without a pack to whack against my palm, I had no clue what to do with my hands. *Eighteen years old today, Matt, and no clue what to do with my hands.* What ho! Two white guys straggling down the sidewalk. The lanky guy's t-shirt was drenched, and the other, Mr. Pecs, didn't bother with one. If either had a backpack or the rumpled exhaustion that said, "Well, that was fourteen hours on the bus"—if any of that were in play, I'd swap info, guesthouses and places to eat for a smoke. Plenty of times, I wouldn't have to swap. White guys, man; that's a straightforward undertaking. Wink, "Got a cig?" "*Siygaryah?*" That's how Nadav met me. No backpacks and straggly in the afternoon, though, that pair was straight out of the whorehouses of Pat Pong, fuck them, but I still needed a smoke.

The rain shook out its last. At the end of the street was a neighborhood wat and a monk, a different, orange-swathed monk. His bald head reminded me of a cabbage. Chances of a cigarette, double goose egg.

Relieved by the rain-cleared fresh air, I crossed a bridge over a grey-green river—

bridge grey-green water down there; rocks?

—landing on a tree-studded market street where a zillion barbecued ducks hung by their headless necks. A man with a brisk air about him called, "Noodles?"

No way I was eating all that fattening glop. The next stall was produce. A Barbie-pink kimono paraded to the front. The person wearing it carried a pure white rat and batted—his?—fan in time with his downcast eyes, blinkity-blink. I stared down the pet's pink eyes. Did he dress to match his rat?

"Hallo, pretty girl. *Rambutan?*" High-pitched but he-sounding voice; he waved a radish-bunch of fruit, each piece golf ball-sized with spiky red rinds, moving the rat to his pink shoulder as he cut open a rambutan—"Ten baht"—deftly but carefully peeling away the spiky stuff to offer the milky-colored flesh, peeling and fleshy flesh, asking where you from, where you go, where you husband.

"I'm not married."

Matt, he made the face they all make when I say I'm not married. Like they suddenly noticed I had a charred limb.

"But you pretty. Pretty body."

My sister had the pretty body.

The man from the noodle booth leaned across. "He ladyboy. You get? Ladyboy," and teased the ladyboy in gunboat Thai. The ladyboy took a girly swing at Noodles with his fan, but as he turned, blinkity-blink, he pulled me flash into his life, a ladyboy because he didn't know how to be anything else, his fingernails, their swishing, the old, white men and their saggy stomachs, when all he wanted to do was die.

I became the white rat, staring from his sweet pink Barbie-pink shoulder, then I bounced to the top of my old Barbie's Dream House—Mom got rid of that when I was about ten years old— staring at my own bed in my own room at home, staring at a man's shape on my bed, a man who filled one hand with the soft bulb of thigh near my crotch as he jerked off; it was pulling, the string that pulled up, pulling my head off—I wouldn't let it. Slam, a five-baht coin on the counter. I thunked it down hard enough to hurt my hand—

"Pretty girl, you say ten."

—on the bridge, not exactly hearing him say, Okay you come back, then, clearly, Eat shit—let me feel for you—Chakrapong. And corner, same corner. Khao San and Chakrapong Roads. String tugged.

Stay here, birthday girl. Stay. Look. Look at Khao San Road. Backpackers, now, and vendors. Tug tug, no, no—

Stay.

There were guys winkety winking at me, guys to bum from, there were *Tracey Chapman* t-shirts and pirated David Bowie tapes and Levi's, I can't—

I can't breathe Chakra—

I can't brea—

"Miss? G'day?"

It was a guy. A normal traveler guy, backpack with sleep roll up top, his shirt on and the whole thing.

" . . . a good guesthouse?"

Of course I knew a good guesthouse. "Jalan Jaksa."

No. Jalan Jaksa was the backpacker neighborhood in Jakarta. That was six months ago.

How did six months happen?

"I'm disappearing."

"Miss?"

"K'I bum a cig?"

The string won.

The Bangkok air carried the tinge of coconut oil.
Every day got stickier than it started out.

City street solid under my feet. *That's good, Matt. Means the white space is clearing. This is our guesthouse. Don't ask me how I found my way back, but here I am, knock knock.*

This is the room I share with Simon. No windows, no mirror, our little room. Simon, stretched out on the bed, a cigarette in his mouth and a sheet wrapping his pelvis. *Every time I see him thus-trussed, I flash to Christ in a drugstore frame.*

Simon raised his head. "Love." Almost as soothing as nicotine. I sifted down to him. Simon never asked why I ducked out before the afternoon rain. He used the time to get high.

He stroked my arm. "I say, we'll need more."

Simon meant hash, but he was British, so it was: we'll need more. Like I'd had so much as a hit.

I should have made him go find hash and, while he was away, gone to that island with the Israelis. Vault: Nadav.

That stoner psychic Simon could always tell when I was thinking about Nadav. He leapt naked out of bed.

"My queen! A boon!"

I coughed with laughter. "Who are you? Robin Hood?"

"Allow me to—"

"King Arthur?"

"—protect you from these Bangkokian streets!"

"Is that even a word?"

Simon flailed madly, faking a sword fight. The only thing floppy on him went flop. "That blasted cow!"

"Cow?"

Oh, man. Something else went on that I didn't remember. Obviously last night, with one of the sacred cows kept by the local wat, mammoth creatures continuously wandering into the surrounding streets. I chewed deeply into a fingernail to keep from screaming, "I didn't drink that much." How was I on the street? A young boy was selling sarong—who was Simon anyway? Some guy I met a eleven days ago on his way north hoping to drop a coin into The Golden Triangle.

"Please buy sarong, lady," said the sweet boy *Little* I turned away from—

Almost bumped into two white guys, jerked my chin, "Hey, man. Got a smoke?" Nice enough guys. Cheap cigarettes, *siygaryah siygaryah*, but nice enough guys, bye bye—Lise flew home. Malaysia Thailand blowjob. Bangkok north, north.

I'd gone north, did what had always worked, got Simon, had a new guy lined up, Golden Thai tip top Triangle. But there was no more north. Where was I supposed to go next? I couldn't write in my head to Matt: Where was I supposed to go?

South.

From Bangkok, the train left at dusk, sunset jungle outside my window doing nothing to fix what felt like hawk talons—I knew what would, but I would not ask. Two women in nearby seats, wouldn't peg the Asian one as a traveler—who wore white to travel in? Great look; they took out rice wrapped in banana leaves and strange dried meats. That spicy meat smelled good.

I found my smokes and lit up. Simon and Tallie left to blaze it on the platform between cars and, presto, Nadav, his eyes like sex on the move, unearthed an amber-filled bottle. My tension was the plastic seal, cracking. Nadav tuned his guitar, sang high and clear, yum yum, golden hum; I babysat the Mekong and the harmonica—*Can't like Dylan as much as me without playing harmonica*. Across the aisle, the tall white lady smiled, a smile like she was singing along. That time Lise licked me, it was not to get me; it was to get the men. Laurence, song about rain buckets, army-green tank top smooth meat shoulder blowjob—

Conductor, white jacket, black pants, seats pulled into single sleepers upper, lower. Move-your-hips song. Simon announced that he would take the top bunk. When did—he came back?

"You will not." When did I?

Tallie took out her guitar. "No fights. Let her have it, Simon."

" . . . can sleep on top of me any night."

Nadav looking at me. Simon looking at me. Simon shoved his backpack into the bottom bunk. Nadav still looking at, me. That shark-catcher metal rope hauled me toward Simon. Closed the curtain, bye bye Nadav mad eyes. Simon stroked my arm. Twice since we met, Simon undressed me the way the ladyboy peeled the rambutan. When Simon was blunted, though, Tallie was right. His hand would never slide farther nor grope harder. Oh, man; Nadav's would.

Simon and I became the clatter of the train.

Put the moment in a glass jar.

Keep it forever.

At still-dark the next morning, crisp white jacket and black—ow, lights on—snappy taps on bunks, up and down the aisle. Simon and I lagged after fifteen or so backpackers who transferred to a bus. The Israelis sat at the back. They didn't save us seats. As we approached, Nadav plugged his Walkman into his ears; coming off him, the scent of lonely sleep.

Behind him, a tall lady stood, the white one whose smile sang at me on the train. She indicated her friend.

"If ya'd prefer to sit with your mates, I'll shove over."

She rolled her *r*'s like bells ringing, totally Scottish. I said, "Cool"—goddamn, my head hurt—as Simon turned down her offer as if refusing one too many tea cakes. It all happened anyway. The Israelis stayed non-communicative. We drove to a pier, where whatever God was pressed the "Commence Sweating" button.

The tall lady with the long r's was next to us again. "We're waiting for the train due in from Malaysia."

Tallie asked her, "How long until this train?"

Simon did his *Appear* thing. "I say, you've made this trip?"

"I say," Nadav snorted through his cigarette.

The tall lady said, "I'm Ava. You-lot are bloody good on the guitar—Cho!" Ava waved over the Asian lady. "Come 'round."

Cho came 'round at a pure dally. Ava chattered—their destination was the same as ours, Haad Rin Village on the island's south side, but their plans included the tai chi school that was just up the hill from the village. Having seen old people waving their arms around in parks across Southeast Asia, I knew what tai chi was.

Deducing that these were not the smack-dealing womenfolk he sought, Simon reverted to elementally bored. Nadav did that thing with the pack to flip up a single for Cho goddamit *siygaryah*. The flint against my heart could have lit her cigarette, but Cho gave that honor to Nadav, nothing like kindly, more like he was a folder of data she'd seen before. While Ava and Tallie talked about tai chi, Cho's eyes found me, then Simon. Reaching Simon, a smidgen of revulsion moved under her skin as far as her cliff-like cheekbones.

At last, she introduced herself. Her accent was pure American. Cho Yamashita. First traveler I'd met with a last name.

Cho interrupted Ava's bright banter, "Maybe these people don't need to know our whole lives," with an amiable little poke.

"Oh, deary me, has the aimless prattling begun?"

The sun was now well into the sky. Even conversation between Ava and Tallie hung by its headless neck. The waiting part of traveling; man, all there was to do was smoke and—

The air felt free.

She should be calling for money about now, Patrice.

At least one of us got ten grand out of them.

—the boat jerked into a launch. We roasted for over four hours before reaching Phangan's main town, Thong Sala. The six of us got into an old red skiff and spent forty minutes low to the water and cool from the spray. We puttered around a southern tip that reached into the ocean like a beckoning finger. The sunlight was so bright, it was like living in yellow. I grew into a ribbon the color of the velvety blues of the water surrounding us, stunning against the greens and soft browns of the nearby beach lined with cliffs. We rounded a bluff to come into a vast, sapphire-blue bay, then came up on a sparsely populated beach, perfect in its vanilla-colored sand, its fringe of palm trees. There was no warning. The string simply lifted me into the clouds.

Phangan glowed purple below, a closed fist turned to the sky, the one, long pointer its only extended finger. It guided me back to my body.

Matt, I wonder why that wasn't scarier, like if all the booze was wrecking my mind.

I took that back. Matt didn't need to know that part.

A movement to my left drew me into the intensity of Ava's gaze. She appeared to know what had just happened. I busied myself with the wade through hip-deep baby-blue water to a beach the color of my hair. The waves were mere ripples.

Its sand under our feet, Phangan appeared standard-issue traveler-island: gorgeous. Except for the stringy white women with darting eyes who wandered the beach in nothing but bikini bottoms. They scratched a lot. I spotted cats.

Ava gestured over a hill rising to the south. There was a Leela Beach Resort they always stayed in. "No bigger than a postage stamp," Ava said. Tallie decided on it for her clan, and I was whatever, but Simon wanted to stay in town. "Where the action is." *This should be it, Matt, where he goes his way and I go north—south, now; wherever, not Simon*—but there we were, Nadav and Tallie gone Leela Beaching and me and Simon, Jesus-hair tosses, a sweaty hour squabbling, it was gonna be what Simon wanted to do or what Nadav would want me to do. I was about to buy a Diet—Oooooo, ice cream, vanilla with caramel running through it; they had popsicles. I should have one of those instead. Only ninety calories.

Simon dropped into whispers with a beefy man by a shack they called Hello Hotel. I overheard, "Full Moon party." Simon's new best friend's laugh was as thick as muggy weather and he strode away, a confident invisible towing Simon after him.

And that was that.

Stay, birthday girl. Look at the—what? The path, the hot dirt path, up and over the jagged hill behind which the sun was beginning its descent. Look, a narrow beach, a wooden footbridge. Ava was hurtling my direction.

"Hey ya, wee mucker, babble babble."

There was something appealing about Ava that I was starting to hate. "Where'd the Israelis go?"

"You mean your new fella?"

"I'm so sure." Truth be told, Ava gave off a joy that resonated like the bells of her rolling r's.

"Now, lass; don' be crabbit."

"What does that even mean?" I had to hustle to catch up with her leggy skip.

"That strapping young gent oodles prettiness. Heaps better'n—"

"Man, half the time—"

"—that bampot Brass Monkey."

"—I can't understand—" I'd never met anyone who celebrated dips in the path, as Ava did now, with a "Tra-loo!" Or who capered the up-hills. Capered. I kept waiting for the ironic part.

In the dusk, Ava had me at a bungalow. Cho perched on the porch, tidier than ever in a fresh sarong and white tank top. When Ava said, "Your mates went along to Sunset House," Cho's "No room at the inn," recalled Simon's disinterest on the boat, and Nadav's not entirely sober "sleep on top of me." The uneasy combination prompted me to offer Cho a smoke.

Ava climbed into the hammock as Cho surveyed my bribe. She said, "Ava's allergic."

I lit up.

Cho maintained an even expression. "How old are you?"

"How old are you?"

Ava said, "I'm thirty-three, the age Christ died."

"Are you always this weird?"

Ava crossed her arms like armor. I didn't expect that strength out of her. She said, "As you asked, a mucker is your mate. An' a Brass Monkey is what we Scots call a heroin addict."

"He's never even tried it!"

"Gi' him until full dark."

Cho added, "After which, you will never see him again."

I was so out of there, flinging my own cigarette, a missile, at the rocky cliff bordering a wooden-planked footbridge, I was almost above it, Simon at the base of the finger pointing him toward he won't shoot up, won't shootup wontshootup, running straight to our hotel, why grateful for our door, our room? Dark.

"Simon?"

No answer. I snapped on the light. In the glint of time before

I turned it off and ran—a syringe, a belt. Cotton balls dotted with blood. His puke. The string didn't have to pull.

Somewhere in there, I bought a fifth. Three quick glugs. I wasn't enough to stop him. Two more. The drunker I got, the more I hated life on the new hand of Phang—I wobbled to Haad Rin. On the main beach, the party came into view. A band played from an open-air restraint, maybe a hundred travelers writhed, writhed to a Bon Jovi cover, splashing phosphorescence over each other in the shallows and drinking and smoking lotta hash on driftwood logs. There! My Israelis, coming toward me with a new group of friends. They, checking. I'm good, I'm good. I leaned toward Tallie, teetered into Nadav, who took my hand, into the squirming human mass, now raucous Irish rock. The Pogues battered away all *whoosh*

Red, red wine, white people were screaming along, and to the next song, *Mar-leee!* My hips and shoulders round and round, a kimono lady with no kimono. The Israelis' new friends watched with Tallie from a rock. Another girl, a zero-fat blondie with gravity-resistant tits, the bottom halves practically peeked out every time she took a drag. We had a kitty when I was a kid. He came to me most. My sister, my Patrice, her eyes became little slices of fury. Blondie, slice, when Nadav, forearms around my waist—I let kitty out, knowing he would never come back. There was no cat to let out now, when slice when Nadav guided me into his chest, my nose and mouth against his shoulder.

" . . . do mushrooms with me?"

Bam. I was back.

Nadav steered me to a quiet log, where he fished a fold of paper from his pocket. They looked like regular old, dried mushrooms. I hesitated for the barest moment before holding out my hand. Tasted like bitter wood. I guzzled his water and waited for Technicolor cartoons.

Nothing happened. "So, how long does this take?"

"Could be fifteen minutes, could be more. Drink water."

"Let's. The beach." This time, I took his hand. We climbed the hill. By the time we came down the other side to the narrow beach, the wind was so like feathers that each hair on my body clarified silver. I saw the stars. I could taste them. A giggle. That couldn't be me; I didn't giggle. "Nadav, can you taste the stars?"

He giggled back. "Carlie is tripping." He lifted me easily and swung me around, newlyweds across an imagined threshold except there was no bed—only sand and sand, endless sand, endless sea, endless sky, endless night we fell all over each other near some rocks, half in, half out of our clothes. His mouth and skin were strange-meat delicious. With guys, this was where I started doing whatever would get the thing over with but tonight, tonight, I wanted the sensation forever, to last and last so I could keep feeling Nadav on me and the sand under me, every granule as I ground against him, up and up. Tonight. Tonight. He whispered, "Carlie," and over the brink I was riding close, free-falling. Heat pulsed from my center down my limbs, swirled into the last little tingles between my fingers. I couldn't believe it. I came, too.

Still kissing. Our breathing slowed. Nadav pulled up my clothes, devoted, caring for me. "You were amazing. No girl ever loved it like tha—"

I shot above. It was not my eighteen-year-old body down there. A child, maybe fourteen years old, I could barely see her skinny legs splayed under my father. Flattening me—I couldn't breathe. I was above; I couldn't breathe. My father made me come. *You loved it.*

Down a tunnel a trainload of shame. Smash. No one would ever make me come. Ever again.

"Carlie! What?"

Nadav was trying to calm me, saying it was the drugs. He was way bigger, but I was electric with the need to stop men. It was everything in the world to shove him away. Down the shore, a dip in the beach was a good reason to throw myself onto my stomach—cold sand, harsh breath. "Matt! Matt." I rolled over, stared into sky slipped through my fingers I wanted to miss Mom to miss Patrice but I never did. Not once. Not really. It never got easier. I must have passed out because I started from some dead zone to find the black softening into gray then pink, pink, blinkity-blink, time-lapse photography. Someone stood over me, troubled face, determined bones. Tallie?

Mom.

She was Asian. She said, "Boy, you don't look great."

What's-her-name, the clean lady who hated me.

"You're Carlie, right?"

"Jen! My name is Jen."

She sat on the sand, her arms draped over her bent knees, her back curved like a spoon. I could fall off the world. No one would notice. Maybe my thoughts were really loud, because she said, "I would, Jen."

"I didn't answer, before. I'm eighteen. Double goose egg—oh, Jesus. I was just a little kitten."

More might spill out, my birthday, my father—did she just say, "I believe you"—all the men, the mushrooms, the ladyboy; "I am him," I said, I knew I said that, "and he is me." When I was finally totally silent, she watched me until her hands slid down her strong calves to easily reach her polished toes. Her gentle rocking ebbed into the part of my body left vacant by the weight of everything I'd never told anyone.

Seattle

I was watching myself from beside myself. I saw myself crouched in the dim light of the hall stairs, eavesdropping on my father and Lyle, one of my father's best friends. They were whispering about my sister.

"Patrice has gotten mighty curvy all of a sudden," Lyle said, not a compliment, and my father agreed in the carpet voice he used only with Lyle and Ted. That was when I left for the ceiling. I was light, looking down at myself on the stairs—same Catholic uniform as all the girls, but I knew it was coming. For three years, they'd left me home to take care of Little when they took Patrice to Lyle's cabin in the mountains. I never asked, and Patrice never told, but each time Patrice came home, she looked swollen.

Next time they went, they left Patrice at home with Little.

It was Friday night. Lyle's cabin was brown and boring. I watched from beside myself as Lyle, Ted, and my father played pool and drank. My father and Lyle bellowed, "You never forget your first girl." Ted was a lizard. They were the stupidest people I had ever seen.

"Rack 'em!"

Ted removed his ring. He said, "Looks like we are out of beer," and with a gesture like a monarch of yore leading troops, my father placed his pool cue in the holder on the wall. He fetched a green bottle with a narrow neck, "Glenfiddisch" printed on the rectangular black label. Mom drank that stuff. When I was little, I thought she drank "Glen fishes."

Lyle removed his ring. I went into the smooth sides of the Glenfiddisch bottle, exactly like the cool thing I stroked when I was young and Mom drank. At home, my father never got drunk. In the forest, his mouth opened and closed before anything came out. He took off his ri—

It was Patrice they had here. It was anyone but me. I was home. "Rack 'em." My father had no chance of winning, everyone knew that. The contest was between Ted and Lyle.

Ted won. I was gone. After Ted came Lyle, then my father. The next night, Lyle won.

It was Sunday morning. Everything was pain. Lyle helped me pull on a sweater. Its long sleeves hid the bruises on my arms, gray smudges, purple, I didn't notice until right then. Those marks were on my thighs, too. Some big. I saw them the first time I changed my pad. My father had given me a full box. My sister got her first period when she was about my age, just about the time Lyle's daughter started looking curvy. Patrice didn't get it again until, like, a year ago. Mom told her a girl's cycle didn't always regulate right from the beginning.

Patrice didn't get her period that first time.

In Ted's jeep on the way home, they smelled like cologne. We pulled into a truck stop—big orange sign, Truck Stop Seven—where they encouraged me to order anything I wanted. I gobbled two vanilla sundaes with caramel sauce and puked in the parking lot. Oh, the fuss! They sponged off my face, carried me to the jeep. Lyle clicked me in as if he were caring for royalty. Ted told my father to give me a mint. We drove by a pay phone. I could call someone, call the police? Help me.

They wouldn't believe me. My father wiped my face one last time. Did any of that happen, at the cabin?

As we passed through the last tunnel into Seattle, my reflection in the car window stared back at me, swollen.

At home, Patrice called me a bitch. Like she did when our kitty loved me more. There was nothing to do but watch her dress for school, her sweater tighter than usual, her mini more mini. I couldn't eat. On my bed, I curled this way then that, refusing to leave my room, refusing to go to school or even ballet. Across the room, my first pair of toe shoes dangled on the wall by their long, pink ribbons. I was so proud to buy them, back when it mattered who moved up to *pointe* class. Blisters formed before *barre* exercises ended. They popped during *adagio*. By the time you got to jumps, your blood dried your pale tights to the insides of your toe shoes. Removing them after class was tricky work. I loved the pain, the blood, the proof that I was working hard. As of now, I was done with pain and blood.

That night, I listened to Patrice get calls from boys. I could tell they were boy calls because when Dad or Matt said, "Patrice! Phone!" she answered, "I got it!" in thrilled ups and downs. Three got-its. I dropped into my chest, an interminable hole, the bottom of the universe, its empty, cold weight on top of me. I went to that speck of light. It kept me alive.

When Mom returned from her business trip, she hovered over me, smoothing her already smooth hair. She asked, "Hon, was Jen like this all weekend?"

"I don't thi ... Maybe it's—you know. Starting."

Mom took my temperature. Dragon snort of rosé and cigarette smell onto my face. "C'mon, Jenny-Jen-Jen. There is nothing wrong with you."

My mother, Earth First Cosmetics' top outside-sales rep, had decided there was nothing wrong with Jenny-Jen-Jen.

Receiving no response, Mom turned to my father. He stroked her arm. "I'll swing her by the doctor's tomorrow."

Lyle was our doctor.

Lyle was our doctor. My father gave him the lead on the cabin, and Ted was their lawyer. Our families spent Christmas together. Christmas, Easter, Fourth of July. These were our friends. These were our only friends. The sole answer was to spread my wings and fly to a land where kind people danced in temples as the sun rose and set.

My parents left. I stared at the ceiling, sometimes down from it. Little Matt came into my room. He didn't knock because nobody knocked in this house, but he hesitated for a respectful three beats in the doorway before embarking on a cautious path across the floor, a sub in enemy waters. He pulled onto the edge of my bed. We sat like that, unable to be anything but mute. A stench like a sewer welled up inside me, pressed hard against my throat. I locked my jaws against it and wrapped my arms across my chest. I would not cry. They would not make me cry. It was Patrice for three years. Now it would be me; not only the weekends Mom was out of town, but also the many nights a week she worked late. A pall would descend on the house, horrible and sticky, and we would wait—me, in my room, and Little and Patrice in Patrice's room, in the fort they built of pillows and blankets. Because each of us felt it during Patrice's time, each of us would feel it in mine, our father moving: kitchen, den, kitchen, patio. He would stare at Puget Sound and the Space Needle; each of us as protected as we could be from the moment he could no longer fight himself and came into my room.

Finally, I understood why Patrice never fought him, why she knowingly waited, a flower to be plucked. There was no way out. Those men would do to my body what they wanted, but they would never never never get to me. I would keep them out until I was old enough and strong enough to make them stop, and one day I would make them hurt, too.

Little put his hand on my knee. He was only eight. In this house, where did he learn empathy? I couldn't take it. I hit his hand away. I said, "Get out."

Koh Phangan, Thailand

The Great Ultimate

I jerked awake, no idea where I was or when. The angle of the sun said early afternoon, but, as far as I could tell, I'd been on Phangan less than twenty-four hours, half of them out of my head, so I couldn't be sure. My hands automatically sought the comforting bulk of the fanny pack at my waist. Where'd it—there, on the nightstand. Money, passport, ticket; just like when I bought the Mekong before the Full Moon party.

This room. It was nicer than the places I'd been sharing with all those guys. Those had a sense of smallness. This room might not have been much bigger, but the woods were polished and a sarong draped around the window, a flower, there, gave it grace. A candle waited for night. This wiggly familiarity was undercut by the sensation of wearing another girl's clothes. A rustle from the porch. The Asian lady with the amazing cheekbones came through the door, ducking to miss the low frame, saying, "You're up," saying it with the same confident yet questioning expression she wore when she found me on the beach, when she said she believed me. She believed me.

After a moment, she said, "Sorry, I'm not sure of your name."

"Carlie." I must have told her Jen. Cho, that was her name. Why did I tell her all that stuff, doing mushrooms with Nadav, doing Nadav, doing all those loser guys from the last six months? Did I tell her that I stole the money? I'm sure I told her about my father. What about Ted and Lyle? She believed me. She said she,

she—said so.

Cho did not sit. I dug my hands—whap whap no smokes—into the thin blanket. The blanket and I pressed against the wall. "Man, everything hurts. Where's . . . what's her name? The skinny one."

"Ava." The slight displeasure in Cho's tone made me understand that I'd intended to piss her off. At the same time, I intuited I was wearing her t-shirt.

Cho said, "Ava wanted to be here when you woke up." To my dragon's exhale, Cho continued, "I know Ava can be intense. Boy, does she get that. She can't always control—anyway, she's at tai chi practice. You and I need to speak alone."

I squeezed even harder against the wall. Cho perched on the edge of the bed. "Is there anyone we can contact for you?"

Scratchy blanket. The entire world, a cat's tongue covering my knees.

"A relative who's not involved, like an aunt?"

There were some. New Hampshire. Connecticut. I'd met a couple of them like, twice.

"How 'bout a teacher?"

"I am a stray cat."

Cho smoothed her loose, onyx-colored hair into a short-lived ponytail. "That guy, the Israeli—"

"Nadav?"

"He came looking for you this morn—"

"We were together when I freaked out. I mean, man, it was"—I actually blushed; I don't blush—"Like, I've never . . . Never. You can kind of see why guys . . ."

There was no end to that thought. The next, "I was above," made the world spin just like it did when I came. I came.

Across the bed, Cho offered me her handkerchief. She carried a handkerchief. "Boy, Carlie, we need to find you some help."

"Why can't you help me?"

Cho moved her gaze to the wall as if it were a window. "That's really more Ava's purview than it is mine."

"I don't want her."

"Well. You see, I left social work years ago."

I said, "You're so mean. You're just gonna let me—"

"I'm on vacation."

"Just—just—"

Out of frustration, Cho found, "Just come to tai chi."

Cho's "Okay?" didn't wait for my, "Okay." She was out the door. I skulked after her, furious enough to catch up so that I could say, "Can't I get a drink first?" with the same piss-her-off feeling as when I'd said, "The skinny one." Between us felt like a cigarette lighter about to spark. We were climbing the dirt path, when who should appear at the top but a long-legged form that could only be Ava?

"Hey, ya," she sang out. "You lot didn't put in an appearance. We can't have you missing your first lesson, Carlie. Tai chi is pure dead brilliant. It changed my life."

For a moment, Ava's forehead drew toward her eyes, like she was sadder than anyone could articulate. In a heartbeat, all that melted off. She swooped in, linked arms, her Scottish r's sticking to me like wet flaps of seaweed. I shook her away. In the fifteen-minute walk over the hill and along a cliff, I don't know why Ava took it upon herself to reveal the entire history of tai chi.

" . . . in the wee town of Shao Lin, which is in China."

I knew that, China. I glared at Cho.

" . . . temple monks were a fat, lazy lot . . . developed exercises based on yoga . . ." Then something about nine years in a cave. Stick Ava in a cave. Though her sentences were scrubbed of indigestible Scottish slang, all those words were too many to come out of one mouth. I searched my pockets for my cigs.

" . . . five basic styles . . . most widely known are *Chen* and *Yang*. We do Yang."

"Got a cigarette?" I asked Cho, who shocked me by handing one over. The sensible girl smoked Camels. Ava was almost boogieing along the footpath.

" . . . in Yang you find Chen strength, as there is romantic splendor in Chen." She twirled. "The natural polarities pull in opposite directions, leaving space for you in between."

Sounded like *Star Wars* to me. And, by the way, Ava was bats.

We turned off the path and continued down a set of steps cut into the hillside to confront a large clearing, a packed-dirt beach licked by kitten waves and fringed by palm trees. Three rickety bungalows sat at its southern edge. A few feet from the beach—cue the next set of travelers—about twenty white backpacker-types practiced Kung fu-looking fighting combinations, all done super slow. The guys had nice muscles and more earrings than the girls, who were skin-and-smoke or just fat enough to look best in baggy shorts. I caught myself assessing the men.

Little. I could break right open.

Before I could back up the steep staircase, Cho hugged and then introduced me to a woman whose hair was a cape of brown curls. Gemma, the American who ran the school, shook my hand with both of her sturdy ones. Her New Jersey accent was harsh but welcome. I could not bear one more ounce of Ava's happy-crappy woo woo. Gemma was old, forty or something, and lived in the chicken shack buildings, leading morning and afternoon practices. She indicated for me to follow her between the palm trees at the back of the clearing, where she showed me how to tuck my pelvis and depress my chest, forming a soft half-circle with my upper body. It went against years of ballet training.

Gemma tied her curls into a knot. "No biggie. Most of us have to learn to chill."

Next, Gemma told me to pretend to hold a beach ball. She called it the tai chi ball. "Palms face each other, a foot apart. Right hand above, left below. Breathe. Rotate the ball so the left hand is above and the right below. Palms face each other," she reminded me. "Rotate again."

I rotated, I reversed. When I remembered to breathe, a

pleasant rhythm took over. When I messed up, Gemma got me back on track. About the time I registered the all-over headache as gone, Gemma interrupted with two claps.

"The form, please."

The hippies lined up facing the ocean. Since I had no clue what Gemma was talking about, I crept to a palm tree. The class stood silently, backs rounded, chests depressed, knees slightly bent, arms dangling at their sides like an upside-down horseshoe without that rigidity. An impossible position. They were all doing it. Gemma stood between the group and the sea. She faced everyone, her right hand forming a fist about sternum level. She moved her left hand to rest with the palm softly over her fist. The class gestured identically.

I thought, *May the Force be with you.* I couldn't help it.

Gemma turned so that she, too, faced those teeny, tiny waves. A sterling stillness passed, then everyone began moving with the unity of a school of fish. They rotated the tai chi ball as they turned. They dipped to the ground and punched, spun on one leg, wonderfully able to maintain their balance, then slow-mo kicked with the other leg. After what must have been fifteen minutes, they stood as they had to start, facing the water, come full circle. So that was the form. I was holding my breath.

"What d'ya think?"

Ava popped up out of nowhere. For the first time since the train, she came across as sweet, those skies of eyes filled with all that hope. I said, "Kinda cool."

Her arm came through mine. "Tai chi gives you strength. To do anything. You know that, don'cha? You can tell me anything?"

Her father.

I ran, not fully aware that I was running until I heard "Carlie!" from behind. I charged the steep steps leading from the practice area to the path along the cliff. My smoker's lungs caught up with me half-way up the stairs. Two guys from the class—they were cute—were passing a water bottle. One winked.

"K'I have a sip?" I barged in with practiced, graceless panache, interrupting the easy patter of Swedish or Norwegian. Asking in that flirty way soothed me. The guys: one of them would pass the water and the other would have the smokes. Everything would get back with the program.

The guys exchanged a nod, both of their mouths down at the corner in a way I'd seen a lot from Northern Europeans. The smiley one handed me the bottle. I peered into his eyes with the right amount of chin tilt.

The other said, "Do you smoke?"

Ava dashed up. "Carlie, I need to speak with you. Privately."

The guys took to the steps. With the cig that was supposed to be mine. I said, "No, wait—" but they were gone, leaving me with this creepy madwoman. "Butt out!"

Cho arrived. I was still shouting at Ava. "Man, what is your problem? And you!" I swung a damning finger at Cho, who started to speak. "Shut up! You told her!"

Cho all but whispered, "That was really unprofessional—"

"Well, you're not much of a professional, are you? I was only twelve. How could anyone do that to a twelve-year-old?"

Ava reached. I pushed away. "No!" To Cho, "Answer me!"

"This is why I left social work, Carlie. There are no answers."

"There are," Ava said. "Carlie knew about me the way I knew about her. That's God, Carlie. That's God. I was wee, as well. Fourteen. But mind you, Carlie. Do tai chi. You build joy."

"I'd settle for a stiff drink." I hoped my harsh tone would wound her as much as it shredded my heart.

"I know ya would. You don't have to."

The rumble in my ears was a rockslide, only silent. Into the quiet, Ava said, "Tai chi translates as The Great Ultimate."

"More like the great ultimatum." But it was like when she crossed her arms yesterday. Something made sense just when you were about to bash her over the head.

With a rather grumpy look toward Ava, Cho assured me that

tai chi demanded no ultimatums. "In fact, it is the opposite of ultimatums." When I refused to loosen my spine, she said, "Carlie, would you like to have dinner with us?"

I gave her my cruelest dragon snort. Cho climbed one stair. With an impish, not-very-Cho grin, she climbed another.

During dinner they ordered Cokes, not beer, Ava a diet, Cho a classic. I sensed I should do the same. My diet went in a flash, and I had no cigarettes, leaving me with nothing to do but eat my damn food. Cho devoured hers. Ava sorted the vegetables and squid from their fragrant sauce and paid no attention to her rice. I tried the same but couldn't battle the comfort of those soft mounds or the coconut curry like velvet. Impossibly full, I leaned back. Every other table in the place held a chirpy group swilling beer. A blond guy, maybe the guy from the tai chi steps with the cigarette offer, I let him catch my eye. God, I knew how that would go; great for the first few—you're drinking and screwing, okay, so now that I knew what coming was like, maybe not coming but at least he was there against the night, until he wanted me to get high with him—where was Nadav, anyway? He should be trying to find me.

Still in eye contact with the cigarette guy, I heard Ava. "Why ya cryin', wee mucker?"

With my pointer finger, I smeared up a few drops from my cheek and gazed at them. "I'll never make anything work. K'I bum a cig?"

Cho said, "How old are you?"

I reached for my empty glass. "Twenty."

"How old are you, Carlie?"

"Just turned eighteen."

"Eighteen-year-olds buy their own cigarettes. Anyway, Ava's allergic. We don't smoke where there is no breeze."

I looked to Ava. "You two are the weirdest couple."

"Speaking of which," Ava's voice sailed over the touch of a scowl Cho shot my way. "Our room has two doubles, if you'd like to use one tonight."

"Oh, man. I forgot. A room." I led us out of the restaurant before another lecture could land on me. They crashed as soon as their heads hit the pillows. The longer I didn't, the clearer it became that I was about to sneak out of this double bed and find me a drink. I could feel the Mekong glide across my tongue and burn a trail to my stomach. What I couldn't conjure was what I really wanted, the shady golden hum, the brilliant blurring of painful edges.

There were no ultimatums. I could drink if I wanted to. Just slide out of bed and along the cliff, down to Haad Rin.

Go.

A reddish gleam. Ava's hair. Plenty of passed-out guys in my former bedding situations. Not a one expressed the restful bliss coming from the next bed over. I wanted how they slept more than I wanted Mekong. Tonight, anyway, I was willing to live with the twitching legs, that way-old pressure behind my eyes. I breathed it quiet. If I didn't move, it couldn't find me.

Voices engulfed me like the hum of bees. Slowly, one came clear. *You'd better not tell.* Three tigers circled me. *No one will believe you.* The voice lightened, became feminine. *Do you think I believe you? I know what I saw. A hickey.* Yelling now, wine breath, nails digging into my upper arms. *You make them do it! I'll kill you!* And their voices again, *We'll kill you if you tell.*

I jolted from sleep. The cliff, go to the cliff. Oh, my God, and I couldn't drink. On the porch, peaceable dawn. Ava in the hammock, long fingers in Cho's hair. Cho on the wooden deck, back curved like a spoon. I lunged, collided with Ava in a way that almost hurt. As thin as she was, she felt solid and, for the second time, real. I maybe pushed her away, maybe told her. But still not about Ted and Lyle. I knew I didn't say that. Because whatever I did say, it was enough to turn everything stupid.

" . . . babble your feelings . . . "

I didn't want feelings. I wanted a goddamn cigarette. We appeared to be having this as an actual conversation because Ava looked like I had knifed her in the eye. Cho interjected that the best thing for me was to go to tai chi, and when did she decide what the best thing—

"I am not going near those cliffs."

Clearly spoken. By me. In the end, a Camel from Cho. "We do what we can." She held my hand as I braved those jeering rock faces and took the steps to the tai chi beach.

Again, Gemma led me between the palm trees. Hands on hips, she assessed my ability to rotate the tai chi ball. "Right on. Now, Wave Hands Like Clouds."

"Everyone else gets to do the form."

Hair into knot. "Everyone else has covered the basics."

"What about that?" I point to two girls facing each other, circling back and forth with their right wrists crossed and touching. "Why can't I do that?"

"Push Hands? Push Hands takes listening."

"Screw it, just— show me this thing . . . what's it called?"

Wave Hands Like Clouds started in the same position I'd practiced ALL DAY yesterday. Hold the tai chi ball. Right hand floats to eye level, crosses the face without touching, then floats down as left hand moves to eye level, crosses the face, and floats down. Unending circles, up, across, down.

"Hands are clouds sailing across the sky," Gemma said as I practiced. "Blown by the wind. Nope, too tense. Flow with it."

I coasted on a warm pulse that started in my palms and circulated dawn-calm through my body. When Gemma clapped twice and called out, "The form, please," I took up residence near the palm tree. As the form finished, a spot of army-green descending the steep steps ended up being Nadav's tank top. Mother of God, he had gorgeous arms. He met me between the palm trees, his dark curls lolling like happy puppy ears. Right away, I tucked in my chin. "I ditched you."

In his guitar-like accent, he said, "I am here to find you," said it as if I were a normal girl, just traveling. When we got together, he made me come. I wanted to make him come. That was normal. I wanted to be normal. Nadav was pulling a shroom-sized fold of paper from his pocket, "We try more carefully," when Ava showed up to save me and Cho arrived to say, "Stop it, Ava. She needs to work out for herself if her life means anything to her."

I slapped my hands against my things. "She?"

Cho pulled her ponytail. "I'm done with your moods, Carlie."

"Are you now, you holier-than-thou dyke?"

"Why don't you leave?"

"Maybe I don't want to!"

"Maybe I don't want you around anymore."

"Cho, stop," said Ava.

I said, "I bet you were a shitty social worker."

Nadav took my hand, and the two of us were up those stairs. On the downside of the cliff toward Haad Rin, it hit me that Nadav had a pocket full of drugs and expectations—confirmed at the turn-off to the beach, when he told me he got my backpack from Simon as if he deserved a big smooch. He led me to the rocks that had secluded us, where he pulled me to him for that kiss. Still kissing, we found the sand. The last time I sat on this beach was when Cho took me into her and Ava's lives.

Nadav's mouth felt dry. He must have sensed it too because he pulled out the mushrooms like a question. He used my name. "Is Carlie ready?" I'd had men inside me who called me, "Carrie," when they came, but I could not answer Nadav's simple question. He ran his hands down my sides and asked again, then again. When he cried out, "What do I do wrong?" I couldn't even say, "Nothing." And Nadav was gone. I watched his footprints blow away, bit by bit, as the sun coasted into its two then three o'clock position. Couldn't reach for Little Matt. This same sun would soon slip like a deserter below the horizon, and I didn't have anywhere to sleep. I knew only one way to solve that dilemma. I didn't even have my own clothes.

The breeze was giving off the initial hint of sunset before I allowed the decision. I went into Haad Rin for two packs of Camels. Then I passed the steep tai chi stairs and—breath held, success—skirted along the cliffs with those rocks below, and approached Cho and Ava's bungalow. On their porch, two forms. A conference. The compact one waited while the tall and fair skipped to me.

"Hey, ya," crooned her brogue.

"The two of you are missing afternoon practice?"

"They'll be loads of practices, Carlie. There's only one you."

Hard to believe she actually said that. As if sensing my doubt, Ava said, "I'm an incest survivor too, Carlie."

Her string of babble was a tsunami against the shore of me. "Do ya know, Carlie, my father was a postman? Claimed that delivering the post was a position of public trust. Enough to drive you right 'round the bend."

"Could we just, not, for once?"

After another knife-to-the-eyes, Ava linked our arms. Man, could she bounce back. She suggested we return to Cho.

"Like she's ever talking to me again."

"Don't fret yourself. Cho's a right hothead, but—do ya know, *cho* is an old-fashioned Japanese word for 'butterfly?' Not a girly one. A hunting insect that enjoys snatching at you, sharp!"

We found Cho in the hammock, poised nothing like a bug. She was an empress, regarding the file folder of me as if the shredder was imminent. As Ava disappeared inside their room, my eyes locked on the lip of the cliff, about twenty feet away. Somehow, my voice creaked out, "I bet you weren't a shitty social worker." I couldn't make myself say, *Sorry*. Got out a look at her. "I bet you were great."

"No. I'm not particularly nice. Look, I'm not sorry for what I said, but I could have said it more gently. For that, I am sorry."

"Would you like a cigarette?"

Scottish brogue. "Can I come out now?"

I tossed Cho her pack. With Ava on the porch, conversation was energetic, even fun, all that Scottish slang that I couldn't track—minging?—but made me laugh. They lived in Tokyo. She'd washed my clothes, she taught English at a community college but was considering a position at the English Conversation school, recently opened by Cho's department store. Ava said, "Where our determined butterfly is an important body."

Cho waved her hand near her ear. "Not that impor—"

"The store's bloody called Yamashita's. Who else, may I ask, is the heir apparent?"

I said, "No way! We have a Yamashita's in Seattle. Japanese import store. That's you? Why are you guys staring at me?"

Ava flopped next to Cho in the hammock. "My bonny lass, we have a self-disclosed fact about Carlie."

Cho said, "She's from—"

"Don't say it," I said. "People could hear."

Cho said, "It's one of the first things travelers tell each other."

Ava kissed her. "It's right there in the book."

"Rules for a Lonely Planet life."

"Stop making fun of me. I ran away. I stole their money—"

"You stole money?" Ava demanded at the same time that Cho wanted to know, "Is that why you changed your name?"

"Ya changed your name?" Ava asked, before she turned to—on—Cho. "How'd you—?"

"Don't fight, you guys." To stop them, I'd tell them, but to tell them, I had to move. We took the path along the cliff, circled the bungalows, and then climbed the hill to Haad Rin to its crest. Ava cringed when I described the men playing pool. Cho took her hand, all the while asking questions that led directly to the money part. I recounted the details the way I stole the dollars, cautiously at first, picking up speed as Cho made me go over the good parts. She crowed unstoppably when I outsmarted Shelly at the third bank.

Ava was quiet.

We were back at the bungalows, hushed in the twilight. Cho gave my shoulder a strong, brief squeeze. "Fuckin' A, girlfriend."

"How else would anyone deal with—?"

A single-syllable hacking sound from Ava stopped me in the hurt I felt for her. I said, "You seem happy, now, though. How do you deal?"

Ava forehead-squinched-to-eyes until she came to "Wave Hands Like Clouds."

The days took on the rhythm of Wave Hands Like Clouds: up, across, down. Up at seven, cross the cliffs to tai chi, down for a nap. Up in the afternoon, evening practice, down for bed. Cho established ground rules: no yelling, swearing, or stomping off. There were times that I showed up to tai chi not speaking to her, but I always showed up, and half-way through the class, I never failed to notice that whatever mood had followed me down the steep stairs ceded to the feeling of something I could only woo-woo call energy being freed. It came from releasing tension when I reached from a targeted area, such as between my clavicle and shoulder joint. It amazed me that I could feel so specifically, could feel anything, in my body. However, my commitment to the twice-daily practice stemmed from my fear of what would happen if I didn't. No one needed to know the number of times, man, each hour, that stretching my arms to the sky while I pushed my legs into the earth was the only thing that kept me from a bender. The time I came closest was the afternoon I found my backpack on our porch with a slip of paper tucked into my Lonely Planet. It was Nadav's address in Israel.

My brain pulled from the rest of my head. That part was already down in Haad Rin, drinking. Somehow, I stretched my arms to grab myself back, didn't even tell them. I didn't want to "process." I was just getting a grip on not running to them when I woke in terror, *I'll kill you if you tell*, then Mom, her nails gouging my arms as if they were a carpet runner. *You make them do it*. She knew. Of course, she knew. *We'll kill you if you tell*.

Up, across, down. Gemma started me on learning the form. Ward Off Right: an opponent comes at you from your right side. Block the blow with your right arm. Rollback Into Press: use both hands to grasp your opponent by the shoulders and pull towards yourself, then push into his chest. I asked Gemma how long it would take to learn the whole form; I had just over two weeks left on my tourist visa.

Gemma said, "To know the form takes a lifetime."

I opted for a grin. "How long does it take to get a straight answer out of you Buddha guys?"

That night, I marched myself to the cliff, took a seat far enough from its sheer edge, and focused on the sound of the waves hundreds of feet below. It came to me to write to Little in my head, but I chose instead to let the stars draw me in. I never did this, never sat before going to bed and let the stars absorb me. I never even noticed they were there. On our way to morning tai chi, I told Cho and Ava, "I'm gonna get my own room, sleep by myself." To cover my pleasure at their proud astonishment, I finished, "You two sleep with anyone you want."

But then it jabbed, the way they took hands.

The time left on my visa crossed the one-week mark, then six days. At dinner, Ava poked around her carefully sorted plate. "We leave in two days' time."

Man it killed me, how she could not eat stuff. My plate was wiped clean.

Cho asked me, "Any idea where you're going next?"

To divulge my plan to teach English in Japan would come across as desperate. "Maybe India. Flights to Delhi are cheap from Bangkok."

Cho's eyes glistened like warm oil. "It is my opinion that you should come to Tokyo. With us."

There was a pause, during which nothing bubbly came from the Scottish corner. I skewed my chin toward Ava. "Got a vote?"

"Maybe India, maybe Tokyo. With money you stole, Carlie."

"That is hardly your b—"

"Having it makes you a victim, not a survivor."

"Maybe I'm just not as good a person as you, Ava."

Cho broke in. "Wherever you travel next, at some point, you'll need to go to Hong Kong for your money." She pulled from her fanny pack some business cards and a bunch of those scraps of paper covered with hastily scribbled travel tips that always ended up in there. She passed over two cards with a nod to the top one. "Stay at Tan House. Boy, does Mr. Tan know the form."

"You carry around his business card?" I asked.

"Someone from tai chi's always asking for a good place."

"And you aren't particularly nice." I had to laugh when Cho waved her hand near her ear, dismissing my irrefutable logic with, "Now, your money. You should invest it. How much is left?"

Over Ava's subtle, damning grunt, I said, "Just under eight."

"Take three to get set up in Tokyo, and in Hong Kong, go see my broker. His is the next card."

Chinese characters on one side, English on the other. Cho continued, "I'll warn you, Liu's aggressive, likes high-risk funds." She noted my expression. "I'll write it all down."

Ava did her own breaking in. "I understand why you stole it, Carlie. Of course I do."

"Do you think she knew? My mom?"

"I know she knew. They all do." Ava reached across the table. "Come to Tokyo with us."

This time, I didn't decide to grin. It blossomed.

In Bangkok, Cho and Ava's flight departed four hours after we reached the city, giving us only enough time for Cokes before they left for the airport. I had to arrange my ticket and a Japanese visa, so weighed down with the words in my heart all banging against each other that I couldn't find my cigs. Cho slid her Camels across the table.

Clutching the pack, I said, "What if I meet some stoner, get snockered, and blow off you guys and Tokyo?"

From Ava, "I'll wager you keep the cigarettes, then."

Only with a smoke lit, them in a taxi, and the last wave waved did I mouth, "Man, I'll miss you guys."

Tan House was a rattly old structure the color of mint chip ice cream, located down an unflustered street on the Hong Kong side. I tugged a long red rope to the left of the scarlet, four-paneled door, ringing a bell that echoed like the Addams Family's. The door unfolded. A plump rooster shot out. A gentleman no taller than me with strong wrists and an old man's belly took my backpack with a bow and a grandfatherly cluck.

"Tan," he said.

That settled, Tan turned me over to his daughter, Eleanor, who had his apple-like face with half the wrinkles. Eleanor led me to a hot nook of a room on the fourth floor. She apologized for its size all the way up then all the way down, then into the dining room for tea.

"Especially you are friends with Misses Cho and Ava. You practice *tai ke*?" Packaged slice of cake in one hand, empty teacup in the other, Eleanor mimicked a tai chi Ward Off. "Please ask Old Tan practice with. You will make him pleasure."

I finished my tea with a cigarette instead of cake. Then, Mr. Tan took me to the shaded, red-bricked courtyard outside the sliding glass doors to the dining room. Amidst the clucking of chickens, we went over the first third of the form that I had learned on Phangan. I was accustomed to white guys fitting their height into the movements. Tan's body made way more sense.

He started me on the first posture of the second half of the form, Embrace Tiger, Return to Mountain. Turn around, reaching to the back-left corner while bringing the left hand overhead and the right up from the earth, like tiger's jaws. The arms got a gorgeous stretch.

An hour later, the dining room began to fill, couple by couple, group by group, with what looked to be the usual assortment of Europeans, Aussies, and Americans. When Tan finally allowed me to go to dinner, not one guy offered to buy me a beer. A girl said, "Dude, I like your hair"—which had grown enough to run my fingers through if I was flustered. Which I was when she started the what-did-you-do-today. I couldn't answer because my day consisted of not drinking and missing the only people on this lonely planet who cared.

The dude girl turned to the traveler on her other side. I overheard the making of evening plans. I was not invited. I did my sagging-flirty best, asking a British guy for a cigarette even though I smelled menthol—yet there was something as different about me as there had been when I was light, looking down on myself on the hall stairs: same Catholic school uniform, still set apart. I sipped more tea and tolerated bummed menthol. The room emptied, traveler by traveler. Man, I would sit there forever, would solidify and compact, becoming a statue. Maybe then I'd understand what the hell Ava meant by "victim, not a survivor." In the morning, I called for an appointment with Cho's investment broker, going so far as to iron the crumpled Ralph Lauren dress exhumed from my backpack. It was about a size too big for me—thank God. I'd been eating so regularly that I was sure I would be too fat to wear it. I didn't know why I felt so nervous, except that I was about to tell this investment guy my real name. I had no identification for any other.

At the address printed on the business card, a secretary in a yellow suit quickly led me to a modest but well-appointed office with a harbor view, fresh lilies in one corner, and a tank with a goldfish in another. My fish!

A slim man entered, not at all the "Buy! Buy! Buy! Sell! Sell! Sell!" type that Cho's description had led me to expect. The file folder he carried already had my name typed on the tab. His glasses breathed prudence.

He bowed. "I am Liu."

"I am Jennifer Brewer." Man, my name sounded like something to be snatched back. I reminded myself not to say, "Man," with Liu.

In clipped British English, Liu offered me a cigarette from a cloisonné box. We sat so that Liu could explain stocks versus bonds and tax-exempt something-or-other. Tax exempt? I didn't have a job. Maybe it was like sex. The guy knew where he needed to get and, hopefully, I wouldn't get more damaged.

As Cho predicted, Liu nudged me to make a riskier investment. He tried twice. Taking care not to whine, I said, "Look, there's no family, no home. No friends really, except Cho and Ava. I need to be careful."

We both seemed embarrassed, and so took refuge in the depersonalized process of paper signing. Once we were officially cohorts, I was emboldened to adopt the Chinese—and, to me, grown-up—way of calling someone by their last name.

"So, Liu." When he didn't stop me, I continued, "This account is mine, right? I mean if people claiming to be my parents or, like . . . oh, I don't know"—I sped up, here—"the police or something wanted to see it, you wouldn't let them, would you?"

Liu pressed the tips of his fingers together. "Miss Brewer, I would need to know nothing more about the source of this money." He escorted me to the door, where he hesitated before handing me his card.

"Miss Brewer, you are certainly a sensible young lady. Occasionally, however, things do happen. Please call if you ever have a problem."

Dear Little. A man on my side.

I wanted to write those words on a postcard.

Returning to Tan House in the heat of the afternoon, I told myself the cool, empty common area would be most comfortable. Underneath flitted the knowledge that my room wasn't so hot. I was steeping myself a cup of tea when Eleanor entered. She dusted a row of photos on the corner altar. Then she knelt on a flat pillow and lit a bundle of incense which she placed in a rectangular vase filled with sand. The scent wafted toward me: sweet as candy yet a touch burnt: a more gentle version of the fragrance that hung in all those Balinese temples.

Next, Eleanor clapped her hands into prayer position and pressed them to her forehead, remaining there for some moments. In that pause, I expected—what? Assuagement. An explanation. Something along the lines of Ava. But there was only Eleanor, now adjusting the position of the largest frame.

"Eleanor, who's that?"

"Is mother. I miss. But ancestors take care for us."

"What if they don't?"

I didn't mean to sound like such a victim. Eleanor turned, still on her knees, folding hands I'd never seen idle into her lap. Her voice came as if from the bottom of a well.

"Miss Carlie, we don't need understand ancestors. We trust for our best good."

"Why?"

"To have hope."

She hadn't had to pause or think. I asked, "How do you pray?"

She patted the flat square pillow next to hers. I edged over as she said, "Direction to east. Light come first there." She inhaled. "Hold Quanyin in mind. Think what you want her to hear."

"What's Quanyin?"

"Goddess of Mercy." Eleanor gestured to a gray-flecked marble statue of a female Buddha with rounded cheeks. "See skinny bottle she holds? Is tears of all people."

"Man. I thought that was a bottle of *sake*."

I inched toward the figure, moved so close that I could clearly see this Quanyin's beautifully wrought face. This was no tourist-shop souvenir. She was almost alive. I said, "I am really trying." Then I breathed myself into her kindheartedness and said, "This new me is starting out weird. Man, I'm scared. I'm scared I won't ever get to the me that's in here somewhere, but I keep fuc—I mean, messing up." I barely said aloud, "I'm scared I'll drink." Closing my eyes, I went to an untaught place inside. What came out was: "I am afraid no one will ever love me."

"Miss Carlie is already loved," said the voice from the well, and I saw myself on an urban avenue with cars and people getting on and off busses and neon signs with Chinese letters reaching over me. A blurry-faced Asian woman in white called, *You dropped your wallet.* I said, *Not mine,* but it was mine, I just forgot—creased leather and brown and soft with age, folding open in my hands to disintegrate, leaving me holding a ruby-red object the size of a piece of fruit. Sweet-smelling, pulpy. Precious. I covered my eyes with my hands, grieving.

Onions in the Tea Garden

Oh, man. I left my smokes at the boarding lounge, Hong Kong to Tokyo, so on the plane, it was super hard not drinking. As soon as lightly-accented English announced that the in-flight beverage service was ending, I chowed down the peanuts I'd somehow avoided throughout the flight.

Narita Airport, an orderly haze of white tile. I passed through Japanese Immigration and Customs—Mother Mary, was that beer in a vending machine? Swiftly, I looked to buy some Camels. Six dollars. I settled for a random brand, about three bucks, and found a pay phone. In accordance with directives issued in Bangkok, I dialed Cho at work. Someone female and polite answered with a lot of Japanese.

Hesitantly, I read aloud the Japanese sentence Cho had written out for me in English. "Yamashita"—her last name; easy enough—"Booch-o-u"—whatever—"ee-maska?"

My words sounded fat. A moment later, Cho was in my ear with, "Girlfriend! Boy, I'd love to—but I'm going into a meeting. Write this down."

Cho fired off the instructions to get me to a train station in Tokyo, Oo-way-no. "West Gate in two hours. Ask for the *nishi guchi*. Write it down."

I had the startling desire to hug her.

In the long line for a ticket, I nearly panicked with the

understanding that the train, spelled U-e-n-o, would cost me nearly 50 bucks. Man, I didn't spend 50 dollars on two months of transportation in Thailand. For an hour, overcast sky and patches of green and brown earth crept by, those legendary smooth green hills in the distance. Smooth green hills, a couple of kimono ladies, and cash pouring in from teaching English, these were the stereotypes I retreated to if the bus ride got too long or the guy too dull, if the night ended before I was drunk enough. *Finally, Little Matt, I was really headed into those hills.* I wanted more peanuts. The acres of tilled earth gave way to towns, a metropolis, and eventually, Ueno Station.

There were a zillion people. There was the rumble of mass transit, a diesel smell, all familiar reminders of Southeast Asia with two notable variances: brisk air and beers sold from vending machines. I asked a uniformed guard for, consulted my scribbles, the nishi guchi. West Gate. I expected crimson, wooden largess. Turned out to be turnstiles. Leaning my backpack against a post, I had a not-Camel, wishing for a warm hat, watching well-dressed men wearing gray or black suits and carrying briefcases—had to be the proverbial Japanese salarymen—and fewer women in dark blue or black, an endless sentence punctuated by neon green pay phones. After two smoke-long epochs, one of the purposeful, passing Japanese carrying a briefcase broke away from the sentence with a brisk stride and a familiar, "Girlfriend!"

I didn't expect Cho to embrace me quite so hard or for as long as she did. It was going to be okay. I was going to make it.

"How was Hong Kong?" she asked as we pressed our way to the mobbed sidewalk. When I bit my lip, Cho unloosed the impish grin I'd only seen once before.

She made me giggle, and I don't giggle. "Man."

She hailed a taxi. The driver wore white gloves. We inched through a congested shopping street, storefronts as well as open-air stalls. Not a single jaywalker. Cho lit a Camel and used it to light one for me. I relished its almost-vanilla sharpness. As the neighborhood became department stores and high-rises, Cho pointed out the post office, the natural foods store; who but Cho could locate a natural foods store among the high-rises of Tokyo? The busy street circled past, oddly enough, a lake.

"Our tai chi group practices there." Cho's nub of a cig indicated a clump of trees next to a shrine so grand and red it should be the West Gate. Her nails, polished a self-possessed maroon, conflicted with the moody rat-tat-tat she beat against her briefcase.

I said, "I saw beer in vending machines."

Cho did not disagree. She waved to an arched stone gate. "Tokyo U. B-school. Why I am where I am at the tender age of thirty-nine. Boy, do I let motherfucking office bullshit get to me."

"Do you ever pray?"

"Save it for Ava." She patted my knee.

I dragon-whimpered. All Cho did was fire up a new smoke. Guess if Tokyo didn't work out, there was always India. The high-rises disappeared, to be replaced by imposing Japanese-style homes regal against the gray sky. At Cho's command, the driver halted before a simple wooden gate. Behind it, a stone path through a crisp-cold garden, bushes and trees, a fairyland, even a short, rounded stone lantern so self-possessed that being mad at Cho was stupid.

The entry was eight by ten feet. Stairs led off to the left, a hallway to the right. Copying Cho, I removed my shoes, placing them toes toward the front door. Felt so Japanese. We padded down the cold hall—no central heating in old Japanese houses, Cho explained—past several sets of sliding doors that Cho told me opened into the living room, dining room, and kitchen. Pushing the next set to the side with a satisfying *whoosh*, she brought me into the soft light bathing what was now my room.

Oh, man. Smelled of warm hay. Half the floor was inlaid with straw mats. The other half was dark, shining wood. In the center of the room rested a low, rectangular table. Sliding the doors closed behind us, Cho informed me they were *shoji*, the mats were *tatami*, and the low table was a *kotatsu*. She opened the closet with another *whoosh*. "Futon! You look freezing."

She pulled one from the stack of thick quilts. I expected to wrap myself in it. Instead, Cho removed the top of the low table. She had me drape the futon over the frame, then she replaced the top. The ko-toast-o or whatever was now skirted. She reached under. There was a *click* followed by the electric hum of a heater.

"Ko-tat-su," Cho corrected. As with the shoes, I followed her lead—I sent my bottom half beneath the futon, into warmth that felt like my best dreams of Japan.

"My grandma made these. On my mother's side. One of the first things she did after they were released from Minidoka." Cho stroked the pattern of red, pink, and peach against a restful blue. With her straight, dark hair, her torso rising from the material engulfing her, Cho was a modern kimono lady.

Made me want to drink. "Could I have some tea?"

Cho banged around the kitchen. " . . . can't believe I'm making you tea when this morning, I nearly threw a cup at a farty old man who told me to—" Slam, boom. In my room, clean lines and the smell of warm straw. "The Board treats me as if—yet who raised revenues at least forty-seven percent each year for the past five yea—" A *whoosh* brought Cho into the room. "They touch themselves. Before negotiations. Got my price list, got my calculator, got my dick."

"Do they check after meeting with you?"

When Ava came home, she greeted me, "Ya didn't drink!" The "so proud of you" that came with her ample hug felt like the day she missed practice because "there's only one" me. Which was super marvelous. Then, Ava segued into more babble than anyone ever needed about teaching English in Tokyo. "The job board at my college is loaded with adverts, looking for private lessons. Sixty dollars an hour, Carlie. Imagine how quickly you'll pay back your debt."

"Debt?" And I'd wanted to talk about praying.

"What do you call it?"

"Justice."

Cho said, "Come smoke with me, Carlie. Back porch." We stood in the dark cold of the glassed-in hallway overlooking the skyline-lit tea garden. Cho told me it was a formal tea garden. "*Teien*. A regular garden is *niwa*. It wouldn't have those. *Toro*." She gestured to three short, rounded stone lanterns, reminding me that Cho was great. Her girlfriend was the lameass. Cho's hand ended up on my shoulder. "Ava's trying to help. Like when she insisted you return the money. She's not moralizing. We both believe that any needs you have of them, you're still a prisoner."

Futon-soft Japanese made us turn. Cho introduced my new landlady. Under five feet tall, face a mass of folds, and a full head of hair, pure white and wispy. Cho had to walk me through the syllables of her name: Ka-shi-wa-ba-ra. And a "-san" on the end, for propriety's sake. She had the whole of the upper floor.

"Where we do not go unless invited," Cho instructed in sharpish English.

"Supper!" Ava chirruped.

The ko-tat-su on the kitchen floor was set with plate after artful plate, lots of veggies, none of which I recognized, cut into unusual shapes and sprinkled with white sesame seeds. All made by Ava. Fine, one in her column. Except that across my flat pillow of a seat she'd laid the Monday edition of an English-language daily, *The Japan Times*, folded open to the first of many pages advertising teaching positions. The next morning, fresh, white tofu sprinkled with black sesame seeds and minced green onions came with steamed brown rice and miso soup. Green onion garnished them, too, all accompanied by the most recent edition of the paper. Not only was she insisting that I get a job, pay them back, she was trying to make me fat.

"You can't expect not to work," Ava whined after me as I

stormed to the back porch. I could rip those short stone lanterns out of the earth. With my teeth. It was my money. I more than deserved it. Anyway, I was never going back to the States, so how could I return it? I was crying. I would never pray again, weeping so hard that I didn't hear Ka-landlady-san until I was bawling uncontrollably into her shoulder. Her stiffness implied that she would like to comfort me but had no idea how. Look at her perfect garden. She would never get it.

When the squall subsided, the landlady loaned me her hanky. She took me through moist, low bushes to the back wall, where she pointed out several thin plants growing about a foot high. Then she gestured as if chopping with a knife. *"Negi."*

I leaned down to sniff. Green onions, like Ava had dotted everything with. "Negi," I repeated.

My landlady set her lips with gravity, returned me to my glassed-in roost, and was off before I realized, I had no clue what it all meant.

Cho worked most of the weekend, disappearing after morning tai chi practice in (Cho talked me through the name again) Ka-shi-wa-ba-ra-san's tea garden, the only time Ava and I relaxed around each other. I didn't ask how she spent her time. Man, why I was in Japan if Cho was going to ignore me and Ava was going to embody sanctimony? A storm bejeweled the round stone lanterns, bringing with it a longing for beach breezes and inexpensive travel. Tallying the yen spent since the outlay to get to Ueno Station came to just over a thousand: two packs of Camels from the vending machine down the hill—I caved. Other than that quick trip, I didn't explore much of the neighborhood. Ava said it was called Hongo—side streets of wood-and-paper restaurants emitting savory scents, a main street of fast-food joints. And bars. I ignored *The Japan Times.* Bitch. Until Sunday night. On Sunday night, I poked my head into their room. Cho was still at work, and I couldn't wait. Ava looked up with surprise from the stack of papers she was correcting as she hummed at her large, wooden desk.

"Ava, I think . . . I mean, I'm itchy. You know."

She removed her glasses. "Is it a yeast infection?"

I hated the sound of that.

Ava smiled, a nice teacher flipping through her Rolodex. "You'll see my gynecologist. Her English is pure dead brilliant."

Can't be that bad, I reasoned, if Ava can do something so ordinary as roll the hell out of an *r*.

Writing out the doctor's number Ava said, "If I may I ask, do you use protection?"

"Protection?" I sensed myself inching toward the ceiling.

"Condoms."

"Condoms?" I was gone.

With concern, she returned her glasses to her nose. "Carlie, you've been having unprotected sex."

"I guess." When Ava inhaled with alarm, I rushed in, "I know you're not supposed to . . . but, man . . ." What, ask the guy?

"You're bloody lucky you've not been pregnant."

I didn't need a symposium from Ava about how one ended up pregnant. I said, "I don't get my period."

Oops. I didn't mean to tell The Veggie Queen, over there, about eating less to stop my period. All I'd admit was, "Like, four times in my whole life."

"And you slept with Nadav a bit more'n a month ago." Again, Ava took off her glasses. "How do we know you're not pregnant?"

The *r* on that one could wrap around the world.

"You'll see my OB, lass. She'll right you. And Carlie?"

I almost refused to turn, but I did, only to hear her say, "You might ask for an AIDS test, as well."

Early Monday morning, a phone call determined that it would be two days, forty-eight endless hours, until I could see Ava's gynecologist to find out if I had AIDS. I retreated to the back porch. Ka-shi-wa-bara-san tried to tow me in the direction of the what's-it, the green onions. At least she paid me some attention. Neither Ava nor Cho would take what Ava called my "moaning" seriously.

"Not until your test results come back," Ava said, prepared to drag me like a hostage to Ueno Park for tai chi. Cho couldn't go due to work, but both thought it best that I get out of the house.

"Or what? You kick me out?" My bravado was real, but so was the vision under it: me, homeless and dying on the hot streets of some mammoth Asian city.

Cho pulled her loose hair into a ponytail, where it remained for less time than it took her to say, "You're a survivor, girlfriend. So go to practice and start surviving."

Feeling more wet kitten than survivor, I followed Ava across the broad, busy street in front of the large pond that was fringed on the opposite side by trees. Ava said, *Shinobazu Ike.* Ike means pond."

She pranced in a wacky dance, nearly splashing through puddles, yelping if she managed to skip over one. I had to enjoy myself. Too bad she couldn't be this delightful all the time.

We arrived at a sun-filled but soggy clearing deep enough into the park that we couldn't see the street, only a section of the pond now behind a small-scale wooden shrine with a stone gate. The distant hum of traffic remained audible through the trees. Ten or so—what does Cho call non-Japanese people? *Gaijin.* Stretching. Like on Phangan but with more layers of clothing. Lanky guys and solid women. A few thin. I wasn't the thinnest. That badge went to the single Japanese person here, a woman I guessed was five years older than me. Some of the gaijin were paired up and circling back and forth as they practiced Push Hands, the great mystery someone had yet to explain to me.

Ava big-hugged the leader, a broad-chested but not tall American she introduced as Doug Lee. I caught myself going *Man* about his good looks, kind of Asian, framed by shoulder-length hair with more red under it than Cho's black, but still black. Until I remembered that he was probably the same as every other itch-spreading shithead out there.

At ten o'clock sharp, the probable shithead started practice with two claps. He had us stand with the trees behind us, the large pond in full view, skyscrapers in the distance. We saluted each other as three thousand years of tai chi tradition dictated: right fist in front of the sternum, the left palm curved softly over it, power and the correct use of power. Doug then warmed us up slowly by having us swing our arms forward and then drop them—"ropes with large rocks tied to the ends. Let the rocks fall"—plus some other gentle stretches before taking on the form, which Doug called the *kata*. After twice through, the more advanced students lent a hand teaching the newer ones the postures—that's what Doug called each movement.

A heavy-set Canadian with beige curls escaping the colorful, concentric rings of her Rastafarian beret, Margot, as she introduced herself, showed me Repulse Monkey. "Arms go like you're swimming. Crawl stroke, eh? But walking backward at the same time."

We tried it. I was bad. With less than Gemma's patience, Margot took me through it again. I continued to shank it.

Doug came up. "If it's okay, Margot? Carlie, right? So, swim forward at the same time that you walk forward."

We did. In the middle of it, he kept swimming his arms to the front but switched to walking backward. I followed him easily. He said, "Keep going," his brown eyes on me like fingers.

I stopped. Every man on this continent sucked ass.

Doug backed away. That's when I noticed the swing in that shoulder-length hair.

He called for the class to do the kata one last time. We finished the form right fist in front of sternum, left hand curved gently over it—power, and the correct use of power. People broke into talky threes and fours. I had no one to talk to.

Until Ava sidled in. All she had to say for herself was, "Fancy coming to my college? We could look at the job board."

"Man! Would you butt out!"

I walked away so fast that I practically smashed into Doug. Deflecting with instinctive grace, he invited me to tea. "We all go after practice."

For the second time, Doug retreated from my alien seething. The sun brightened the group's backs as they crossed the mire of the clearing: that Canadian lady, what's-her-face, wide-set with determined shoulders topped by circles of color; the guys, mostly tall and lean; Doug, the shortest and the most muscular; Ava, gone. Good. "Wait!" rolled behind my clenched teeth. As I envisioned the class laughing over tea, it occurred to me that Doug hadn't been checking me out, some dickwad. The guy had been watching me the way teachers do their students. I pulled out my cigarettes. The rain started again.

I didn't want her to, I certainly didn't ask, but Ava took time off to go with me to an area of the city called Roppongi, to see her OB. In the waiting room, when they called my name, she found a way to give my knee a squeeze without making me want to sock her in the nose.

"Thank you," was all I could say. In the end, though, I faced the doctor alone.

Dr. Imura was probably in her late forties. Square face, a bit plumper than most Japanese females, all of whom appeared as finely rendered as those in *The Tale of the* goddamn *Genji*. I described my symptoms. She inquired how long it'd been since my last OB exam. Naturally, her next question was "How long have you been sexually active?"

I decided to answer, "I was twelve."

A penciled-in eyebrow went up. "Do you use a prophylactic?"

"I'm beginning to think that would be a good idea."

She closed my chart. "We must do several tests. First"—she handed me a plastic cup and sent me to the bathroom to collect a urine sample for the pregnancy test. Ick. Once again in the exam room, Dr. Imura had me on the table, legs spread—no; my father, he; I can't—feet in stirrups, bottom half under a white sheet. I disappeared into a similarly milky blur as she explained the pelvic exam, which involved "putting speculum inside vagina." She held up a nasty-looking metal thing.

"Mother of God."

I became aware that Dr. Imura was poking around down Virginia way but was blessedly numb until I heard something like, *"A-ra!"* My mind leapt to the headless ducks I'd seen hanging in Chinatowns across Southeast Asia. I was a dead duck.

Dr. Imura came out from under. "You have Condyloma."

"Is that Japanese or English?"

"That is Human Papilloma Virus. Vaginal warts."

"Oh, man." Then, "Am I going to die?"

"Of course not. I will burn off with solution including trichloroacetic acid. Sadly, it is very painful."

"Very painful" does not begin to describe having warts acid-burned off anywhere, let alone the region in question.

Dr. Imura finished. I sat up. "I will never have sex again."

With a serious face, Dr. Imura set up to draw blood to test for AIDS and a couple other choice diseases. A nurse popped in. I was officially not pregnant. I hardly had the chance to rejoice. Dr. Imura was instructing me to return in one week for my second treatment. Given a certain throbbing, it took me a moment to fully get it.

"Hang on. Second treatment?"

"I must burn again any warts that have grown back. After that, if you do not have intercourse with infected person, they should not return. Also for next visit, we will have all test results."

On the back porch with Cho. Our smoke melted into the fog floating through the mist-draped tea garden. She told me she'd set me up with an interview at her department store's English Conversation school.

"You'll start working, you'll get your test results back, it'll all settle down.

I was too agitated to listen. "Man, if I'm gonna die, at least I want to know who gave it to me."

Cho patted my shoulder. "Girlfriend, you're not going to die from Condyloma."

"AIDS."

"Don't future-trip. The Condyloma pamphlet said once you're infected, it takes three months to show."

"That was Christmas-time. Malaysia. It might be . . . oh, what's-y-hoo-dit, that surfer guy with the baseball hat."

I heard what I'd said and broke into tears.

Kashi-wabara-san chose that moment to join us in the conversation. Through Cho, she insisted that we return to the negi. Cho translated for her.

"It was the war. We had nothing to eat. We did not complain. In Hiroshima, in Nagasaki, Japanese people lost everything. My husband did not return. They sent home his sash. I placed it on the family"—Cho stumbled for the word— "altar, but it could not feed us. We had this garden. I could plant the negi. I was young and strong. I could eat only bitter negi and survive. But my baby"—Cho repeats this in Japanese—"my *aka-chan*. She did not survive."

We were quiet in the mist until Kashiwabara-san spoke again. When she finished, Cho translated: "Each year, I must plant negi. There are always onions in my tea garden."

Rollback into Press

Test-result day. Ava couldn't take off a second time. Alone yet armed with a color-coded map of the subway system, I took the dark blue Mita Line to the gray Hibiya Line. Transferring at the underground quagmire called Hibiya Station took twenty minutes longer than expected, as four subways rolled in, and half the women in the station seemed to be wearing kimono and clicky-clacky wooden sandals, both of which made them walk super slowly. Lots of boys, too, wearing half-kimono over navy-blue shorts. In perfectly clear English, a kimono'd lady who volunteered to help me find the Hibiya Line explained that today was a holiday called Boys' Day.

Did not seem auspicious for my purposes.

As I left the lady, an unbelievable number of men nearly crashed into me. Being so outnumbered by the despised species was repulsive.

Little Matt! The posture was Repulse Monkey.

I imagined forward swim-walking to the train. My flow state was upended by the sight of brightly-wrapped mini bars of chocolate, gold bullion, stacks of it, shining from a kiosk counter.

Little, I don't eat chocolate.

I made it to Roppongi. Struggling to locate the doctor's office among the gray buildings and weather of this Boys' Day, what I was about to learn hit home. It was all Ava's fault. In the examination room, Dr. Imura greeted me with such normalcy that my doom was beyond question. She promptly said, "Remaining tests, negative *desu*."

Relief akin to peanuts flooded me. I was up in the stirrups in no time. "Merely two," said Dr. Imura from under the sheet. The searing pain sent me above, where I contemplated which convent to commit myself to. Definitely a Buddhist one.

When Dr. Imura was done, she sat me at the edge of the exam table with a hand mirror and showed me how to check myself. Not so embarrassing. After all, we all had one—Dr. Imura, Cho, Ava. Even Kashi-wabara-san had one. Bagingo!

The doctor leaned on me to, once a week for three months, give the ol' box a good gander. "If there is no reoccurrence, you have no need to fear for re-infection. Would you see cervix?"

I was not sure what my cervix was. Dr. Imura re-inserted the silver thing. With it snugly in place, I bent down and looked into the mirror. Expecting a gross, hairy mess, it was a surprise to see a pink button with one horizontal and one vertical slit.

This was me.

The core of me.

Clean and pink.

I gazed at my perfect cervix. For the first time since my father started in on me, I understood how filthy I'd felt.

When I was done with my cervix, Dr. Imura loaded me up with condoms and pamphlets and stuff. On a thriving street of one of the world's busiest cities, in front of all those people on the sidewalk, I took the time to reach to the sky the way that guy, Doug, had us do to start practice. Man, the gray afternoon was lovely. I couldn't imagine descending into the subway. My color-coded map indicated that it shouldn't take too long to walk home.

Tokyo was cement-colored with brown wood at the edges. A few new leaves in corners. I ambled down streets and up hills, between tall buildings and through back alleys as quiet as those in any small town. A string of red lanterns and a piquant smell led to a noodle stall where rough-looking men sat on equally rugged benches. A different scent—elegant; I recognized it: Bali, Hong Kong, Eleanor—drew me to a corner graveyard crowded with tombstones less than a foot wide, as tall as a person. I breathed in my old friend, incense.

From that block, a busier street. I took my coat off. Plump ladies in faded pink wraps clucked over customers at their vegetable stalls, and boys, suddenly, little boys churned around me, navy-blue school uniforms with dark blue derbies. As if pinched, their cheeks bore rosy circles, and chatter and chatter and chatter.

Two hours later, I arrived home. Within minutes, Cho had me on the back porch, We smoked while she bitched with analytic passion about the males at work, an *Imai-san* in particular. I loved her. Ava called us to dinner. Her own lavender apron emphasized how slim she was. I almost loved her, but man, I wasn't going to eat all that food. Tonight's feast was udon noodle soup, topped with grilled shrimp and Ava's notoriously ascetic vegetables. I ate every bit. Ava had maybe two noodles.

Then she had to bring up it, didn't she; big blue eyes spewing innocence, the English Conversation school.

"I will be taking the head teacher position as soon as my contract at the college ends in August. You're an ideal English Conversation teacher, Carlie."

Cho threw in, "Cute and white."

"What does 'white' have to do with—" I began, when Ava cut me off, practically yelling at Cho, "It was your bloody idea for me to change from a proper college to a conversation school!"

Cho twisted her hair around her right hand. "I shouldn't have said that." She gave her ponytail a tug and then let it fall loose.

Ava chewed a noodle. As if realizing a poisonous error, she pushed her bowl toward the center of the kotatsu.

I said, "Don't fight, you guys. I don't even want a job."

Ava sniffed with indignation. "Rent."

I said, "This is blackmail!"

"This is reality. Man." Cho wiggled her fingers in a peace sign before adding, "Tell them you're growing out your hair."

"What's wrong with my—"

"—and be *genki*."

"What the hell is—"

Ava chirped, "Happy and cheery." I could have brained the two of them.

The next morning, Cho hustled me through Shinjuku, a vast train station/shopping arcade on the west side of Tokyo—some shops classy, others flashing neon. I was hard-pressed to keep up despite the spike in Cho's mahogany high heels. She slowed us up as we approached a brass-trimmed set of glass doors. Posted on either side were two girls a little older than me in identical blue uniforms with caps like flight attendants. They bowed in unison to the throngs passing into the store.

Mid-bow, one caught sight of Cho. Her mouth froze in a smile. Then Japanese flooded out. Cho inclined her head modestly. As we barreled through the first floor, every employee we encountered responded the same way—astounded eyes, earnest amounts of Japanese.

I asked, "Why are they so nice to you?"

Cho nodded pleasantly to a sales clerk who, it appeared, might faint dead away at the pleasure of seeing her. "I'm a *Butch-o-u*. Department manager. Ava calls me the Booch."

We reached the elevator. Outside it, a different flight attendant pressed the call button. Like, her job? Once inside, still another pressed the necessary buttons and announced each floor as we arrived. Man. Her job. At the twenty-seventh floor, Cho nudged me. Phones jangled as we progressed down the hall. Cho bowed variously: most people got a slight bob of the head or neck, a few qualified for the upper chest. She coached me, "The only people I bow lower to are the *kaicho* and the *shyacho*. The kaicho is like the chairman. A Yamashita grandpa has been kaicho since"—she waved a hand near an ear— "boy. *Shyacho* is the general manager. My uncle. Then come us Booches. *Ah! Imai-san!"*

Cho bobbed to a nattily-dressed man she introduced as the Sales Booch. Her English to me carried a hint of derision that she masked completely in the face she showed Imai-san and the Japanese she used. Bows ensued as we backed away from each other along the blue hall.

Cho said, "Next time, you should bow lower. About fifteen degrees shows respect."

"So, Imai-san outranks you?"

She glowered.

"You bowed lower!"

"He bowed less than he should have, the slimeball motherfucker. He's been out to get me since the first time I was promoted over his sad ass. He's my cousin, by the way. We're in a dead heat for shyacho."

I was trying to recall what shyacho was when Cho stopped. Across a frosted glass door, "Achieve English Conversation School" was stenciled in plain black script.

"Achieve English?" I'd rather press elevator buttons.

"Talk to marketing." Waving her hand near her ear, Cho led me into a neat lobby carpeted dark blue, past a reception desk monitored by four stewardesses with no hats but identical black hair: straight to the shoulders, bangs. Then the staff room, smoky and crowded with metal desks, photocopiers, and traveler-aged gaijin yakking it up. They paid no attention to Cho—Hey. She was a Booch—who told me to address the woman we were about to meet, Mrs. Saito, as sensei. Cho offered a pat on the shoulder— "Don't say, 'man,' and you're growing out your hair"—before depositing me in the office of a middle-aged woman in a powder-pink power suit. The head teacher asked a few questions: my hobbies, travel experience, how long I planned to stay in Tokyo. Saito Sensei was pleased that I spoke no

Japanese.

"Students must use English to you. But lack of experience, *ne*. Even with good recommendation from Yamashita Butch-o-u."

She sucked air through her teeth. "Can you teach sample lesson? We can pay money."

Barely waiting for my "Now?" Saito Sensei made a phone call, and we were off. To a warm closet of a room dominated by a six-foot round table, around which were seated three of the four receptionists. Saito Sensei introduced Ritsuko-san, Satsuki-san, and Akemi-san. "Office Ladies are not students. OLs will learn for sample lesson only."

All three bowed. I returned it, hoping I didn't look as if I were mocking them. Saito said, "A sensei does not bow."

I said, "Except to you," and hit it. Fifteen degrees.

Saito Sensei's raised eyebrows showed approbation. She motioned formally for me to sit, handed me a floppy red plastic folder, and settled herself pinkly into a chair in the corner.

Emboldened, I proposed that each OL choose an English name. Saito Sensei titled her head. Approval? Ritsuko and Akemi giggled, sweet butterflies. Satsuki declined. I fanned myself with the red folder until Ritsuko asked to be called Lisa. Akemi picked Marcie. She touched her own nose. "Family name, Masumoto."

Despite her seated stature, she bowed. Fifteen degrees.

I opened the folder. I almost said, "Man." We were supposed to warm up by practicing consonants: B-b-b-b, k-k-k-k, ch-ch-ch-ch. The butterfly girls giggled. Satsuki looked up for it. Genki? The ballet performer I once was shook herself out as if from the bottom of a backpack and overcompensated with clown-like *b*'s and *ch*'s. More giggles. Allegedly prepared, we advanced to the main lesson, compound verbs. The folder suggested a list.

Marcie got "run over." She blinked. She blanched. No giggle.

"Don't be nervous, Marcie. What happens when something gets"—I gestured—"run over?"

Marcie closed her eyes in concentration. "The cat is flat."

At the lesson's end, the three OLs bowed and filed out. Saito Sensei assured me I got the job. "You are so genki!"

And white.

Saito Sensei signed me up for twenty teaching hours a week at—again, I came close to saying, "man"—240,000 yen a month, something like two thousand dollars. Saito Sensei finished with, "Personnel office will process paperwork for visa. Please take there your passport and university diploma."

Over dinner, Cho all but spat, "She doesn't have a diploma.'

Ava said, "She turned eighteen the morning you found her."

"She hasn't graduated high school."

"Ooch, immigration can't issue her a work visa."

"I'm going to lose face!" Cho had never looked so furious.

I said, "No, you won't."

They turned to me. At long last. Man. I poked my chopsticks into the strips of toasted seaweed stacked on a rectangular plate that fit the narrow pieces perfectly, and took one. "I'll find an American, photocopy her diploma. Maybe have to pay her. White-out her name, type mine in, copy it again."

I dipped the seaweed into soy sauce and used the damp wrap to scoop up a bite of brown rice. "I'll tell Immigration I was traveling and didn't want to risk losing the original. Bam. Visa."

Ava let out, "That is completely illegal."

Cho stayed neutral. Maybe impressed. I popped the rice ball into my mouth. She remained dispassionate. Through rice and seaweed, I said, "Simon told me everyone does it in Taiwan."

Cho said, "Solid junkie logic. Girlfriend, try convincing Immigration that you graduated college when your passport shows you turned eighteen two months ago. You're going to enroll in a Japanese language school. They'll sponsor a cultural visa, which allows you to work twenty hours a week. Legally."

"Yeah, but how much will it set me back?"

Cho had no answer, which her grimace showed she hated, and Ave was vague: maybe fifty thousand for three months? "Margot will know," she assured me.

After the next practice, I followed the Rastafarian beret on the chubby Canadian to her Japanese school in Shibuya, another Shinjuku-sized shopping arcade two stops along the Yamanote, the train line that made a big loop around Tokyo.

"The University of the Rio Grande?" I questioned the arch of Old West letters above the graphic of a cactus on the door. As if guilty, Margot rotated the stud in her nostril—a purple gem so small that I hadn't noticed it until this minute. The classrooms, however, were reassuringly professional: bright, and spacious if a tad refrigerated. I signed up.

Waving goodbye, Margot pulled off her cap. "You might even learn Japanese, eh?"

My training began at Achieve English, after which I started work promptly at seven a.m. B-b-b-b, k-k-k-k, ch-ch-ch-ch. I mingled moderately with the gaijin in the smoky staff room, even lunching with Joan, a serious Korean Canadian, until afternoon Japanese lessons kicked in, adding daily classes and three hours of homework each night to the twenty hours of English I taught every week. No more lunches. Plus, tai chi every Monday, Wednesday, Friday. To Shinjuku for work, to Shibuya for Japanese school, back to Shinjuku to teach evening classes, then home. Four rides a day. Six, on tai chi days. When the rainy season set in, I looked up the cost of a flight to Bangkok, bought Camels instead, six dollars, plus a postcard of Tokyo Tower; refrained from writing *Dear Little, I light up the instant I'm off a train, suck it furiously through long, underground transfers and across crowded platforms to noisy, sometimes rainy, always sweaty streets—so hot, June, incessantly hot.* Ripped up the unwritten postcard before the final thought dragged me in: always, always past kiosk counters stacked with mini bars of gold bullion I never used to notice.

Toward the end of my first giddyap month at the University of the Rio Grande, our sensei, Ihara, stood before the students, mostly Australian, Chinese, and Korean, who filled the large, unpleasantly cold classroom. Ihara Sensei dressed in various shades of cocoa and orange, unknowingly providing me with ideas to augment Achieve English's ridiculous red folder.

Ihara Sensei glanced up from her own folder. *"Carlie-san. Tenki wa, do desu, ka?"*

"Ten ki wa, do desu, ka?" I repeated, splitting the question into understandable lumps. "How is the weather? Wet as hell."

The class broke up. Ihara encouraged me to use Japanese.

"Ame," said Dennis, the too-smart Aussie who sat behind me. Ihara Sensei continued to probe our enthralling topic, aided by photos clipped from magazines. *Tenki wa ii*: perfect weather on what could be a Thai beach. I used to be there. With a chilled beer anytime and plenty of cute guys. Now, I was forced to compete with Dennis when all I could think about was how much I'd eaten for lunch. The glistening display in the same restaurant window seduced me every day. In the red compartments of a black-on-the-outside bento box were two plump pieces of fried shrimp, a moist square of tofu sprinkled with minced onions so green you could practically taste them. And rice. Thick pillows of it. One hundred percent plastic, utterly convincing, and the real deal on sale for only six hundred yen. A thousand calories, easy. Scarfed it in less than ten minutes. Would have to skip whatever dinner Ava tried to shove down my throat.

"Carlie-san?" Ihara Sensei wanted to know something about wind. My stomach—oof; too much rice. Dennis answered for me. Sensei brought out the next set of pictures. Food. I couldn't even take notes. Everything belly and below was in pain. I raised my hand and asked in English to be excused.

"In Japanese? *Nihon-go de?*" Sensei said. I blasted past her, out the door. On the toilet, I stared at four viscous splotches of reddish-brown in the crotch of my panties

The machine in the ladies' room ate my ten-yen coin without

dispensing as it should. I crammed some toilet paper into my undies and waddled to the front desk, where, euphemistically, I begged the two Office Ladies for help. The OLs conferred in Japanese—sounded like water trickling downstream—until the taller murmured, *"Aaah. Seri-chu desu."*

"Sure. I don't have any . . ." I flapped helplessly.

She flowed toward her purse, handing over the necessaries with an edifying whisper in faulty but welcome English: OLs often called in sick at this time of the month.

"Can I borrow your phone? How do you say that, again?"

I dialed Achieve English and delivered my first complete sentence in Japanese: *"Seri-chu, desu,"* hoping to sound weak and menstrual. Ava would be home by now. Fixing dinner. I stormed to the station, fat enough to have a period. Passed a kiosk. Ripped the gold foil off a mini bar before the guy had my hundred yen in his register. The next day, it was two—one on the way to Shinjuku, another on the way home. Ava never ate candy bars. Unable to deny myself the numbing sweetness of chocolate in transit, I took a later evening shift at work so that I could skip dinner. Cho didn't come home until after ten. Ava accepted my late homecomings, my "studying." Leaning into my cigs, I hewed it to one mini bar a day. A person should be able to eat anything that was only one hundred yen and one hundred calories without getting fat or going broke.

Smoking on the back steps. Cho dropped next to me. "Hey, girlfriend." She was blushing. Cho's like me. We don't blush. She waved away my proffered pack. "I'm quitting. For Ava. Boy, don't say, 'Cut back.' I'm not the type. We could call each other at work, to check in."

I ashed. "Since when did this become a Communist Utopia?"

"Carlie, please. I could use your help."

When a Booch from a major department store chain says, "Please," it is flattering. We kicked it off the next morning. Instead of smoking, I spent my train platform-crossings fantasizing about the chunky satisfaction of a regular-sized bar. At my first break, I did it. I headed with startling automation for the candy machine in Achieve English's blue lobby, paid three hundred yen, over three dollars, breathing hard in anticipation. Snuck to the bathroom, barricaded myself in a stall and downed that sucker in two minutes. Then I called Cho.

She started right in. "I'm nic-ing like a—and that little mother, Imai-san . . ." Cho riffed for a bit before getting to, "How are you doing with it?"

Putting food into the place the cigarettes used to be. Anyway, I could skip lunch.

Cho trashed herself for another minute. On my return to the classroom, I bought a second bar. Why did I volunteer to be the person Cho phoned when she wanted a cig? Once, she mentioned that she was eating more. I mumbled, "Yeah. Me too, I guess,"

On my train rides home, I poured my imagination into ice cream. Even though I wasn't able to read the label, I knew: one pint, four servings of 260 calories each. Within the week, I couldn't refrain from buying that pint. I did it every night. Alone in my room, I ran my hands over my clavicle, no longer sticking out in true ballet fashion. A pad across my stomach. Bigger boobs. I wanted to slash them off. Tomorrow, tomorrow I would stop. But every tomorrow: absent the benefit of a cigarette, should I reach Shinjuku in the morning without eating breakfast, should I manage to avoid the bakery on the first floor where the lemon-, cream-, and cherry-filled soldiers lined up for the assault; should I then squeak past the candy machine in the lobby and make myself call Cho, some Achieve English student was bound to have a cold. Trapped in the small, hot classroom, she'd rip open a pack of tissues. Sounded like a bag of Oreos. Cough drops smelled medicinal but cherry enough. Break was in ten minutes. A pastry. Five hundred calories. And that night, four servings of 260 calories each. *Oh, Little Matt, I did it every night.* I finished the ice cream, hoping to get to the bottom of the carton and find, for once, something besides the bottom of the carton.

One evening, late July, I finished the ice cream and in total resignation, I went again into the muggy night. A different store, another pint. I ate the ice cream while walking, ate it with my finger, as ludicrous as Simon had been when he left me for the beefy laughing man on Koh Phangan. Once home, I practically ran to the bathroom, stuck that same finger down my throat. It wouldn't come up. I thought about Rollback into Press, grabbing the enemy's shoulders.

I pressed. It hurt, the rush of food.

Good.

Step with an Empty Foot

I knew exactly what I was doing. Ballet girls did it all the time. If I hadn't known, there were plenty of articles to instruct me. Two thousand yen for English-language magazines. Sixteen bucks. I bought them anyway, read them while bingeing, read how vomiting destroyed stomach lining, teeth. Oh, get to the important stuff: how much weight did so-and-so white girl from the wealthy family with the controlling mother lose, and how quickly? Tell me when Tokyo became the capital of kiosks, supermarkets, convenience stores and fast-food; how to skip breakfast when Ava came after me with long *r*'s and steaming miso soup; low-cal enough, but—man, those cushions of brown rice she was forever shoving at me. 120 calories, and once I ate carbs, it was over: I was a ferocious stallion, finally let run free.

It was humiliating.

I did it anyway.

And the money. Dear God. I blew right through what was left of the three grand I brought to Japan. My salary went toward rent and expensive organic vegetables I bought, swearing, "Tomorrow." They rotted in the fridge as I flushed what I should have been banking. The articles never wrote about that.

In Japanese class, trying to focus on other than Snickers bars, I imagined a slim volume, *The Care and Feeding of Your Bulimic*. Chapter One: carry a toothbrush. Duh. Two: eye drops, for those burst blood vessels. Three: fried and baked foods hurt coming up. Soften fried with Cokes and baked with ice cream or milk. Always, in the last moments, finding the nearest toilet, I thought, I cannot go stick my face where anyone in Tokyo can put her butt.

And then I did.

It was worth it: I lost the weight.

It was a lie.

There was no imagining that Cho wouldn't pick up on it. No more break-time visits to her thirty-fifth-floor office. And Ava, forget it. Concerned by my rapid weight loss, she fretted over my protein-to-carb ratios. Best to avoid her, humming as she corrected quizzes in the evenings, best to quit tai chi—no; my only peace was my morning session in Kashiwabara's now blooming *teien*, and Doug's practice at Ueno Park. It was only then that all that existed was me and the movement.

In the supermarket one summer night, buying ice cream. A bottle of sleeping pills in my shopping basket. I didn't put it there. Right? Outside, hand in pocket, holding the bottle. Pit-stop in the restroom of a fast-food joint, after the last French fries I could cram into myself. Finally, our simple wooden gate. The stone path through the fairyland that was my daily homecoming: bushes and trees, my short, rounded stone lantern. Japanese beauty I could no longer feel.

The front door, the genkan, shoes off, toes pointed toward the door. A least I grasped this part of Japan. Ava, coming down the hall, bell-ringing, "Did you eat a proper supper, wee mucker?"

My "Yeah," as evasive as my bedroom shoji sliding closed. From the closet, I pulled out a futon and unfolded it across the floor, then sat to open the pills.

They were red dots. I pushed the bottle to just beyond reach on the tatami. Out of nowhere, hot rain against the window. Ava, fussing in the kitchen. One, big ear, I bet. A feeling from five years ago, Rome, a sunny bridge. At least then, the bridge held me. "Little," I begged the ceiling.

"Carlie?" Ava was on her way through the door. Despite my tears, I scanned the room for telltale food wrappers. Her eyes locked on the pill bottle. I lunged. She got there first, held it out to me like a question. I stopped crying at her to leave me alone and started crying at my aloneness.

"Carlie, talk to me. I'm an incest survivor as well—"

I did not want to hear that word. "Ava, shut up. I am not you. I puke."

Ava dropped the bottle. Red spots bounced across the pale straw mats. She leaned as if to gather them, then turned to me. "It's not your fault, wee mucker. It's a disease you have called—"

"I know what it's called. I know, I know, and I know. Knowing doesn't help."

"I know."

Her forehead-to-eyes made it so that I was not utterly taken aback when she finished, "I'm bulimic, as well." Then, "Whyn't ya tell me?"

"Why didn't you tell me?"

Ava was wearing indigo-blue batik sundress that wrapped, making her look super thin. Her hip bones poked out. Insult to injury when she said, "I haven't purged in three years."

"Years? I barely get through three hours!"

As soon as the words left my mouth, Ava went to def-con helpful. " . . . we have a breakfast every Saturday . . . someone from tai chi . . . terribly important to share with others who have issues with food—"

Man, I hated that; issues. I hated it. What a lemon of a choice, to tell Ava. Clearly, she was as screwed up about food as I was, despite the pithy gallivant through Tokyo and the humming and the "sea vegetables." It was seaweed, goddamnit. But she'd mentioned someone else. The next morning, I spent the practice in surveillance. Elise was skinny. Not as thin as I used to be. I used to be so thin. Waaaaaaaaa. How did I used to be so thin? Right: I ate nothing but cigarette smoke all day and drank dinner. Totally unfocused on the form, I almost lost my balance. Just as Doug was watching, of course.

He came over, his dark hair held off his neck by a blue bandanna. "Don't shift your weight so soon. Step with an empty foot. Sink into the standing leg. Really root, so that the other foot has no weight. Let the empty foot find its place, then step into it."

"It's hard to root when there's no . . . earth." Across the grass, next to the slim gusto of her girlfriend, stood the one person I knew with real ground beneath her. Who I lied to. For months.

Ditching Doug, ditching practice, I pulled Cho to the shrine, where solid brown beams and the vigor of red trim gave me the ability to admit, "I've become bulimic." Cho lowered her head with a, "Sheeez."

I wanted to tell her how I knew my failure had to do with quitting smoking. Ripples quivered across the slate-blue surface of Shinobazu Ike, lifting then lowering the browning lily pads fringing its edges. I really wanted to.

Cho said, "How did I not put two and two together? Especially when you lost weight."

"Do you want me to move out?"

Cho reached to twist her loose hair around her hand and then let it fall apart. "I was pissed that I'd gained. Boy, when you brought me over here, I thought, here we go, I've been too bitchy. Girlfriend is leaving us."

Cho was willing to listen but didn't require much filling in. "I've been in love with a bulimic for four years. You going to Saturday breakfasts?"

"Man, it's so . . . My name is Carlie, I'm an alcoholic."

"You are an alcoholic."

On Saturday morning, the coffee shop Ave led me to was one of those Western ones that also served Japanese food. When a familiar bulk with a Rastafarian beret approached our table, I discharged my foulest glare at Ava. This breakfast was supposed to help. Margot was *fat*.

To Margot's clear interest in my presence, Ava said, "Carlie will join us, if you've no objection," and ordered the Japanese Morning Set: miso soup, fish, white rice, and a tiny salad. Six hundred calories, if Ava would use salad dressing rather than a shake of vinegar, would eat her friggin' rice. Margot ate it for her, after consuming a stack of pancakes and a side of sausage. I picked at one of two slices of dry toast and waited for Margot to "use the restroom."

Never happened. Instead, the Canadian described "this week's humiliation." At the junior high where she taught, she entered her classroom to discover on the chalkboard, a cartoon, huge stomach and breasts, wild curls topped by the colorful beret. "They even got my," Margot indicated her nose ring.

"It sounds awful," Ava said.

"That's jokes, eh? They're kids. You finished there?"

It was clear from the brusque way Margot waved with a sausage link to one of my untouched slices that she knew we did not believe her. Her butter knife clinked against the jam jar each time she scooped.

Onto my toast. I asked her, "Why don't you eat less?"

Margot's mouth dropped open. I could see my toast. Luckily, she laughed. Loudly. "I cannot seem to cultivate the necessary denial. Where's the creamer?"

Ava passed it as I pressed Margot, "But when you . . . after a certain number of . . ."

"Twelve hundred," Ava said.

"Five hundred." I ate less than her. Ha.

"What are you talking about?" Margot summoned the waiter, hail fellow well met.

Ava didn't hesitate. "Calories before you might as well purge."

Margot let out an "Ah," and rotated her nose ring with

uncommon understanding. Mortified, I tried to clarify, "It's better not caring, but, *boday-con*."

"Japanese slang," Ava said to Margot—even though I could have. I had to add, "For 'body-conscious.' Guys at work say it about their hot students."

Margot muttered, "I guess we fatsos aren't conscious of our bodies," as Ava took on the look of a dinosaur, seeking prey: elongated neck, eyes on fire. "Is that going on, at the school? We shall put an end to that."

Of course, the coming week had to be the one that Ava started at Achieve English. When Saito Sensei presented Ava as the co-head of school, man did they make a pair: Saito Sensei, the sturdy epitome of the Japanese businesswoman in a powder-pink power suit, and Ava, wearing an eggplant-purple dress. Its cling emphasized the lean, long line of her, and the color turned her fair skin to snow and her strawberry-blonde hair into a dawning sun. Also entrancing were the traveler touches. A jade pin from Burma (Cho's) peeked from under a batik scarf. From the moment Saito introduced their new supervisor, the teachers loved Ava—every gaijin I knew not one whit better than when I had started last April. Ava was as generous and—well, as goofy-loving as she had been in Thailand, once I got to know her. Teachers could hardly wait to yakity-yak—her "mates," as she called them; though not "muckers." I found myself pleased.

No. Relieved.

Even in the face of the curtain-thick smoke in the staff room, Ava was Lady Equilibrium. If a chat went on too long, she'd take care of herself as well as them by bowing out with a, "S'not your-lot's fault I'm allergic. I'll be in my office. Door's always open." That bell of a laugh. "Euphemism." At home, she told me that, to address the smoke, she took Chinese herbs Doug gave her when she saw him for acupuncture. I didn't even know Doug did acupuncture.

Ava said, "You should see him for treatments, Carlie. It so

helped with my bingeing. Especially in the beginning."

And out the window went my interest in freshening our friendship. At the office, I felt pressure to eat nothing except for the lunches Ava provided: bean products and leafy summer vegetables, brown rice that left me obsessing over the sesame seed garnish. Individual grams of fat. Man, I couldn't pop a Diet Coke without her peering over the tops of her glasses, checking and checking. She wouldn't trust me to work this out, even though a new volume replaced *The Care and Feeding of Your Bulimic* on my internal best-seller list.

How To Keep Your Head out of the Toilet.

Chapter One: "Studying." One Saturday at breakfast, I revealed hesitantly that my primary binge time was when I hit the Japanese books. Ava asked me what my desk looked like when I studied. I hated her subsequent idea so much that, on the way home, I stopped at a convenience store. However, when I set up in my room, I went ahead and did what she suggested: took a moment to take in the top of the low table. A literal half-moon: pint of ice cream, notebook, three candy bars. Then a space I had literally left empty, to fill after my second trip to the store.

I forced myself to cram the ice cream and candy bars into the kitchen trash. When it persisted in calling to me, I poured dishwashing liquid all over it. I'd put food in the garbage, before. Then I ran down the tatami hall to Ava. "How did you know?"

"I used to work that way, as well."

I heard myself say, "How'd you stop?"

"I prayed beforehand. When I couldn't pray, I asked for help."

"Who do you ask?"

"I simply ask."

A puzzling relaxation crept up my legs and into my belly, which pooched out in relief. I might be able to open to a something that was nothingness. Getting in the way was that I was not willing to pray.

As if she could sense it, Ava scooted me to the kitchen. Even before I sat cross-legged at the low table, the binge food in the garbage beckoned. I would wash it off.

Meanwhile, Ava launched into brewing two cups of green tea with toasted brown rice. She hummed and nattered in a way that distracted me nicely. The tea offered the same relief as pooching out had. I took a moment to close my eyes and breathe into the memory of the Quanyin woman in white calling to me about my wallet, to bring again that precious red object into feeling, this time pulsing in my heart area. Not grief, anymore. Pain-filled joy. Tea and a Quanyin check-in became my study ritual.

Over the weeks, Margot helped me identify my trigger foods, mostly creamy or cakey things. Kid food, she pointed out as we ambled around Shinobazu Pond after morning practices. Margot always took the time, if I asked, which I tried to do, if I'd binged. During one such stroll, she told me about dropping out of her Ph.D. program in Applied Math to travel Asia with a guy who dumped her along the way for a sex worker he claimed to have fallen in love with.

Slowing my steps, I decided to tell her. I didn't mention Lyle and Ted. I said only, "I'm an incest survivor."

Right away, she took my hand. "Like Ava?"

It would have been so easy to shrill out, "Not like Ava. Like me." Instead, I sat on a nearby bench, where I found myself lifting my feet off the ground, one after the other. "We're just, both incest survivors."

Chapter Two: no counting calories, no weighing myself, the rule I'd have given my right lower leg to ignore the March morning tempting me to try on the rose-colored skirt it had been too cold to wear since autumn. I loved this mini. My smallest. Chapter sub-heading: Who Needs a Scale to Weigh Herself?

Again, I fled down the tatami hall. All resolute sparkle, Ava assured me that I had a lovely, healthy body. Meanwhile, she ate, like, sprouts for lunch. I phoned Margot.

"Wear the forest green with the tiny buttons down the front.

You're a doll in that. And throw out that pink thing, eh?"

I left the house verdant. The subway smelled like sesame. On the platform, kiosks' counters offered stacks of gold bullion. I pretended I was at Ueno practice, sending shoots into the earth, and arrived at work unsullied, despite the radiant cherry battalion in the first-floor bakery.

I didn't have to walk by them.

I could have gone through Accessories.

I hated accessories.

And the packed elevator. For twenty-seven floors. And the staff room. Hot, crowded, tobaccoed. Ugly blue carpet. I wanted a Diet Coke but not Ava's pop-top concern. Distracted from lesson planning because a red-haired Australian, Brian, was showing off for a pinkish Brit by the name of Felix. With me sitting right there, Brian said, "New student, mate."

I knew they would before they said together, "Boday-Con." They actually high-fived.

It was going to be those pastries. I had to wait until my next break and then had to negotiate my way out of the office. Ava would know just by looking at me—How dare they talk about our bodies like that?—just by looking. The forty minutes before I could sink my decaying teeth into the flakey, carmine delights were murder, but, man, the high; the high lasted until I was no longer eating but stuffing frenetically—How dare they; as if we existed to be assessed—furtive appropriation of co-workers' yogurts, their egg salad sandwiches, slinks to the vending machine, let the wild horse run free. We are not objects. I am a person. I was a child.

No wonder I made myself barf. It hurt.

"Oh, Carlie," Ava said when she found me that evening, pale-faced in the kitchen.

"Three days! It was the longest I've gone since this whole thing started."

Ava put down her book bag. All I needed was for her to hold

me, and that was all she did.

First class of the next morning. B-b-b k-k-k, zzzzzz. I introduced an ice breaker about hobbies. Most of them "played ski."

I couldn't resist the endearing phrase. "I play tai chi."

Impossible, then, to convey why a white girl would study a Chinese martial art. In Japan. My "It's grounding," only served to confuse them further.

The young woman who was the best speaker in the class, Ihori, said, "I sing in the church choir. Miss Carlie? Would you explain about the Easter? Why is the Easter?"

I erased the board. The four young women and one young man around the table remained motionless.

What was a white girl to do?

"Well, Christ"—this Catholic school drop-out's first use of that word as other-than-epithet in quite some time—"died. Then he rose, proving God's . . ." I clutched my eraser.

Ihori clapped with delight. "That is why he leaves eggs!"

Made as much sense as anything. From then on, I couldn't make myself do it when I practiced alone, but each time we started the form at Doug's class, as I held my right fist in front of my sternum and curved the left palm softly over it, power and the correct use of power: *Okay, whatever you are that's in charge of all this, show me your stuff.* One Saturday, while I was on the lookout for miracles, Doug came close with the subdued grin that no longer masked a true teacher's strength of mind.

"Carlie's standing around doing nothing. Something's up."

"I am seeking proof of God."

Doug used a solid hand to shield his puzzled expression from the sun. "You don't come across as super religious."

"This is the problem."

Hard to tell who laughed harder, me or him. A few of the others looked our way, looked back.

"I'll tell you, Carlie, sometimes, God, you gotta wonder." Doug's eyes appeared, if possible, to darken. He shook away the mood. "My friend, a lotta people come through these practices. Not many get what you get out of them."

He called me his friend. The feeling took a while to identify: a spot of light, right after the first time at the cabin. Watching the purple fist of Koh Phangan from the sky. The silence after Ava said, "I know ya would. You don't have to."

When I came back, Doug was still waiting.

"I feel—I don't know . . . in the center of myself? Guess that's it, after practicing."

"Sounds like a good place for God."

Across the spring grass, deeply focused, Ava trusted her weight to her standing leg before stepping into her empty foot. But when I came home as afternoon was tapering, no jolly whirlwind was plating up low-cal organic delicacies in our kitchen. Spying a reddish gleam on the back porch, I made toasted green tea and brought it out in two palm-sized cups on a varnished tray. A blue Air Mail envelope was on the top step, open but with the letter tucked inside. Ava sat next to it without seeming to see it. As I put down the tray, however, she gestured.

"That one arrived today. Full of Ma's usual. Sis got the kale to come up early. There are new ducks, I haven't written back in two years, Carlie. She appears not bothered. Fuck, are you sure you're not slippin' out for a smoke every now and again? This porch is positively clatty."

I heard myself ask, "What's that mean?"

"I can'nae believe I said—and you're so crackin', making me tea. It means 'stinky,' ya wee mucker. Each time a letter—that's when the doubts truly upend me. 'Did it happen? Di' it really happen?' You seem so certain."

Deliberately, Ava ripped her mother's lightweight note in half. "When things go well, like this new job, and I'm good at it and the teachers like me, well! I hear, if they knew, or, if Saito

Sensei knew, well! So I push, and I push at it. It can't have happened. It can't be real. Not my Dad."

I dropped next to her on the steps.

She continued, "I don't have the memories you do, Carlie. I have strong emotions that come with shadows, images that I've learned to trust. Dougie and his acupuncture helped with that. I don't know that I'll ever have more than those to hold in my hand, to stamp me as a real survivor."

"I started purging because I quit drinking and smoking."

Ava didn't appear to hear my painful admission. She stood to kick out her long legs, one then another, like a colt. "The days I up and claim it, life is so much more clear. Cho says I'm a textbook survivor, right down to the way I attempted suicide."

"Oh. Man."

"It was a year or so after I met her. I wrote a note"—Ava made jazz-hands—"lit candles all around, and ate a bottle of your wee red sleeping pills. Then I got scared and threw up the lot. Which is worse, a successful suicide or a failed one?"

"You're not a failure, Ava. You just wanted more."

"Than what?"

"Than what we got."

After a pause, Ava used her toes to sweep together the shreds of her mother's letter. "Under Dougie's guidance, I stopped writing Ma back. Despite Cho's, I have yet to bung a letter into the bin unopened." Ava ground a scrap of paper into the dirt. "I should write to them, tell them I know all about it."

"Guess what happened at my house, the morning after my sister ran away?"

"They called the police."

"Why would they call the police?" I asked.

"Their daughter went missing!"

"Why did their daughter go missing? What happened the morning after my sister ran away was that my brother and I went to school, and our parents went to work."

"Are you sure your mum knew as well?"

"Under the guidance of my friend, Ava, I say: Of course she knew. They all do."

Ava's eyelids quivered. After a time, she asked, "Does it ever seem as if life responds to your beliefs about it?"

"Let's practice."

I backed onto the grass, took the starting stance, and rotated the ball the way Gemma had me do a year ago on Koh Phangan. The basics. I raised and lowered it. Up and down. The movement surprised me, growing of its own accord, becoming up, out, and down. I crouched, smelling good dirt, scooped up more and stronger chi, reached for the sky—a late-spring afternoon sky, a day I knew but couldn't name. Five years old? No; eight. On a beachy knoll overlooking Puget Sound right before Dad and Lyle and Ted took Patrice to the cabin for the first time.

"Carlie?"

We three, Patrice and Little and I, were at Carkeek Park, on the rocky beach between the play area and the Sound. The air glimmered, and the water was vast and steely blue. How could we have known what was going to happen to Patrice? The sky was empty of anything except its vibrancy, but we knew, we three. We all knew.

"Carlie!"

Ava's urgent tone told me she could see my legs trembling. I almost opened my eyes, but that would send me into what we knew was going to take place. In the back yard, I stretched toward the water. I could smell drying seaweed. Waves far bigger than Puget Sound allowed surged to meet me. At each wave's apex, it shimmered silver-white over me and circled back to the sea, where it dissolved, only to form again. I hovered above the self who was scooping and reaching as I simultaneously hovered above us three children on the beach—above but also part of what was about to happen, which was not what we deserved. I could smell sunscreen and feel the breeze and the warmth of the sun against my cheeks and across my nose, yellow and green— and me able to trust the beauty, the safety.

Next to me, Ava took the form's opening position. We began. Halfway through, she was stepping onto firmer ground than I feared I would ever find. I didn't feel the envy I'd battled all along but acknowledged only now because, for one moment, I got it, too. For that moment, I was swimming in God's soup.

Crashing

When we finished practicing, I told Ava to relax so I could make her more tea. Waiting in the kitchen for the water to boil, I flashed to a different time my family was at the beach. In this memory, I was nine years old. My father was taking pictures of me, and I felt like a movie star. My cover-up was Lifesaver green with inch-wide shoulder straps that I loved the color of: crisp white. I played catch with Little and Patrice, but, for once, I was the movie star. My straps slid pleasantly back and forth as I dove for the ball. We'd bought it at the drugstore, the ball, along with my father's film and Juicyfruit gum that would fall out of the pack and to the bottom of my mother's purse. I was sure that Mom knew when I snuck the flat, foil-wrapped sticks from between the pennies and loose cigarettes. The gum never tasted only sweet. It always had tobacco flakes in it.

The kettle began to tremble. I remembered that the sand between my toes felt scratchy, a grown-up feeling, almost painful, but even that rough sense pushed me toward beauty. The air smelled exactly the way beach air should, like waves crashing. The wind held just a touch of sunscreen. My father's fancy camera focused on me, for once. I loved the attention. I was beautiful, a movie star. I was green, I was mirth; I was everything they wanted me to be. My shoulder straps had a round white button on each, a big round white button. A button.

In the kitchen, the kettle shrieked as loudly as my mother ever had. That one-moment God invited me to let it in: what my father would do with the pictures, once developed, do to his body while he watched mine, and my hand reaching for the kettle shook because I'd brought back the button and the ocean and the waves. The waves, crashing.

Precious Brocade

I got through Thursday and Friday by ignoring the memory. I even got through most of Saturday. By Saturday night, man; as I kneeled at the kotatsu in the kitchen, unable to ingest even my tea, I listened to Ava and Cho in their room, giggling as they dressed for a date. They came into the kitchen—"What ya up to, tonight, lass?" "Renting a movie"—and I was face down in food. Two days. To crawl out of the hole, I went to Ava. She should write, *On Crawling Out*. All we needed was a haiku: Establish mealtimes/Moderate serving sizes/No second helpings.

Phone calls with Margot let me unpack the emotional overwhelm—Matt, little sub in enemy waters—and tai chi righted the physical blowback. But to dig into the actual pain, there was no one for that but Cho. I asked her to our favorite spot in the house, the back porch, sliding open the glass door to allow in the best part of May: the air. It felt like what I imagined air would feel like if we'd gotten to be three normal kids.

"Do you think I should contact Matt?" I asked Cho.

"Carlie, girlfriend, you just spent two days on a bender. Now is not the time to contact anyone in your family."

"But I ran out on him. I want to—to save him. Is that dumb?"

Cho held me, let me cry, wiped my tears before saying, "Maybe one day. Just, not today."

I didn't reply, unsure I agreed until Cho, Ava, and I came up on the pond on our way to the next tai chi practice and Ava said, "The lotuses are coming back."

It was true. The dried remnants at the edges of the pond had sprouted low, flat leaves that ducked under and over each other, organic support for the exquisite blooms to follow. But you had to believe in flowers.

Monday. Wednesday. Friday. At each practice, the lotus occupied more of Shinobazu Ike's surface than they had the previous Monday, Wednesday, or Friday. Apparently, Doug was observing our progress with similar stealth, because with the heat of the June rains came his diagnosis: our form lacked chi. Loosening the blue bandanna from his dark hair to wipe his neck, Doug introduced *chi gong*.

"It's like tai chi with no martial application. We do it purely to develop chi."

He started us learning the *Ba Duan Jin*, the Eight Treasures, also called Eight Pieces of Silk or Eight Precious Brocades. "Eight postures done eight times apiece. Simply put, each one governs one or more of the body's organs or systems. The first is the Triple Heater. It balances the metabolism between the lower, middle, and upper body."

Doug inhaled, bringing his hands to mid-chest, turning them over, and pushing them toward the sky as he went up on his toes. He stretched fully, into the air and into the earth. Then he lowered his heels and arms as he exhaled. He demonstrated eight times at a comfortable pace, fluid through the different parts of the posture. Nice arms.

The Second Brocade, the Archer: arms slowly opened as if shooting an arrow, first to the right, then to the left. Eight times total. Stretched the chest, stimulated the lungs. The Third Brocade started by reaching the right arm toward the sky and the left toward the ground. The arms then floated to briefly hold the tai chi ball, then reversed, left up and right down. Eight times. Separating Heaven and Earth.

The Catholic school drop-out in me dragon-snorted. "If I'm not sure about God, I certainly don't believe in hell."

Ava's tone came easy. "Not hell. Earth."

I shook off my annoyance by re-focusing on silky movement. The shifts through my chest allowed the muscles to open, releasing the shame and fear around yesterday's binge, my first in two weeks. After practice, I told Margot about it, but I didn't want to tell Ava. Not because I didn't want to process. Because I didn't want to tell her.

The Fourth Brocade: Wise Owl Gazes Back to Let Go. Arms at your sides, palms facing down, look to the right while breathing out. Then inhale. Exhale while looking to the left. Eight times. Over the weekend, my frail-looking landlady with the full head of white hair came across me practicing what I could remember of the Eight Treasures in her again-spectacular garden. My Japanese was still jerky, but Kashiwabara-san's was less incomprehensible. Maybe she spoke about her son, a reporter living north, in Aomori, and the trip they took to Hawaii in 1974. On the other hand, it could be that Kashiwabara-san was leaving for Hawaii on the nineteenth for seventy-four days.

"This summer, does Carlie-san plan to return home to visit her family?"

No mistaking that question. Kashiwabara-san had let go of more than I could even look at, yet I could barely breathe.

I could.

Kashiwabara-san left me to what she called my "work." I stood with my arms at my sides. I looked to the right while breathing out, then inhaled and looked to the left. The air filled more than my nostrils, more than my sinuses. More than my neck and lungs. More than me.

Entering the house, I found Ava, her body aimed toward the place in the garden where Kashiwabara-san and I had our conversation. "What was that all about, Carlie?"

"She asked if I would go home for a visit this summer."

I was confident that empathy would surge through Ava. Instead, she crossed her arms into full armor. I was able to blame not her but one of her mood swings.

At our next practice, the Fifth Brocade: Wild Horse Swings Its Mane. Head led the torso in a sweeping circle to the right, then to the left, then in a circle, then the reverse. Eight times, total. I became a pendulum: I am fat. I am beautiful. Men in and out of my bed while traveling, barely even glanced at a guy for the past year. In front of me, Margot swung her wild mane strong. A great friend and a cool chick, but there was no guarantee that Margot was a Tokyo lifer. Cho, Doug, even Ava; their heads should lead my torso. Ava was no Cho at Japanese, but she understood how to work the food in this country. Cho read the business section every morning, phoned Liu constantly.

Doug touched my shoulder. "Stay focused."

The Sixth Brocade was the Angry Fist. Slow-motion punch with one fist, slow-motion punch with the other. This brocade was too easy to connect with.

Deep breaths between each punch.

I breathed.

Oh, man.

The Seventh Brocade, unromantically titled Reaching Down to Dissipate Disease. Hands on what Doug termed our buttocks. Exhale as you bend forward, sliding your hands down the backs of your legs to the ground. Then a big inhale. Doug said, "Draw energy from the earth. What overwhelms you, she will carry. As you stand straight, pull her strength up your legs."

Earth chi blasted through me, a geyser. I listed to the left.

Doug gestured to said buttocks. "You're swayed. Relax."

He tapped my coccyx. The contact dazed me. Doug repeated, "Relax." Despite the clean, sweaty scent of him, I managed to. My spine, neck, and head found alignment.

Doug's eyes shone. "You were a little out of whack, that's all."

"That's where I need you."

We both froze in the hot sun. Oh, man. But, whole year. I said, "You always get the bigger picture, when we talk about the form."

The confusion left his face. "Hey, I'm a tai chi teacher. That's what we do."

After a moment, Doug said, "Okey-doke," and crossed with unhurried grace to the new German guy. Horst winked at me, but I wanted to feel Doug's fingers once more against the base of my spine, wanted to trace the shape of his dark eyebrow. Without cigarettes or alcohol, I had no idea how to flirt, so I spent next few practices allegedly breathing; to take a mouthful of that solid neck. When Doug concentrated, his face took on an engraved beauty. Something funny didn't get the guffaw it would get from Margot. His head went down, and the corners of his mouth reached for his eyes like the sun breaking through.

Oh, I was ga-ga.

"Coming to tea?" I asked him after one notably humid practice, hoping no one could guess about me.

"Lemme check with Akiko." He called over to the girl who appeared occasionally, the only Japanese student. Always in black: large sunglasses, sandals with clunky heels. She toed them off before every practice to do the form barefoot. Doug and Akiko discussed the tea issue; rather, she told him, in Japanese that I understood every word of, that she didn't want to go out with the rest of us. She wanted a lunch date. She wore no blush; the sole splash of color her wine-red lips.

Oh, man.

She was his girlfriend.

Fuck.

Goddamn it. She was his girlfriend.

Shit.

I skulked away from the practice area, fantasizing their lunch date. Doug, perspiring lightly. Then dinner: Doug, not sweaty. Smelling good. I took them home. His hands ran under her tight black top. I almost bought cigarettes. I hated Doug. At the next Saturday breakfast, Margot reached for, then stood firm against, Ava's rice as I said, "Is Doug one of those loser white guys who go for Asian women because they can walk all over them?"

My words boomeranged with an ugly clang. The Eighth

Treasure, the Spinal Jolt: raise up on your toes and drop. Hard.

Margot said, "Doug is Chinese American, eh?"

I said, "He thinks I'm some dumb kid."

Margot and Ava purposefully did not exchange glances. The Spinal Jolt done eight times was supposed to be a mind-blowing chi-o-vator. At work, Brian, the Australian ginger and key *boday-con-noisseur* asked me about the language games I had started using to enliven classes. Didn't matter. On a phone call, Liu implied there was cash to be made in software, should I invest thusly when my CD matured in September. I wound the phone cord through my fingers, trying to recall if he'd had photos of a wife and kids on his desk.

Professional recognition didn't matter. Stocks, big whoop. Love was the Eighth Treasure.

Three weeks passed, no binges. It mattered. We sweltered toward August. We raised to the sky and lowered, shot the arrow, separated heaven and earth. I couldn't do anything for Little Matt, could barely let it go, but gamely swung my horse's mane. Margot got together with Horst. When she and I circled Shinobazu Ike after one practice, I said, "I wouldn't mind a date."

Margot rotated her nose-ring. "I could name five guys from tai chi who are dying for your attention. Horst thought you were sugar, eh?"

Since he'd been dating Margot, I had noticed how dashing Horst was. That beard. "How come he didn't he ask me out?"

"Carlie. Five. This minute."

My mind ran the roster: Canadian Steve, Australian Johnny. What's-his-face, the super-tall one who talked to me too much. None of them liked me. I studied harder, read the paper, reached down to dissipate disease. Shinobazu Ike was all green leaves and white flowers with yellow centers. The lotus had blossomed.

It mattered.

Liu called from Hong Kong. "An American concern, went public March of eighty-six."

"Any signs of a split?"

"Already has done. September of eighty-seven."

"Man."

"My thoughts precisely. And again, April of this year."

It seemed an obvious investment. Plus, the name tickled my fancy. Microsoft.

September and new teachers at Achieve English. One of them, Yvette, was a not-quite-Ava-thin, gray-eyed Brit who clicked with another newbie, this one from New Zealand. What this one lacked in the pedagogical department she almost made up for with incomprehensible good looks: creamy cheeks, sapphire eyes. Great boobs. Her name actually was Mona Lisa. She moonlighted as a nightclub hostess, a job which involved drinking with and lighting the cigarettes of Japanese customers. Yvette teased Mona Lisa non-stop about her rich Japanese boyfriends. The two of them whispered in a way clearly designed for other people to almost hear. By the time the lotus across Shinobazu Ike receded and browned into a fringe at the pond's edge, Yvette served as proxy queen of the staff room when Ava retreated to her office due to the smoke.

I was flattered the day that she and Mona Lisa waved me over for lunch.

"There's a pretty number," Yvette shot my way, examining the well-ordered bento box Ava had packed for me. It was. With the change in seasons, eggplant and snow peas had given way to Japanese pumpkin and chestnuts stewed with persimmon then sprinkled with black sesame seeds. I almost teared up with the memory of how terrifying those individual grams of fat used to be. These days, not only did the meal go down easy, it stayed down—and the solidity of it warded off another binge.

"Did you make all that?" Mona Lisa asked, opening a box of red licorice and chewing in the ugliest way possible, with a strip drooping out of the side of her mouth.

"Ava did." I sounded like a high-voiced child.

"Co-head Ava cooks for you?" Yvette asked. Something about the way she said it brushed my skin as false.

"You're not as skinny as her," said Mona Lisa.

"Shut it, Mona," Yvette said. To me: "Tell me, Carlie. Are they planning to bring in an assistant head teacher? Aren't you thick as thieves with Yamashita as well?"

"Yamashita Butch-o-u," I had to say. It was too rude, not using the title Cho had turned herself inside-out to realize. Besides, Yvette's obvious ploy burned like three heaters. Though there were riches here, too. Over the next weeks, as Yvette continued to shine on me, I didn't have to fake focused reading by the window, the way Serious Joan from Canada did—even if I did have to continually turn down cigarettes, licorice, and, man, offers to join them for pints after work. I prided myself on not binging over it. Following one too many evasions, however, Yvette insisted, "It is Friday night, dear."

Mona Lisa said, "Let's go to Tengu."

I was familiar with the restaurant. Too familiar. Their pumpkin croquettes were as sweet as fried cake. I should go home, as I had for all these months, get some silken sleep. Have Saturday breakfast with the old ladies.

Damn it, I was going to do what nineteen-year-olds all over the world did on Friday nights: shake my mane.

Wild Horse Swings its Mane

We traversed Shinjuku—an admired three and we knew it. Stepping from the crosswalk onto the sidewalk, we ran into Brian from work.

"Carlie's coming out?" bellowed the redhead.

I said, "Do alert the media," drawing a laugh from someone I hadn't noticed at Brian's left, a Black man with a shaved head, a small gold hoop in one ear, and a marvelous olive-green tie.

"One of me rugby mates. Az," Brian introduced him. Az's glance lingered on Mona Lisa, who answered with an offhand smirk. Even when Brian presented me as "a Yank as well," the buccaneer's attention stayed on the fairest of them all.

Brian invited himself along. "Best way to meet women, go out with women."

Az said, "Brian, bro."

"They trust you more!"

Yvette and Mona Lisa were already overlapping each other, having no problem saying right in front of Brian, "He's revolting." "Obsessed." "At least Az appears to be a gentleman."

The last surprised me by being from me.

Approbation flashed, a match, Yvette to Mona Lisa, who didn't sparkle in return. Instead, she turned to Az with somehow sleek, somehow rounded lips.

"Tengu then, mate?"

The place was mobbed: lots of Japanese yuppies, more gaijin. We piled into a smoky corner booth, the dim orange light making Az's suave scalp—man—glow. A waitress appeared. Yvette said, "First shout is Brian's."

Az asked the waitress to put the beers on *Akage-sama's* tab. Akage meant "red-haired." Using *-sama* rather than *-san* indicated reverence. I was the only one to laugh, signaling the waitress before she left. *"O-cha dake, kudasai."*

"What'd you get?" Mona Lisa asked, whapping the end of her pack of cigarette hard against the table at the intrigued look my request pulled out of Az.

"Just green tea." I spoke louder to be heard over Steve Miller Band on the sound system. "Some call me the gangster of love."

Yvette's glossy red lips drew wide, as if she were all emotional support. "Carlie is a terrible swot. Forever studying Japanese."

Mona Lisa's mouth became plum flesh. "Or she's got her nose in the newspaper. *Man.*"

"And this is the first time you've come out with us, isn't it, dear? And you don't even have a drink-y." Still lustrous, Yvette indicated the ladies' room with a tilt of her head. I trailed her and Mona Lisa, grateful to be included, pathetic pony.

In the restroom, fluorescence glared against the white-tiled walls and floor. Through the fiery grimace of unneeded lipstick application, Yvette instructed Mona Lisa to shag Az.

Mona Lisa shut herself into a stall. "That Black? Anyway, I'm due at the club in forty minutes. Carlie kin have 'im."

Yvette leaned her hip against a sink. As if biting into one of those long, twisty donuts from the store's bakery, she said "Tell us about co-head Ava, then, Carlie. Isn't she like that?"

A ping at the base of my spine told me I understood, confirmed when we heard Mona Lisa, from her perch. "She wears make-up. You'd think she was normal."

When we returned to the smoke-plagued booth in the corner, the table was laden with beer, fried food, and one prudish tea. Az played eye games with Mona Lisa. After about ten minutes, she pushed her plate to the center of the mess we'd made.

"I've an engagement." She reached half-heartedly for her bag.

"I've got it," Az said.

"Cheers." Everything round about Mona Lisa—cheeks, eyes, boobs—went demure. After she left, Brian said none-to-quietly to Az, "Steer clear, mate. She's good but strange."

I didn't care what might be wacko about Mona Lisa. The girl who used to sit alone near the window just craved those leftover fries. My face was three times as hot as was comfortable as I imagined twirling one, dunking it in catsup. I'd smoke it if I could. I'd keep from lighting up if it killed me. Which it came close to doing when Brian suggested sake. I am healing, I am healing, I chanted to myself. How could it be that The Rolling Stones roared "Start Me Up" as fermented liquid poured into teeny tiny cups? As a last defense, I scanned the menu. Steamed soybeans. Safe.

Pumpkin croquettes.

The stallion jumped the fence.

I snuck every fry possible, even the cold ones, waiting for— my croquettes! My plate brought with it a huge liberation, my only thought: everything I got to eat before I had to deal with it.

Engrossed in pumpkin, I was surprised when Az asked about tai chi. Yeah, now that the lovely Mona Lisa was out of the picture. I found myself playing Lonely Planet Carlie to Az's every guy I was going to have to blow to get it over with. As if rehearsed, Az asked if he could get me anything. He meant a drink. I chose an ice cream sundae and ignored the question mark that all but wrote itself across his forehead. The supple bliss of open-ended eating hardened into truth. I slipped to the toilet of glaring white. I was supposed to be healing. The stallion reared in victory.

Back at the booth, Brian was pursuing a butterfly at the bar. Yvette was adding to the pile of money on the table. She said, "Last train."

Missing the last train meant an expensive taxi, an all-night disco, or a Love Hotel, which was exactly what it sounded like. I just wanted out of there.

I had to be back to that weird state I hadn't been in since traveling, where thought happened outside my head, because Az said, "My place is real close."

Yvette's sharp features bowed into the expression she wore when she asked about Ava with her ass against the sink. I leaned toward my pirate's earbob, yet not so near that Yvette couldn't hear, "When's the last train from your station?"

Az ran a hand over his scalp. "About one-thirty."

"When's the first?"

"Six."

"Sure."

Az insisted on a cab. Once we were seated, he interlaced his fingers with mine. If I could just focus on that. "Can we stop at a convenience store?"

"Got that covered, baby."

"No. Ice cream."

Az gawked happily. Unable to clarify, I refused to let Az come with me as I bought ice cream and two large chocolate bars. I was halfway through one as I opened the taxi door. Az's stare was on the meter. "You smell like chocolate."

I sucked a piece into my mouth and kissed it into his. The driver watched through the rear-view mirror. I began to obsess that the ice cream would melt.

"This is it," Az said, showing me his single room with its ribbon-wide kitchen. The immaculate state of the place kicked what I was about to do into the side of my head. Impossible—not with a stomach chockablock full. "Can I take a bath?"

Az's forehead showed the same surprise that it had at Tengu, when I asked for a sundae. All he said was, "No prob."

If an airplane had a bathroom, it would be the size of Az's. The walls, floor, and tub were a single swath of beige plastic. I opened the faucets to camouflage the sound of bringing everything up and was dipping to my knees in front of the toilet when Az knocked. I leapt up just before he came in, carrying several candles.

"Here we go."

To fit into the tub, I had to fold my knees against my chest. I tried not to think about my belly as he soaped and rinsed me. His hands lingered here and there, but there was no space in the tub for much else. We retired to his futon.

Az placed the candles on the windowsills, filling the place with the promise of us. I was warm from my bath, and his face was eager, but my pure fatness booted me out of the room. Like a movie screen, the ceiling played film of me under so many sour-smelling men.

Az stopped kissing me. "Let me know if anything I'm doing over here intrigues you."

"It's late and . . . do you want . . ." My chin made a cursory gesture toward his pelvis.

"You into it?"

"I'm sorry. I'm just really tired."

Az shook his bare head once. "How 'bout we cuddle, for now?"

He fell asleep behind me with his hands on my breasts, his head inseparable from my neck. This was what it could be like. When I was sure he was asleep, I crept to the airplane with the remaining ice cream, stuffed it down, puked, and crawled back into bed.

He murmured, "Where'd you go, baby?"

"To the bathroom." Even now, the binge was not over. My legs against the sheet longed to hack and tear as I waited for the light to grow to the point where I could reasonably leave. When the red numerals of his digital clock read quarter to six, I tried to roll off the futon. He pulled me back. "Stay. I want to hold you."

I had to eat. I could barely wait until his breathing smoothed out, releasing me. Convenience store. Ice cream. Chocolate bars from the kiosk on the train platform. I ate through two more convenience stores and a fast-food joint, purging twice before I found myself sliding off my shoes as Ava and a furious Cho busted into the *genkan*.

"Where were you?" Cho demanded.

"She almost went to the poli—oh . . ." Ava saw my face.

"You could have called," Cho began, but Ava shooed her away and made what she called "a proper breakfast." I panicked at the piles of food Ava expected to go into me. "It'll start again."

"I'm right here, Carlie." *I want to hold you.*

I spent most of the day combating the after-effects of four puke sessions in six hours and arguing over tea with Ava—all long fingers and undulating *rrrrrrr*'s—about apologizing to Az for not sleeping with him, not even blowing him.

Ava said, "You owe no man sex" with such conviction that I could have put a rope around her neck.

"I ran out on him." That's what I do. I run. At least when I stole the money, I had an excuse.

The sideways slide of the kitchen shoji announced Cho's arrival. "Who gives a breathing crap about Az? Girlfriend, are you feeling better yet?"

"Still kicked in the head."

"Call Doug for a treatment, or I call him for you."

And off Cho sent me to talk with Doug about bulimia.

Fair Lady Works the Shuttles

Doug's was a noisy, two-room apartment over a grocery ten minutes north of Ueno Station on the Hibiya Line. The tatami room visible from the efficiency kitchen where he brewed me some tea had a massage table at its center and abundant evidence of tai chi travel—weapons, wall hangings, good quality and placed with care; a wooden statue of Quanyin that it was a relief to make prayer hands to. The sliding doors to the second room were closed. Probably his bedroom. I was staring at those shut shoji when Doug said, "So, what's up?"

My heart bucked. Finally, "I threw up."

"Did you eat something funky?"

"I'm bulimic. I spent the whole train ride here stressing about how to tell you that."

Doug sat across from me and passed my cup. "How long has this been going on?"

"Define this."

His dark eyes were attentive. "Start from the beginning."

Attention on my tea, I began with quitting first alcohol and then cigarettes, left out the incest, and finished up with Friday night, except the Az stuff.

"I was supposed to be getting better."

"It happens, one addiction morphing into another. Still, I see progress. You didn't drink or smoke. That's big news." To better gauge my color, Doug said, he asked that I wipe off the lip gloss (so painstakingly applied) and pressed the fleshy pad between my thumb and pointer finger.

"Ow!" I yanked my hand from his and shook it. "Man!"

"Sorry. I'll need to check the pulses on your feet."

"My feet?"

He reached to prod between my big and second toes, his ebony hair loose around his strong shoulders. All this time of nothing, and in one weekend, the small kitchens of two men. I wished to hell that I could combine the best part of my night with Az with what was going on now.

Doug returned me to the agreed-upon reality by handing me a lightweight robe. He said, "If you're comfortable, take off your bra but leave on your underpants," without discernible interest in anything related to bra or underpants. "Hop on the treatment table when you're changed. I'll be out there, washing my hands."

When we were ready, Doug removed a plastic packet from a wooden Chinese cabinet of sixteen, wallet-sized drawers. He unwrapped a set of thin needles. Stretching a patch of my skin between two of his fingers, he poked a needle in. It didn't exactly hurt, but there was an unpleasant sensation as the tip hit what felt like a flat circle of putty under my skin. Needles went in all over me. I barely felt some of the pushes. Others zinged is if electrified. As soon as Doug said, "Okey-doke. Rest here for twenty-five minutes," my nose began itching.

"Where?" His hand positioned itself noseward.

"On the left. Up a little. Little more. Ah."

A lenient chuckle from Doug. I didn't need to know what that meant. He said, "I'll be in the kitchen if you need anything."

As he left, I closed my eyes and breathed, for how long I didn't know. *Little*—and I was crying the way I'd yearned to all weekend—including Friday night, as normalcy bolted beyond my command. I heard the door slide. Doug said, "It's okay, Carlie," and many more of the meaningless murmurs you'd want a boyfriend to say.

"Are your needles magic?" I asked. Our faces, our noses, were inches apart.

"Sometimes. Mostly, they just do what needs to be done."

"I can't even go home with someone right. I'm fat and ugly."

"There is nothing wrong with you, Carlie. Not whatever you did. Not how you look. I'm here to help you believe that."

Receiving no response, Doug plucked the needles out. He re-checked my feet and advised a relaxing rest of the day.

"What about tai chi?"

"Wanna practice with me? We can go nice and slow."

He took me to a street-corner park under a train trestle. Cars honked up and down as we started the kata. Toward the end, a posture tripped me up. Fair Lady Works the Shuttles. The stately sequence of four separate but similar movements was also called Four Corners because you blocked opponents from four directions. The first action was to fend at the right front corner. Then, a slow, three-quarter turn behind yourself, to the left front corner. That was the hardest, the turn, trying—failing—to reverse effectively, gracefully. It was like wanting to sleep with Az when bulimia was only a three-quarters of a circle away.

After blocking at the left front corner, Doug showed me how to take three easy steps to the left back corner. Here came the specter of Yvette and her lipstick trying to get me to snitch on Ava and Cho. Boom, boom. Finally, from left back to right back corner. There was sure to be blowback Monday, for going home with Az. No way Yvette was going to keep that to herself.

Several times, Doug watched me do the hardest one: right front corner, three-quarter turn, left front corner. He said, "When you fend to the right front, be aware of the attack forming at the left, but don't anticipate. Deal with the first corner, pull to center, find the earth, and *then* defend against the next attack."

"Man, maybe that's the answer. About men."

Doug concentrated on me as if he had never seen me before. "I'll tell you, Carlie, I never say this because patients let me know what they need to let me know, but it seems like more than bulimia is going on with you. If you ever want to talk, I'm here."

I wrapped my arms around him. Doug returned the hug as cars made their noises and a yellow train rumbled above us. After it passed, I said. "Oh, Doug. You are the first man who's ever just been nice to me."

That night, lying on my futon, I placed my hands over my eyes and faced east. It was from the east that light came first.

"God, please help."

Since I'd never asked God for anything, I expected something. Like, something.

Nothing. The next morning, when I entered the already smoky staff room, Doug's muscular arms seemed to surround me, demonstrating Fair Lady. What I feared would be a painful raking-over for my Friday night shenanigans turned out to be no more than the Yvette-led, largely good-natured kind of razzing Brian got for his thing about Asian women. If anything, Brian's lower lip pouched out as he assessed me, as if he respected me more, now. He was best to ignore.

Except that I had to ask him for Az's number. I'd barely blocked the smirk of the all-knowing male when Yvette and Mona Lisa cornered me in the ladies' room. In her New Zealand accent, Mona Lisa asked if Az was "beeg." I wondered if I'd misunderstood.

Yvette oozed camaraderie. "He is Black."

Without bothering to fend off, I broke through them and was out of there. The insinuation didn't make it any easier to call him, though. In the phone booth, before dialing, I rested my head against the neon green apparatus. Again, "God, please help."

From his end of the line, Az threw me into panic by saying, "I really wanted to be with you all weekend." It was intermittent hysteria until work ended and I tracked down the coffee shop we decided on, convinced Az would stand me up. Or worse, not.

He was already there, his tie a sleek pale yellow. As soon as we received our warming cups, I unveiled the apology practiced countless times with the mirror.

"I'm so sorry I snuck out. That was bad. You're a good guy, and I hope you don't hate me." I improvised the last little bit.

Az ran a hand over his scalp. "It would have been nicer to wake up to your phone number."

"You could have asked Brian for it."

"Girl, you walked out on me."

It was simple statement. After a moment, Az touched my knee. I sidled away from his hand. Despite everything Ava insisted, I heard myself saying, "Also, I'm sorry I couldn't . . ."

"You didn't do anything you didn't want to do. I respect that. Besides, we got time."

Here came the part I was petrified he would or would not bring up.

"Carlie?" A tug in his voice forced me to look. "You want this to go anywhere?"

Oh, for a cigarette. Just to exhale. We left it at that'd be great. Be that as it may, later that evening, hanging out on Cho and Ava's futon, Cho's head on my tummy, my legs over Ava's knees, Cho said, "Neckties notwithstanding, I'm not hearing any zing."

The only answer that made sense was: "I don't know."

Ava whipped out an *rrrrr*. "Precisely why one goes on dates."

As winter settled in, Az and I met once a week at the coffee shop. Turned out his name was Azriel, which I liked the feeling of, in my mouth. Better than "Az." I asked him, "Didn't junior high suck, being called 'Ass' 'n stuff?"

"They only did it once," Azriel said, puffing his rugby chest in mock machismo. I liked that, too. The normalcy shimmered, yet twice as great, four times as great, was one more day that I asked God for help and didn't binge or do anything nasty to the thoughtful, intelligent, if increasingly, well, confusing fellow who was into me. Turns out the masculine puffing wasn't a joke. Plus, he rarely asked about me.

During another futon dog-pile, I asked, "Were all the guys I slept with dull, after a while, or was I too smashed to care?"

Cho began, "Girlfriend, from what I recall of your love life—"

Ava finished, "—a bit of tedium might not be such an ill thing. Anyway, if ya don't kip with him soon, he'll end it."

I shuttled to my knees. "Is it really like that?"

"To my aging memory," Ava said, glancing at Cho with an adorable wrinkle of her nose

I didn't want to get joke-y. "Then there's no difference between me sleeping with someone now, just to have someone to sleep with, and doing it lost along The Lonely Planet Trail. Which was tied too closely to . . . you know."

Cho sat up. "You can say it."

"Incest."

Ava flinched. I couldn't take time for her feelings. I was having too many. "I'm not putting Azriel together with the incest. He's coming from the right front corner, and the incest—my feelings about incest, are coming from the left. When I went home with Azriel that once, I mushed all that stuff together. Because my first"—I could barely say it—"time . . . "

Cho took me by the shoulders. "Your father is a pedophile rapist. You are an adult now. He has no power over you."

"I think I just figured out, big picture, why I'm dating Azriel."

Ava coughed out one of those awful throat-clacking noises that she made when she was disgusted with me or with herself. She sprang from the futon and left the room.

"Man. Why is she like that about me?"

"She'll work through it."

"I'm not competitive with her."

Cho gave my arm a pat of ambiguous meaning. All she said was, "Now, you decide whether you want to stay with Azriel or let him down easy."

Two more dates. Azriel caressed my hand regularly and then,

one night, brushed my cheek slowly—

—how was I leaving the coffee shop, and without him?

Later that night, he phoned to let me down easy. "You don't seem to want this to go anywhere." Despite the fact that I was the one who wrecked our thing, I hung up hurt. At least I didn't return to reality at his place, underneath him.

March turned me twenty. I didn't mention my birthday. I told myself I wanted to avoid the cake. Yes, I was getting better. I hadn't binged the whole time I was with Azriel. Didn't drink or smoke, either. Most importantly, those triumphs layered down more faith in God. I had an actual God—although through the kitchen and down the hall, they had each other. As spring peeked out of her cold, dark hole, I spent more and more time deliberating what went on after I peeled off their futon to say goodnight and more and more time enjoying the pre-peel. The first night it was warm enough to leave my bedroom window open, I kicked the sheets off and tried to continue the images.

You can't be gay. You had way too much sex with men—

And never came.

No, once. With Nadav, on the beach—

Out of your head on mushrooms. Seems like anyone would enjoy just about anything were she that out of her head.

With the warmer weather, jackets came off at practice. Sleeves shortened. There were firm arms and the hypnotic curve of breasts into waist. Akiko once again toed herself out of her platform heels to do the kata barefoot. What feet! Goodness, I was as bad as Brian, dawdling with the cute students when a lesson ended. With girls, it went like clockwork. You asked where they bought that skirt then checked out their butts. I was a pig.

"Lovely hair, that Hiroko." Brian whistled as the student's long locks swayed down the blue hallway and into the lobby.

"Yes."

As I'd hoped, my tone brought Brian's eyes to mine. I held his gaze the way I used to when I wanted a guy's attention, held it until right before Brian understood. At which point, I treated him to a pat borrowed from Cho. After a while, though, it was no fun being the only one in on the secret. I pulled Margot into a post-practice walk around Shinobazu Ike.

She promptly rotated her nose ring. "No shit, eh?"

I jolted to a stop, a contraption with a thingy-dingy caught in the gears.

Margot threw her colored cap into the air, that lady in that old TV show. "Carlie, you are a delightful open book of a twenty-year-old. Especially when you imagine you're being subtle."

"Does everyone know?"

Margot took my hand. "I'm not sure who you mean by 'everyone.' We're not a gossipy crowd, eh?"

"Cho and Ava."

"Giggling themselves silly."

"Meanies. Oh, man. Doug."

"Doug wouldn't judge you if you preferred pickles. For the record, gay women do not leer at Doug the way you do."

"Do I still do that? But, man. When he pulls off his sweatshirt, his t-shirt rides up for a second. His abs."

"You Stonewall stalwart, you. Listen, you dated a guy, you're exploring the idea of women. Just what this survivor"—Margot hugged me—"needs to be doing."

The dream began in the mountains of the Philippines, on a mountain bristling with trees. Into the tribe was born an albino child. The people loved their own brown skin and loved her translucence as well. She was gift from God because she was different and precious. They guarded her tenuous life with care. Then to the village came large, white men. They stole the child, burned the homes, scattered the men, and raped the women.

They kept the child in an outhouse, raped her at will. But the people would not be defeated. Under the cover of night, they fiercely butchered the intruders and made of their white hands a necklace that rotted to its bones. I woke still feeling those dead fingers against my neck.

By June, most conversations at tai chi and at work revolved around August travel plans. Ava and Cho were going to the States, invited to visit Cho's family for the first time since Cho came out. That would be twenty years. Less dramatically, Margot and Horst would wander through China. Doug and Akiko were talking about hitchhiking north, to Hokkaido. Even Yvette and Mona Lisa were going to Bali. I caved—I called Azriel, willing to sleep with someone just to have someone. At least for one week of our month off. Maybe two.

Number disconnected. I asked the only person there was to ask. In the crowded teachers' lounge, Brian clasped his hands behind his head with a coarse grin.

"Got work in Nagano. Oy, he said you gave a good gobble."

I rushed into Ava's office. One look at my face and, machine-like, she found a teacher to cover my class, pulled down her shades, and let me cry. For almost a year, I had been the Fair Lady learning to work this shuttle; turned out I knew nothing. I was sure that Ava could make no sense of my tears, my Four Corners and *He seemed so genuine*, but she came up with, "He was. With you. Men are different with they're out with the lads."

"What if they were saying stuff like this about you?"

"Why d'ya think I bunged in my college job for a conversation school? Less money? Fewer holidays? Here, no one can fire me. I can'nae believe we are less than ten years from the millennium, and I have to disguise myself so. Now, open that shade, if you please, or the teacher's lounge will have it that I've been going down on you. Would you like the rest of the evening off?"

For the first time in a long while, my admiration for Ava

kicked in. I felt the same deep respect the following weekend after I found myself hanging around our back porch, jonesing for a cigarette. As usual when I was alone on the porch, Kashiwabara-san approached with lots of old-fashioned Japanese I still couldn't completely understand. She indicated that I should follow her upstairs, my first invitation to her part of the house. The furniture was antique wood, the oblong wall art and flower arrangements magnificent in their understatement. We knelt before the family altar, *"Butsudon,"* she called it, where she explained her relationship to—and I could understand—the now-dead person in each black and white photo. Her husband displayed the same dignity she did.

Kashiwabara-san reached into a drawer holding white candles and incense. She extracted a cloth bundle and unwrapped an old black sash.

"This was his."

The folds of her face showed no pain. Again, I was aware that Kashiwabara-san could look back on and let go of the onions in her tea garden; even as she ate them every day. Ava and I were in the middle of learning to. At our next practice at Ueno, I found myself praying that we both would get to release.

After practice, Doug and I meandered to the station. He said, "Carlie looks sad," said it so effortlessly that I almost brought up the loneliness that was impossible to share with Cho or Ava, even with Margot round-the-pond. Instead, I told Doug, told him as I decided it, my plan to spend August studying tai chi with Gemma on Phangan.

He said, "Well, a month on an island in Thailand. No wonder you're miserable."

Before I could return his yielding grin, he added, "You remind me of my sister."

Of course.

"She died."

A bus passed, then a car. Doug closed like a train door, no

more people in or out. At the turnstile, he stood in his faded tank top as if unsure which direction to defend against.

"It was a couple years ago." Doug pulled the blue bandanna from his dark hair and bunched it in his hand. "Anyway, I'm going to Burma with a buddy. You get your visa in Bangkok. Wanna hang out for a couple days before you head south?"

The downward tilt of his face prevented me from asking the obvious: and ... Akiko? Though not from daydreaming. For the greater part of the five-hour flight to Bangkok, I made believe Doug, next to me, wouldn't be going off with his buddy, a certain Mick. Doug spent the flight absorbed in *Burmese for Beginners*.

After landing, Doug directed our taxi to a quiet place he knew near the massive Lumpini Park, where lots of Chinese Thai practiced, starting at six every morning. Doug's choice of hotel looked like a Thai house, dark wood with swirly, Chinese-style trim painted gold. As "Rhinestone Cowboy" played on the stereo, Doug practically became the hero of the song, swaggering into the entryway, greeting the owner with a cross-hand grip and bro-shoulder, then introducing him as Sinchai. The next morning, six a.m., the older man took us to his tai chi group in the park, after which he returned to work, and Doug and I inched down Rama IV Road in a Sinchai-flagged cab, the thoroughfare choked by traffic. I didn't care; more time with Doug.

"Where are we going?" I shouted over the radio and the rush hour. "Like a Virgin."

"Gotta pay our respects to the Emerald Buddha."

At the gate to the city block of a compound housing the royal palace and Wat Phra Kaew, the temple of the Emerald Buddha, Doug eased us past the tourists—mostly Westerners and lots of Japanese—lined up to take in the sights listed in their guidebooks: a scale model of a temple in Cambodia called Angkor Wat, the Ramakien mural, the Golden Chedi. I wanted to linger over the incredible stonework decorating the many buildings or the whimsical, even frightening, statues—half-human, half-animal—along the stone walkways, but Doug was all business.

"We've got maybe twenty minutes before everyone else gets there."

"There" was the oblong building Doug called "his chapel." Bronzed lion-creatures guarded the door. Leaving our shoes, we were the day's first visitors to the high-ceilinged space, which was relatively temperate. The wall at the far end of the room was built out with a multi-layered altar draped in gold cloths and set with a multitude of figures I now knew were not the Buddha. There was only one Buddha. The rest were bodhisattvas, the enlightened beings who put off entering paradise so as to help others attain enlightenment.

I thought the Emerald Buddha would be fat, glowing green, a Chinese restaurant deity. I almost missed him, a jade-opaque dot at the pinnacle of the gold statues. Doug dropped to his knees and pressed his forehead to the glossy wood floor.

We sat. I tried to tap into whatever Doug, now in a relaxed lotus position, had going. Too distracted. The heat grew in proportion to the hum of Bangkok traffic; tourists trickled and then poured into the hall. The murals on the walls surrounding us, starburst swirls against dark green, implied universal order. Why, then, did the Buddha feel so far away?

"What's with that big sigh?" Doug wanted to know as we left the crowd in the chapel and joined the throngs outside. There were so many happy families. I couldn't put it into words, not as we wandered the temple complex discussing the existence of God, and not as we wandered the markets outside the temple, debating the consequences of none. Not when the afternoon heat forced us to nap in our separate rooms, and not later, when, in the hotel's restaurant, Sinchai set down a pot of jasmine tea to end our dinner. "Rainy Days and Mondays." Not even when it became clear that debates over the existence of God had no effect on the existence of God. All that mattered was how lonely you felt. Travelers at the other tables must assume: a guy, a gal, normal. I was more normal than the girl who came to Thailand the last time, a closed palm, the fingers of which were allowed to open, one at a time, at the right moment for the right experience. Then again, I didn't get how the no-longer-child I was now would become the adult I needed to be.

I found myself telling Doug the only truth I could find. "I do not want to get on that train tomorrow afternoon. Not alone."

"Are you worried about stuff?"

"I'm not worried that I'll drink. I am, a little, about food."

"Must be tough. Food's so always there." Doug ran his palm against the pink tablecloth. "You know, I thought about asking you to come to Burma. Mick can be . . . I dunno. But it's not like you have to be alone. We men aren't that hard to get in bed."

Doug's matter-of-fact tone startled a laugh out of me.

"Just, you know, be safe," he finished.

I did pack a whole bunch of condoms, thinking there might be a God, after all. Recalling the scent of night wind across a beach, the consciousness-blowing grate of sand against my bare back, a small "Hmmm" escaped. Doug's eyes opened like I'd never seen.

"I've never done it when I wasn't wasted." I flushed in a way that I hoped was not too ugly.

Doug's look vanished. He was again my good friend. "It's better. By a lot. You can really be there for her. And for yourself."

Silence. Doug drained his already empty cup. He gestured with his thumb and, mouths still stitched shut, we went upstairs. Our arms brushed. I felt myself color once again. Foot on the top step, Doug said, "You know, me n' Akiko, we might break up."

"Don't you love her?"

"It's not Akiko. She's past that age when Japanese women kind of have to get married and I won't let . . . get honestly close to any wom . . . not since . . . you know."

I wanted to be empathetic the way Cho could be, to give him,

"You can say it," but didn't think I could pull it off. We hovered in the hall between our rooms. His eyes once again expanded. They stayed that way as my lungs shut down.

"I should get to bed."

"Okey-doke."

He said it simply, not "Me, too," or "See you in the morning," just as I didn't say, "Go to sleep" and the door to my room was closing behind me and I was leaning my forehead against it. Which one of us said no? And to what? At least I didn't screw him. As much as I wanted to believe that it would have been something real, as long as Akiko was in the picture, I could only get screwed. The next morning, I was doubly grateful, as Doug treated me with absolute normalcy. If it was anything, it was his confusion over Akiko. If it was anything. That afternoon, I said "You don't have to," when he offered to accompany me to Bangkok's main train station, Hua Lamphong.

"I want to."

As I climbed aboard, he took my backpack, double-checking the straps like a concerned brother, holding it the way I wished he'd hold me. The fateful whistle blew. Doug passed my pack. He watched me tame its weight with last night's appreciative eyes. I considered shaking hands, but that would be so dorky. I settled for, "Take care, man."

"You, too. Man."

"I will never say 'man' again."

He said, "Expect the miracle."

"What does that mean?" I had to raise my voice because the train was pulling away.

"Things mean what they mean!" Doug waved until he was as distant as the Emerald Buddha. I located my seat, clutching his last shout closer than my gear.

"The miracle!"

This time, it was a sharper-looking red skiff that put-putted around the southern fingertip of Koh Phangan. There was a dock to the white sand of Haad Rin Beach now, and the village had grown into more than two sets of cross streets, but the rocks of sex-with-Nadav fame had not changed. At tai chi, Gemma's chicken-shack buildings listed by the familiar palm-tree-fringed beach, and her New Jersey accent remained as intense as her cape of black curls. In tank tops, however, she was sexier than I remembered. Back then, I dreaded the next group of all-the-same travelers. This current tai chi bunch was easy to like. Some danced with their souls. Others were content merely to practice.

Between morning class at seven-thirty and the afternoon one at four, I had little to do. I fell into the habit of strolling the long, restful beach under the cliffs supporting the Leela Beach Resort, searching for shells; a currency. I was here. Beauty existed. The Full Moon party happened without my participation, without my feeling left out. One hot afternoon, inspiration that had to be shared struck. When I realized how long it had been since I'd thought out a letter to Little Matt, I decided it was best to keep it that way.

Besides, I had a real someone to write to. I settled on the sand near my favorite rocks and started a letter that Doug couldn't possibly read until he returned to Tokyo. *Pain, fear, anger; all make sense to go through alone. But not splendor. Not joy.*

Always, before going to sleep, I sat on my sweet little porch, listened to the waves, and contemplated the stars. This, too, had changed since my last stay on Phangan.

And every night I dreamed. An undisclosed "we" were on a cruise ship. Interspersed with scenes where the captain greeted us, the camera pulled back to reveal the whole thing was a paper-doll book. We were Titanic-doomed. On deck, a wedding. It was my father's wedding, but he was not marrying Mom. He forgot the ring. The napkins were torn and the ragged swatches scattered. Everyone was furious, but I was the only one who said anything. *You always get away with it.*

There was no response. The captain guided me to a banquet room beyond belief. Velvet walls. Chandeliers. Everyone was seated: my father, Ted, Lyle, my mom, my sister. Little. Some wives. They seemed to have forgotten my name. I observed their good time until I pulled from my tiny embroidered evening bag an automatic repeater rifle. One by one, each person fell silent as they realized what I held, how long it had gotten, and at whom I was pointing it. Soon, there was nothing but me with a bead on my father's head.

"Tell them what you did."

The banquet table sprouted goodies of indescribable variety. Everyone morphed into one fat jester dressed in tight, shiny pants. He leapt and posed, promising I could eat to my heart's desire without gaining weight—from this table only.

I cackled in the jester's face, woke laughing. In the dream, my final Ava-sing-songy words were, "Already tried that." And he lost his power.

My third week on the island, descending the steep steps to the palm-fringed practice area, I was struck by the familiarity of a petite blonde holding court over a group of men. When she arched her back to drag on her cigarette, her breasts came close to peeking from under her tummy top. It was the zero-fat Israeli whose meeting directly preceded my doing mushrooms with Nadav. At that time, I was clearly too drunk to realize how stunning she was. I blushed when she beckoned me over with a lofty, "I know you, yes?"

"We were here two years ago, with Tallie and Nadav—"

Her green eyes clicked toward the ocean. Her name was Yifat. I asked about my Israelis. "Tallie is married. Nadav, no." While Yifat's hair was gossamer, circles under shimmering green eyes belied her glamour.

Gemma clapped twice. After the first run-through of the form, Gemma tried to take Yifat to the palm trees to start her on the basics. Being a caliber of good-looking clearly accustomed to getting what she wanted, Yifat demanded that Gemma skip her right to the form. She should be pinched in some non-existent fatty place.

Gemma said, "Carlie, engage this charmer in Wave Hands Like Clouds."

I worked Yifat through up-across-down, hard-pressed to focus on her form and not her form. Another realization, I wrote later, to Doug: *I thought it'd be easier to open up to a woman. Turns out you still have to take the risk. Oh, man!* After the next morning's practice, I beat out a line of six guys waiting to invite Yifat to lunch by asking her girl-to-girl casual. She had side vegetables and a cigarette. Ping, base of the spine, but no proof until our next meal, when she ate far more than I did, including dessert, then left; just up and left. I all but felt her white space.

Her looks, her misery, I finished Doug's letter, from the beach. *I thought that was how you got someone to love you,* and I woke from an afternoon nap screaming, "Daddy!" This was no dream. This really happened, the first night at the cabin. Ted won. He hauled me over his shoulder, a bolt of material, up the stairs. I grabbed each banister. He had to fight me for it. My father's forehead, still downstairs, his eyes.

"Daddy!"

I'd needed his help.

I had been waiting since that night for a man to be there the way my father never could. My sorrow came from the times he said he did it because he loved me. My father tried to resist; he really did. I spent several days so uncertain that even the breeze wafting across the shaded practice area hurt. Finally, twenty-four hours before I left the island, I did the only thing that made sense. I asked Yifat for Nadav's address in Israel and wrote to him—the only one of the two of them that I felt I needed to apologize to—from the rocks on the beach. I apologized for parting in such a selfish way. *No one could have mended me. I needed time. And grace. I've had some and it is better. Not all better, but it keeps getting better. I wish for you the same.*

I thought about it, chose not to leave a return address. And the sand grew solid against my feet and rear, so solid that I lay flat on it. I thought, I should stand, should try sinking and stepping, to see if I would be held. I did not need to. The earth ran deep against my neck and back and legs, stacks and stacks of it, so much more giving than I ever expected.

Sinking Down

Riding the train from Narita Airport to Ueno Station, I thought about how each time you start the kata, you begin by sinking down. You stand with your legs together, rotating them from the hip joint so that your toes pointed out, heels almost touching. Before moving, you take a moment to experience standing, simply standing, pelvis tucked, shoulders rolled back and relaxed, and spine, neck, and head in line and connected to the golden string that attached the best part of you to that great, green god in the sky. If you could do all this while breathing gently, you could do anything.

Still in my train seat, I sank into Japan. Home. Three hours later: our gate. More home. Cho and Ava would not be back for another week. I made it all the way to breakfast the next morning before it occurred to me to check the answering machine.

"Hey, man," Doug's voice came out of it. The message ran out as I jigged around the kitchen, imagining dancing up the walls the way Fred Astaire did once in a movie. I had to rewind.

" . . . man. No, seriously. Wanna get dinner? Mick's here, too. You could—um, meet him? Or, he doesn't have to come with us." A pause, anything but brotherly. "I can't wait to see you."

I rewound about ten times. Then called him, got his machine. Furious, relieved, I left a message, praying, *Please*, believing in God more than I'd ever believed in God. When I finally fell asleep, I floated in the middle of the ocean on a rudimentary raft, just a mast and a flat deck of bamboo slats. The slats were not flush. Approximately six inches separated each. Through that emptiness, I could see strips of green-blue water.

A pod of baby dolphins surrounded the raft. They leapt as they swam, shrinking in order to sail through the spaces in the deck and back into the sea, where they grew.

Snake Creeps Down

"Hey, Carlie!"

Doug's shout stopped me in the middle of warming up. I'd arrived at the practice area fifteen minutes before anyone would logically show. His voice sent me charging across the sun-splattered grass, so full of joy that even the bushes he came around were a blur. "Hey there!" he said over and over as we sunk into each other with delight. Oh, man. Muscles.

Sooner or later, he held me at arm's length. "You look strong and . . . and . . . dang."

You look like polished teak. "The miracle happened."

He came close to not dropping his grin. "Guy or gal?"

"No one," I realized, spreading my arms like a tutu. "I fell in love with me."

Doug gave me another, more tender, embrace. An unspoiled moment later, he said, "Oh, hey. This is Mick—I mean, Michael."

Doug turned me to face a lithe man whose expression, contented panther, could only mean that he'd witnessed everything. I did not know whether to clobber Doug or thank him because Mick, as I continued to think of him, not that I could think, was David Bowie as the Thin White Duke. Tall and poised, alabaster skin, cheekbones. Hair, lucent rather than blond, falling over the eyes in front and trimmed tightly at the back—what a classy neck! He wore his white tank top as if it were a tuxedo jacket, though the armholes opened to his tight waist. Latissimus dorsi like sand dunes.

"This is Carlie," Doug announced from, like, Pluto.

In the nasal tones of a Londoner, the demi-god spoke.

"Hel-lo, Carlie." His voice circled me as if I were a racehorse for possible riding. "I've heard a great deal about you."

Doug turned as red as the trim on the brown shrine. "Let's practice. Mick, you start us off."

Mick zoomed us through a warm-up that had us bending and whipping around. "The style is Korean-influenced," he confided to me. Clean-shaven smell, downy five o'clock shadow. Oh, my.

We started the form. Mick stopped me, almost sharply, at the first Snake Creeps Down. "Face west, legs as far apart as possible. Sink onto your right leg. Left hand to chest as if pulling your opponent toward you. Doug . . ." They went through the ballet, Mick pulling Doug off balance, pushing Doug away. Mick said, "Hasn't a chance."

He made me repeat the face west, pull back, drop, push forward motion again and again. Finally, he allowed, "Thaaaat's better. Now, your hands. Could use more chi." And he gently formed each of mine into the shape he wanted it to be.

It was love. And with a good guy. A master tai chi guy. For days, the music went on and on, so much and so fast that I constantly tripped over nothing on the tatami and once walked into a parking meter. I barely missed Cho and Ava, barely thought about food. Too busy practicing Snake Creeps Down. At Achieve English, I sailed into the smoky staff room, past Yvette and Mona Lisa as they regaled Brian with tales of Bali. Brian took the opportunity to wiggle his eyebrows at me. Like I dressed to impress that lout. I was wearing one of the outfits I bought in Bangkok: an edamame green top with tiny, foam-colored polka dots that matched a mini skirt of tasteful length. The final touch: a bangle from a street stall, black and white leather entwined. As cool as any traveler touch Ava wore. I couldn't wait to wear this ensemble on a date with Mick. The golden fog persisted until Cho and Ava stood in the genkan removing their shoes. The past week of dinners alone in the kitchen and practices alone in the garden, all of it cut through as I cried, laughed, and tried to hold them, all at once.

Cho was wearing her summer whites. She shook me free. "Boy, do you look good! Girlfriend. Did you get lucky?"

Ava and I shrieked like junior high schoolers. I *would not* mention my lacy bra and panties, also purchased in Bangkok.

Ava trilled, "Carlie will share when she feels ready," but her blue eyes peered over the wall of her appropriate reply as if they were nuns dying to escape the convent. Her lovable babble accompanied us to their room, where it was hot but not too hot for a lovefest dog-pile on the futon.

"Cho's family were great . . . her ma gave me a photo of wee Cho . . . had us to supper as if we were a real couple."

Cho's head rose off my stomach. "Give them some credit. Sure, we can live without their approval, but after waiting for so long, it is incredible that it's coming."

"It's like that with love."

My remark stopped all conversation. Then they were on me. "I knew it!" "No wonder you're glow—" "Who is it?"

Cho said, "Carlie, is it—?"

"Doug's friend, Mick—I mean, Michael."

Cho clutched my arm. My "Ow!" overlapped her "Mickey!" And in Ayva's frozen "Oh!" of a mouth, something I'd never seen from her. Real fear.

I said, "You don't even know Micha—"

Cho leapt up to pace. "Of course we do! Michael, is it? He used to be plain old Mick, exploiting what it meant to be God's gift to the fifty-three percent of the Tokyo population with vaginas."

Ava pulled to her knees. "It's been three years, Cho. He could have changed."

"Men like Mick don't change. He went for you when he was

still with—"

"I never took him up on it!"

"You wanted to." Cho's sudden stillness was awful, more awful than her frantic rage.

"Cho, you were my first girlfriend. I wasn't sure. You know I am now."

"So, he'll use Carlie for his love-jones." Cho's head flipped to me. "You crashing into stuff already?"

I sucked air through my teeth. It took a while before I could say, "You don't choose who you fall in love with."

"You do choose what you do about it." Cho slammed the shoji on her way out.

I collapsed on the futon near Ava. She stared at the wall. After a moment, I curled toward her, resting my cheek on her arm.

"Carlie, I can now ruin everything Cho and I have."

"Did you cheat with him?"

"Had I, at least there would have been a reason for the ruckus. I acted as if he wanted me when all he wanted was the challenge of seducing someone in a relationship with a woman. And to take me from Cho, a woman he'd never—"

"I am not in a relationship with Cho!"

"But you could be in one with Dougie. When you said, about going to Bangkok with him—"

I sat up. "You think Michael is pretending to be"—I could no longer say, *into me*—"to hurt Doug?"

"Oh, he's into you. He simply doesn't care about Doug."

"His friend? He wouldn't do that."

"He did that."

"No." I stood. If I stayed close to her, I'd slap her, for sure.

Ava slid onto an elbow. "Mick always kept himself clean-shaven yet somehow managed a bonnie stubble. Does he continue the artifice?"

Even at Ava's most cloying, I'd never wanted to punch her. I did now. I barged to the slid-shut shoji and forced them open with as much ferocity as Cho had hammered them shut. "He smells great! Don't make me any dinner!"

I refused to eat with them, and on Friday wouldn't agree to take the train to practice together. They were already in the clearing with the gang as I cut through the trees alone, viewfinder locked in.

Not here. Doug seemed brusque, but Margot? Transformed. Ringlets dyed russet, sure, but the not finishing other people's meals she'd worked on all year showed up now as significant weight loss. All us girls were gushing when Mick made the scene.

The women clammed up. All the guys who knew him surrounded him with great clappings of backs and other manly expressions. As soon as he was able, Mickey made a beeline for Margot. She did something I'd never seen her do. She crossed her arms protectively over her breasts. Ava armor.

"Mickey."

"Lost weight, haven't you?"

Margot squinted.

He scratched his five o'clock shadow. Oh, to touch it, too. He said, "I meant well, love."

Ping.

Margot was staring Mick down when she suddenly looked startled, as if she remembered something. She became, of all things, kind. "Thank you, Mick."

"It's Michael, now."

"Michael, then." She came across as genuine, although she made no effort to linger in the conversation. She turned away and took Horst's hand.

Leaving Mickey smack-dab in the center of the women. He was polite to the point of disinterest, no roving Casanova there. Man, how could a guy be so slender and still have such musculature? Then I noticed that, as Mick turned from Elise, she received the barest hint of a wink. Then Sara: inattention followed by a clandestine touch on the arm. No no; *no no no*. But there he was tossing a net, hauling in his catch. We eagerly flop-flop flopped, gasping for breath and waiting to be eaten without admitting that Cho was right, all along. He played me so easily.

Cool, slim fingers, caring, on my shoulder. Mickey noticed Ava beside me and tipped his head, as if to someone he recognized from the water cooler. Ava paled, then reddened. I threw off her hand, and those almond-shaped eyes—a jade color, really—shifted to me. Ha.

"Hel-lo, Carlie. How's Snake Creeps Down?"

"Oh, creeping." I tried to dig myself out. "You know. Down." Aaaaaaaaaa.

Mick grinned in a crafty way until Cho gated my other side. All humor left his face. Doug clapped twice for the warm up—Doug.

I didn't know how it got to be the end of the practice. Doug announced that Michael would be leading Wednesday practices. Mickey demonstrated a few postures, that elegant neck, those endless legs and fabulous lats on full display. You could practically hear the women go gooey. The instant the class broke into its usual groups, I aimed towards Doug.

Mickey intercepted me. "The lot of us are off to tea. Do come."

Despite everything I just witnessed, his invitation sucked my stomach flat. I never had a flat stomach anymore.

Cho again, from nowhere. "The store needs you, girlfriend."

The look between them was a declaration of war.

He was fighting for me.

Doug spoke. "Hey, Cho? Carlie can take care of herself. Can't you, Carlie?" In Doug's face was pain that wasn't there when he first came back from Burma. Mick leaned in to tell me the style was Korean-influenced and unplug went whatever could have happened between me and Doug. Maybe I could cork it up. The next practice day, full of hope, I rushed to tai chi. Mick hailed me, and I didn't even say hi to Doug until we all headed to the station at the end of practice. I was a fool. Doug was a Japanese meal,

Mickey, a big, goopy dessert. The meal would sustain me. The dessert would fuck me up. I did not care. I wanted dessert.

Meanwhile, Doug and Mick treated me like any other student. On Mondays and Fridays through September and October, Doug gently corrected my form, receding with a guarded expression when Mick slipped me a sly lift of the eyebrows. For that moment, the world was my whirling nirvana. By the time I returned to reality, his attention had segued to the next vagina on his list. It was all I could do to keep from ditching practice to binge. Every single session.

Wednesdays were The Michael Show. With guys, he taught using effective one-liners. With Elise, it became, "Thaaaat's better," but not until he'd spent a good few moments with her, molding her fingers as he'd done mine that first day. Bitch. When he moved to the next student, however, I saw what I didn't see then, what I did not want to see, once he sent her spinning. I saw the way he glanced back. And then I got to watch the way he gave her the water cooler nod at the practice after the one they left together, half-way through. That same day, he left our after-practice tea with Sara. With her, it lasted more like three weeks— three weeks during which I wondered if I really could punch Sara the way I envisioned. I was not such a cunt, however, that I could ignore how Mick's being with Sara wounded Elise. She stopped coming to practice. Even Doug's.

I would not stop wearing my sexy underthings.

Masturbation was lonely satisfaction.

After, still the only one on my futon, I felt as low and alone as I remembered feeling as a child when my father left my room.

Despite all that, the heaviest stone on my chest, heavier than one more similarity to Ava—a cold wind around the practice area, spying on me spying on Mickey—even heavier than hurting Doug, was Margot. She knew what it was like to lose yourself to the passion he promised, yet his highest-voltage smiles, his most sincere gazes were useless on her. Margot treated him with the composure of a babysitter caring for an entertaining child. Following a markedly affectionate adjustment to her ribs, Margot knocked him right off his horse by asking, like she really wanted to know, "What sort of response do you expect from that, Michael?" Horst grinned into his beard. Mickey's satisfied panther's visage became a hunting one, and I choked on my jealousy. I did not binge.

"In the beginning, eh, he was everything he pretends to be. Nothing anyone said"—Margot indicated Ava's usual corner of our booth at the coffee shop, unoccupied for this special session—"could stop me, just as no warnings on my part nor righteous fits on Cho's will stop you. If you choose to, eh, you will learn there is no greater aphrodisiac than saving a man from himself for the twenty-three days he maintains the monogamy he promises. And then you will learn to look the other way. Even about Ava. Eventually, hopefully, you will see him as no more than the spoiled brat that he is."

"Maybe he hasn't found the right woman."

"Keep believing that. He'll own you."

Margot rested against the brown vinyl seat back. "There are times I worry that he still owns Ava."

"And not you."

"Carlie. I was chubby before I met him. When Mick started stage-managing my pain, that is when I ballooned, eh? Why settle for pure crap when there are good men like Horst?"

Margot would never be skinny, but she didn't need to be. She sat inside herself knowing who she was and liking it. I remained quiet until I arrived at the one question I needed answered.

"How good?"

"He could write one of your books, eh? *How to Go Down*. He could also do *How to Get a Hummer Out of Anyone*.

"It's so unfair. You can get over him 'cause you already—I just want to know. What it feels like. To be that moved."

Margo took my hand. "Then bring several condoms and have a good time. But the more you push toward him, Carlie, the more he pulls back. And pulls you with him."

Snake Creeps Down.

Food was never this all-consuming. Fantasy didn't make you fat, so who cared if you wasted a lunch hour, a train ride lost in it, an entire Sunday morning building an orgasm? There were the bad feelings, after, but planning it, and then during—Mother of God, during; the best part was when I made up that he really, really loved me, loved me so much that when I laid out step by step how he had to change, he did.

As if in pointed rebuke, Mick slithered in late to tai chi with this or that woman. Oh, he still radioed over his enigmatic invitations. I lived for them. At Saturday breakfast, Margot and Ava agreed the answer was to block him out.

I whined, "How?"

Margot rotated her nose ring. "If I had one, Carlie, I'd say, 'Hold my beer,' eh? You have to—"

Ava flat out laughed. "Bollocks. He left the country."

Margot rotated again. Silence followed, highlighted by the merry rattle of plates being set down, by the smell of pancakes and coffee. I heard myself say, "What's so all-fired wrong with sleeping with him one time?"

Ava said, "How many times did you try to eat only one?"

"So? So then we're involved. Isn't that what I want?"

Margot said, "By that analogy, Carlie, you'd be binging."

In the pageant that was Shinjuku Station the very next day, "Hel-lo, Carlie," floated over my shoulder as I waited to pay for my lunch. I'd never seen the man wear anything but workout clothes. Wowed by the look of him in business causal, the blond in the front slicked back rather than flopping over, I didn't care that I could all but hear Margot say, "Don't pretend he was there accidentally." I could see his five o'clock shadow. I could smell his aftershave. I didn't care. That aftershave smelled good.

Mick asked to escort me to work. He took my arm. By the time we reached Achieve English, I was all: Tell work you feel sick. Tell yourself once is all you want.

Mickey took in the plain, black stenciling across the glass door. "Achieve English?"

I was wondering if what he did for a living was superior to teaching English Conversation when Yvette came charging through the door. Her sharp gray eyes whizzed to Mickey. He let go of my arm. I excused myself. They could not have cared less. I kept my back turned to them until I passed reception when I could no longer block the ache.

Through the floor-to-ceiling window to the right of the door, I saw them. If they had been alone, they would have been winding around each other, sniffing.

I headed straight for the vending machine, bingeing and purging for the first time since returning from Thailand. For days, distraught calls to Margot and prolonged conversations with Ava about food replaced most thoughts of Mick. At night, on the other hand, my fantasies made me come more intensely than ever. Slowly, my viscera were digesting that I would never get to experience what it was like to fuck Mick. The torture created the most delicious friction.

As the new year kicked off, attendance at Mickey's Wednesday sessions dwindled. Doug, Margot, Horst, and I were the only regulars. I was tempted to ask Doug why he didn't step in, but Doug was barely talking to me. Ava attended only Doug's practices, unsuccessfully un-obvious when she said, "I don't think about Mick so much when I don't see him." Cho came solely when work prevented her from making one of Doug's Mondays or Fridays.

"Someone's screwing himself out of a job," Cho said on one

such Wednesday as we waited, waited for Mickey. Doug stretched against a tree, the only other person in attendance.

Mickey appeared on the horizon, hand in hand with a darkly-dressed Asian woman. Doug let out a quick, clearly involuntary, "What the fu—" and took off for the pond. He didn't even grab his jacket. Over Cho's shoulder, I used a well-honed viewfinder to identify Mick's latest lay: Akiko.

I caught up with Doug about a third of the way around Shinobazu Ike. In the harsh, shivery sunshine, I could barely keep up with him around the slate-blue water. Finally, he said, "It's not like anything happened between us. You go for anyone who you want."

"Doug, he stole your girlfriend."

He stopped his charge. "We broke up. Earth to Carlie."

It took me a protracted blowing air out of my cheeks before I could say, "You've likely noticed that when it comes to men, I do not seem to prefer reality. And there you were, back from Burma. I fucked up, man, and I am so sorry."

Doug's whole torso moved in a nod. "Hey, if I had a thousand yen for every woman who liked Mick more than—"

"Why is that man your friend?"

"Why are you in love with him?"

"I am not in love! I am obsessed!"

"He goes for women like you."

At that, Doug returned, the Doug who never wanted to hurt anyone, even if it meant he had to have no feelings. He tried to edge past me. I stood in the middle of the path. "Like what?"

"Vulnerable."

A hard breath. "Why didn't you ... do something—"

"That's Cho's gig. Anyway, you think you can fool Death by fleeing to Baghdad, and who do you meet on the road but Death himself. That's an old story."

Doug sat on a wooden bench and gazed across the pond. He surprised me by saying, "In Burma, at this place, Inle Lake, everything floats. The houses, the market. Even the vegetables are rigged up, hydroponic gardens. Guys take you all over the place in boats. They wrap their legs around their paddles, out there on the edges of their tippy canoes, and kick like frogs."

For the life of me, I could not picture what he was talking about. I took a seat.

"It's real acrobatic, real sensual. The whole place is. One time, Mick was off with someone. Akiko and I weren't together, and there were some cool . . . none of them seemed . . . yeah. So I had a guy take me out in his canoe. His name was Zaw. Cool, huh? The air hung super wet and heavy, and Zaw wrapped his legs around his paddle and I thought about you, that night in Bangkok. 'Cross from a kid I've known two years, a kid who had this sweet crush on me, and I'm going, who is this woman?"

Fear shut down my lungs. Doug slid as close to me as he was that night. "What went wrong? When we went upstairs?"

I squinched my eyes shut. "Same thing that's going on now. If things get too real, sexually, I leave."

I peeked. The acupuncturist in Doug was visible. I expected him to ask if I'd been raped.

Instead, he said, "When I got home, read your letter. The way you see things. It's a wow. I was all set to get a new girlfriend so the break-up wouldn't hurt." He stood, kicked the dirt path like a ragamuffin newsboy as he said, "I could have done something when Mick did his thing with you. I just got mad at everybody. Cho always said he . . . you know, I thought she was butting into other people's business. Then he does it to you and you think, okey-doke, the guy's supposed to be my friend."

I was on my feet. "The guy is supposed to be your friend."

Doug sent me one of those looks, like he'd never seen me before. It fed me all the way to Shinjuku, where, in the hallway of Achieve English, I crossed paths with Yvette. She raised her nose. Who raises their nose? And hello, Mick was cheating on her. Or cheating on Akiko with her.

I felt so pleased.

In the cloakroom, a rustle-rustle behind hanging coats opened them to expose an Office Lady in a lip-lock with Brian. He said, "Carlie, we must stop meeting like this."

"We are not meeting like this, Brian."

I slammed the door and arrived in the staff room to find that Mona Lisa, no matter how plummy her lips, how sapphire her eyes, had again neglected to fill out her post-lesson summary. The gaijin who worked here were a gaggle of idiots.

To Mona Lisa, I said again, "It's not fair to our students. I can't plan a decent lesson."

"Don't, then." Mona Lisa chewed her licorice.

"Why do you even have this job?"

Saito Sensei's voice cut in. "Carlie Sensei. My office, please."

Behind me stood our head teacher and Ava. Making myself breathe through a candied wave from Mona Lisa, I followed them to the office. As soon as my rear hit the cushion of a swivel chair, Saito Sensei said, "About this disagreement, you are one hundred percent correct, one-hundred percent. Few teachers chart. We are loosing students."

The oval of Sensei's face went nearly square in determination. "Yesterday, Yamashita Butch-o-u called Ava Sensei and me to meeting. We will soon to appoint assistant head teacher. Butch-o-u suggested you. Excuse me for saying, perhaps I thought you were not best person. So young, not so experienced. However, today I saw. And you bring so many games into classroom. Do you have another idea?"

"Yeah. Cut the B-b-b, k-k-k."

Saito Sensei looked crushed. My torso went into recalcitrant incline. Ava deployed professional objectivity. After a moment, Saito Sensei said, "Perhaps we could improve training program."

I said, "And offer completion bonuses, like Ava had at her college. A hundred thousand yen to finish the year."

It was hard to tell whose mouth fell farther open, Ava's or Saito's. Saito said, "For only completing your contract?"

"Look at our teacher turnover rate."

Saito considered me over her pink-rimmed glasses. At last, she said, "You must come for extra hours until end of semester. To help plan curriculum with Ava Sensei."

Ava's neutrality rumpled into a face that, had it been a sound, would have been her glottal-stop disgust. I was busy saying, "What about my Japanese school? They sponsor my visa—"

"Store can sponsor work visa." Saito Sensei's inky eyes showed not a jot of white. It was not because Ava was in the room that I said, "Actually, you can't, Sensei. I don't have a diploma. So I went to Japanese school. To get a cultural visa."

"*So, nan da,*" Saito hummed to herself. "Then you have grown very much for good."

"Thank you, Sensei. Thank you."

"As for visa, you will be doing something essential for company that cannot be done by Japanese national. Therefore, visa becomes piece of cake."

Ava said, "Yes but, won't administration be bothered that Carlie hasn't—"

"I am administration. Carlie Sensei has the . . . *seijitsu?*"

"Integrity," Ava said.

I knew that. I just couldn't say anything. Everything—throat, heart, stomach, everything—soared on incredulous bubbles. They were purple.

Saito Sensei told us to keep my promotion under wraps until all systems were go. Adamant that my students not have to switch teachers mid-semester, she insisted we plan curriculum around my current schedule. So, mornings. Hearing about my tai chi commitments, Sensei granted me one morning. Wednesdays.

The following Wednesday, Doug, Margot, Horst, and I congregated under cloudy skies. Mickey and Akiko were late but genki. He ended the session with a meditation that had us, eyes closed to focus, gather chi in our *dan tien*, a point two inches below the belly button, and then circulating the energy: down to our crotches, up our spines, over the tops of our heads, down through our sternums, and back to our dan tien. I heard Mickey say, "Women on their periods shouldn't do this one. Your blood contains impurities the mediation could spread."

"There is nothing impure about menstrual blood. It is the most creative force on earth."

All eyes were on Margot. Not as our attentive babysitter. Margot. "Ever wish you had the ability to create life, Mick?"

For the first time, Mickey looked ugly. "If you don't like what I teach, don't come to my class."

Doug said, "Dang."

Margot barged toward the station. Horst followed. Doug and I exchanged a head-bob. He moved to Mickey. I chased Margot. When I caught up, she said, "He hasn't got a leg to stand on!"

"If we believe you, Margot, he has three." Good ol' Horst, he pretended to choke himself.

I joined the Menstrual Showdown Boycott. For a single week. Despite the blue coming at me from Ava's eyes and the—goddamnit—childcare patience from Margot's, not going on Wednesdays meant I would never see him.

Doug was the only other mid-week stalwart. Mick remained fiercely cheerful, greeting me and Doug with a brisk "Hel-lo," as he approached the frosty clearing where we goofed off until he arrived. Frivolity dissipated with the warm-up. These guys were committed. Doug asked if I wanted to learn the long form.

"It's my class. She's not ready."

Mick was looking at Doug. *She* was also in the proximate vicinity, I was on the verge of reminding Mick, when Doug won my heart forever by asking me, "What do you think, Carlie?"

"I'm ready."

Doug turned to Mick. "Okey-doke."

Mick proceeded as if the whole thing was his brainchild. "The short form was taken from the long in the 1950s by the great teacher Cheng Man Ch'ing."

Doug said, "I heard there were thirteen original postures that became the short form, and then the long."

They squared off.

I said, "Let's start, shall we?"

Over the weeks, learning from a different teacher opened me up. Doug strove for yin-yang balance. His big thing was hanging from the string that connected your head to the sky. Mick created chi by generating friction between yin and yang. Push pull, push pull, push, push, push. Though Mick was still the big, goopey dessert, there were times I preferred hanging from the sky.

"Dip deeper into Snake Creeps Down," he said. When I attempted it, he pushed me over. "Lost your center."

He extended a manly hand to help me up. Usually, his touch liquidated my pelvis. This time, I was busy grasping for that string. I moved cautiously into Snake Creeps Down.

"Better. You need more chi in your hands." Mick stepped away before rotating to me at the pace of a furious snail. "I've told you so before."

"Dickhead," I said to Doug as the two of us hurried to the station after class.

"Mick is a fighter. He teaches like a fighter."

"I know someone who manages to be a great teacher without being an asshole."

Doug did a spot-on Michael Jackson spin and crotch grab. "I'm a lover, not a fighter."

"Stop! You're embarrassing me."

He gave an I'm-so-centered shrug. "Mick treats me the same way as you."

"No. There's a difference. I can't name it, I can't touch it, but I can feel it."

I could not, however, make Doug accept it. Later, Ava and I were belly-down on her futon, our feet in the air like fifth graders at a slumber party. Ava said, "If you want someone to agree, you'll have to ask another woman."

"I want Doug to."

Ava raised a pleased eyebrow. I rolled away from her. "Every time I think it might be like that, here arrives our friend Mick and, despite everything I know—"

Ava crashed onto her back, her trademark hack-cough elongating into a moan.

"Let's pay for him to leave the country," I whined.

Ava leaped to her feet as if zapped by a current. "Carlie! It's so simple! We're fighting on his terms! Bloody peely-wally—"

"What?"

She hauled me off the bedding. "Wee mucker, I can'nae teach ya every fart's end of Glaswegien as we're about to—"

"You called me something phallic."

"Him! Mickey! He's peely-wally." She rubbed her arm as if hastily applying sunscreen. Apparently, Ava now counted herself explained because she threw herself into saying, "Right! Do Fair Lady. To the right front corner. Stop." We froze in the first block. "Fight on his terms and"—her foot brushed against my instep—"Over ya go. Stay in the block, and he has to come at you."

"But he won't. He's Snake Creeps Down."

"Which involves him pushing forward. Making himself vulnerable. Get him to make himself vulnerable."

"How?"

We started at each other until she said, "Peely-wally means he's pale."

I went to sleep praying about it. Nothing happened until almost a week later, when Yvette gave me another nose-pass in the hall. I came close to smacking into the wall, that's how desperately I lunged for the elevator to Cho's office, where I had not been hanging out since Micky carpet-bombed Tokyo with charm. From behind her sleek, mahogany desk, Cho kept typing into her computer as she turned her head to greet me.

"Girlfriend!"

I crept to a chair. ""When Ava . . . Mick—was that when she, y'know, tried?

Cho stopped working. She faced me. "To commit suicide. Yes. Get involved with a man like him, Carlie, and best-case scenario, you live triggered. In everything you never solved, as a child."

"Then I have to. I'm gonna get to know Yvette better."

"That one is a piece of work."

"Hear me out. If I re-make friends with her, she might tell me stuff that could really turn me off him."

Cho tapped army-green nails—great look—against her desk. As usual, she could be pleased, she could fire me. I broke the silence. "I'm worried it's manipulative."

"From what I understand about, what's her name? V'yette? She'll be fine. Fucking' A, girl. Bring up tai chi whenever possible. Throw around names she knows."

In the staff room, I was all: Margot, Doug, Akiko. Eventually, Yvette approached with nothing like her usual authority. We found a table in the coffee shop across from the store's demonstration kitchen, where a well-coiffed employee taught a group of ladies to dip fancy chocolates. Warily, Yvette shared that though she was still seeing Mick, he was also seeing "that girl" I mentioned, Akiko. Yvette gave me the details I'd hoped would disgust me. He wouldn't stop seeing Akiko; he wouldn't even stay the night. None of it came as a surprise. What killed me was witnessing this smart woman using her lovely, slim arms to clutch at rationalizations. It caused a strange trembling against my esophagus. I heard myself saying, "Is he worth all this pain?"

"You'd have him in a minute if he'd have you."

"Actually, it's no secret that I'm crushed out on Doug." I permitted a blush. "Anyway, Doug's still not over Akiko." I waved my hand near my ear. "They dated before she was with Mick—"

"You already knew about Akiko?"

Yvette's teeth came together as her lips flared. From beside myself, I feared she was going to bite, my blood indecipherable from her crimson lips as she lunged a second, a third time.

Without a word, Yvette banged away from the table. From then on, she ignored me at the point of a seeming arrow. Rather than intimidating me, her planned purpose caused the thickness in my throat to condense. Mick's always late, "just rolled off someone" appearance on Wednesday mornings made me want to yank out his David Bowie hair by the hank. He should have to feel what we felt. What a relief when April finally came around and my schedule changed. I returned to Doug's Monday and Friday practices. My first day back, there were as many as fifteen students, most of whom I hadn't seen since January. Even Elise was there. She was welcoming; they all were—didn't know I was missed—and full of compliments, after we finished, on the progress in my form. Lanky Australian Johnny gave me an off-center grin. In a voice as flat as Queensland, he said, "I've been going to the wrong practice, ey, mate?"

He had very wholesome green eyes. With very attractive specks of hazel in them.

Mick dropped his arm, nothing but friendly, around my shoulders. "Carlie is a pleasure to have as a student."

Johnny was taller than Mickey, yet Johnny took a modest step backward. I rotated my head to Mick. He looked nothing like David Bowie. He looked peely-wally.

Mickey removed his arm.

I'd blocked.

Light blew through in my heart. I was sailplaning through my friends—Doug's proud eyes—now crouched at the edge of Shinobazu Ike. The sun on the water. Similar silver down my cheeks. Me, twelve, in the beer-hot basement while those men played pool. The three of them were going to rape me.

I told my twelve-year-old to break the pool cue in half and use the jagged end to stab each of them through the chest.

She did.

My father was last. On her own, my twelve-year-old pulled the pool cue from his torso and shoved it through his eye socket to drive it into his skull.

Soothing, that bloodletting. I glided back to the practice area. Only Doug and Johnny remained, going through the long form. Doug gestured for me to join them, but I was as grounded as I'd ever been. I sacked out on the grass to watch strong men move and to enjoy the good, clean smell of the emerging spring. This was a scent from last year. It was soft fresh dirt and new grass. It was April sun on my skin. Spring would spiral into summer, which would bring about fall. Then winter would come, to manifest as spring. Winter always became spring. Faith had less to do with the epic than it did with the miracle of time, passing.

Push Hands

Okay, so the glory of all of it—Mick, eye socket, skull, spring—only lasted two days. The Wednesday following the Monday I blocked, Mick zinged me with a wink—one wink!—and it was as if my triumph never happened. After practice, I headed to Cho's office to puzzle it out. British irritability stopped me at the umbrella counter. In helping the customer with his purchase, I taught the counterwoman a few phrases. Then rushed to Cho's office. "Hey, what if we—"

High heels the color of dandelion center were propped on Cho's expanse of a desk. She stared out her thirty-fifth-floor window. The phone demanded attention. She ignored it. Unheard-of.

I asked, "Did someone die?"

Cho smacked her desk. Instantly, I said, "Your cousin."

"Board meeting. Achieve fucking English. La de da, Imai—did I mention he's my cousin?—he just so happens to have the numbers with him. He says, all offhand, that the school is my job to fix. 'You are the native English speaker.' And what did I do? Exactly what? I suggested that he fuck the fuck off, only not as kindly as such, and the Board saw exactly what he hoped they would see, an emotional female."

I couldn't believe it. Cho's eyes moistened. I leaned across her desk. "Let's teach your sales staff to speak English."

"What are you talking about?"

"We have a conversation school. With a dire lack of students."

Cho's chic shoes hit the floor. I pressed on, "Free lesso—"

"Half-priced." She dove for her adding machine.

Deliberately, I tapped the red "Cancel" button on the top left of Cho's keypad. Over her, "What!" I said, "We can't possibly lose more money than we do now. Try it. One term."

"Fuck it. Seventy-five percent off. But they pay in advance." Laughing wildly, Cho grabbed her phone as she re-calculated a-rat-a-tat-tat. "Meeting. You, Ava, Saito. Now, yesterday, at the school. Get back there."

Standing before Saito's desk, with Ava right beside her, I made the pitch. Ava maintained a fitting neutrality until Sensei's, "This may work very well, very well," when she made her devastated face. Saito, however, was looking at me.

I said, "I have another idea. The demonstration kitchen. We could hold a few sample classes there. Right across is a coffee shop and the exit to the trains, so there would be plenty of foot traffic. We could ask some staff members to be the students."

Saito burst into exuberant Japanese. Behind her, Ava took to a chair. Later that day, Brian rapped on my desk. I lifted my eyes from the computer screen, where I was re-designing the post-lesson chart. His wink thanked me for recommending him, the genki-est teacher, for the demonstration classes. I wished Ava would take it half as well. She avoided me all afternoon and in the evening, at home, I had to poke my head into her and Cho's room to get her to pay me some attention.

"Wanna talk about it?" I asked.

On their futon, Ava slapped her book closed. "I don't understand why you didn't come to me instead of Cho. I'm your direct supervisor."

"You know, you're right."

Without seeming to hear, Ava plowed on. "You don't have a

bloody high school diploma. Why Saito offered you co-head—"

"—assistant to the co-head. I'm your assistant—"

"I've a Masters' from Cambridge!"

"Yes! And I'm a high school drop-out runaway you met sleeping with a heroin addict."

Ava pulled herself to her knees. "I knew you'd bring that up, so smart and strong that so young, you—"

"That is not what I meant and you know—"

"You stole their money. How much have you repaid? Not a *yen* of it, ya wee thief! Get out. Geddout! Don't come back"—Ava flung a pillow at me—"until you're a better person!"

Around midnight, Ava crept into my room, crying like a pipe had burst. "There are times it comes up like a white wall, my rage. Is that why you choose Cho, to go deep? I so want to be of help. I can, about the money, Carlie. Keeping it might feel like revenge, but it will only drive you down. You could end up like me."

"I don't see what's wrong with you, Ava. Even if I do get mad at you, sometimes. You shine with goodness."

"Wee mucker." Ava reached an arm across my stomach and snuggled her face into the crook of my arm, like she trusted me. It was the purest I'd felt since I'd seen my cervix.

The day of the big meeting at Achieve English, Cho Yamashita strode in killer heels to the front of the teacher's lounge. Saito followed her, calling the thirty or so teachers to attention. Cho began by announcing the one-year, one-hundred-thousand-yen completion bonuses, and then masterfully channeled that excitement into interest in the changes. Brian and I received energetic applause. Even greater enthusiasm greeted Ava's description of round-filing the B-b-b k-k-k in favor of conversation games. When the teachers heard they no longer had to complete the post-lesson chart, it was like someone had finally fed the chimpanzees.

Wearing her radiant smile, Ava distributed copies of my re-designed sheet. "Ten questions, mates. Multiple choice, making it easy to assess progress—"

"Or lack thereof," came from the back of the room.

Ava didn't seem to know how to handle the jeering. Fair enough; she'd never had to take shit from these mates. I stood.

"No one is suggesting that you have to make up spectacular results. Just give us the information so we can help you teach more effectively the next time."

Something registered with the teachers, though I totally blew it with Ava. I could tell by the refined hand gesture she used to indicate that I should take over. Oh, man; we'd been getting along so well. However, Saito and I had questions to address. Then Cho made a few more inspiring comments, and the meeting ended. Cho left, mouthing, "Good work."

"Brilliant!" Brian brayed directly into my face. "Co-head!"

"Assistant to the co-head." Several more teachers offered their congratulations before I was facing Yvette. Face like a dart, eye on the assistant head teacher position. She ticked them off on furious fingers. "Akiko. Head teacher. What else haven't you told me, Carlie?"

"Assistant to the—"

Yvette grabbed Mona Lisa and dragged her in the direction of the ladies' room. My eyes followed them, ran into Ava's through the window to her office. She lowered the shades, an accusation. The next day, Saito assigned Ava and me the task of choosing which store employees to volun-tell for the conversation lessons. When I approached Ava, she sang out, "I'm skedaddling off with Yvette and Mona Lisa for tea and a blether. The task's aught but a stooshie. You'll do it pure barry."

"Pure barry," Yvette and Mona Lisa giggled to Ava in big, fake Scottish accents, and then, three together "Stooshie!" What grade were they in? I dove into my work, inviting five of the Office Ladies who worked the school's reception desk. I included the three who took my sample lesson, back when I first applied.

I loved that the two who chose English names still asked me to call them Lisa and Marcie. All three were familiar with the lessons, and with Brian. Others were too familiar. In choosing the remaining two sample students, I left out the OLs he'd messed around with. There remained a slim pool.

Brian displayed a remarkable flair for performance. The demos drew huge crowds. In two weeks, classes were full—mostly with store staff.

"At seventy-five percent off," Cho said, forehead on her desk.

"For one semester."

"You'd better be right."

"I'll be right." With robust classes, the school's atmosphere improved. Teachers' meetings got active. By the fourth one, only Brian arrived late, rushing in as Serious Joan's hand went up.

"The lesson was the simple past. I brought up my childhood in Toronto. No one knew which country, eh? I sent them to find Canada on the map."

"Could they find the map?"

"Thank you, Brian." My function a great deal of the time was to keep the discussion from degenerating into all-out student-bashing. "Any suggestions?"

"Have them look above the United States."

Ava was dedicated to Professional Neutral. The ping at the base of my spine was inconclusive. That said, several head-snaps around the room implied that other teachers thought her remark might be a jab at me. My hands trembled the way they did in the kitchen the day I had the memory about those waves, crashing.

Ava's voice cut through. "What do you think, Carlie?" Was she being kind? Perhaps I responded, "About what?" because the room went quiet.

"I'm sorry I have to—" I gestured in the direction of the restroom and left, not exactly sure I was headed there. In the blue hallway, I heard crying, so barely heard it that I paused. No. Actual crying came from the coatroom. There, I discovered one of the newer OLs. Yuki pulled at her blouse, trying to hide missing buttons. There were red marks on her neck.

I crouched next to her. "Yuki, who did this?"

Her quivering mouth pressed shut.

Japanese were more likely to share personal information in English, so I switched. "Let's go to Saito Sensei."

I wrapped Yuki in my jacket and took her to Saito Sensei's office. I'd never seen a person literally blanch. She said, "This is very big problem in Japanese companies. *Sex-u Har-u.*"

In anger and in Japanese, Yuki let out, "I'm engaged, but now, he'll think I'm dirty." *Kitanai*, she said again and again.

Not waiting for Saito Sensei, I said, "You are not dirty, Yuki. Please tell us what happened."

She did so, haltingly. Brian surprised her in the coatroom. When she resisted, he pushed her to the wall. She used the word *bokan,* an attack that may or may not include rape. Carefully, I asked, "How did it end?"

"An umbrella was to the side. I—" A striking gesture.

"Right on, Yuki," I said in English.

She grabbed my arms. Such tiny hands. "Don't tell another people. Please. All OLs tease Brian fancies me. I have fiancé. I say no. Dirty."

Saito Sensei said in Japanese. "We will find Tachikawa-san an excellent new position."

In English, I said, "We should find Brian the door."

Saito Sensei's eyes took on a flat affect. She used Japanese. "That is the end of it."

Yuki's shoulders were again shaking. To my boss, I said, in Japanese: "We must tell Yamashita Butch-o-u."

Ten minutes later, in Cho's office, she said to the three of us, "Fire him. Yesterday. I will not permit sexual harassment in this compa . . . in fact," Cho settled into her plush chair, a lethal butterfly ready to pounce. "Send him to me."

Saito bowed, a perfect thirty degrees. *"Hai, Butch-o-u. Dakedomo."* After dangling that "however" with a precise blend of acceptance and disagreement, Saito finished in English. "We do not yet know his side."

"What crap." Seeing Saito's shocked eyebrows, Cho reined herself in. "See what he has to say for himself. Yuki, let me make you some tea."

Saito Sensei and I returned to Achieve English and paged Brian. He appeared at Saito's office with a pencil still behind his ear. His athletic chest flexed in surprise when he saw it was me standing next to Saito Sensei, who sat behind her plain metal desk. I did not trust myself to speak.

"Please, take a weight off." Saito Sensei tugged the sleeve-hem of her pink jacket. "We have complaint from one of OLs."

Brian gave a chuckle as he sat. "And I thought I was up for another demo."

"Miss Tachikawa claims you attacked her."

A flush of incredulity swallowed Brian's freckles. "Who?"

"Yuki-san."

"Yuki?" Brian laughed in relief. "You mean earlier on? That wasn't an atta—I'm sorry if she's upset, but I thought . . . then she changed her mind, that's all."

"Miss Tachikawa claims she had to strike with umbrella to make you stop."

Brian appeared honestly surprised. "That's not at all the way it went." When Saito Sensei said nothing, he continued, "If you must know, some girls, to interest a bloke, they say no, but they say it so's you know they really mean yes."

"Did Miss Tachikawa mention fiancé?"

"Yeah, they all say that. It makes you more interested. And they know it." Brian leaned back, clasping his hands behind his head. His arm muscles looked like weights.

Saito Sensei was watchful. Finally, she said, "So, this is the way. You followed Yuki to cloakroom . . ." Saito Sensei waited for his nod. "Why follow to cloakroom? Why not meet?"

"How can I explain this to a woman? Where is Yuki, anyway? Whyn't she telling me to my face?"

Saito Sensei straightened as if she'd been slapped. "In Japan, we do not do."

"You should, ey?"

Saito Sensei allowed Brian to sink into his gaffe. His attention came to rest on me.

"I found Yuki, Brian. There were red marks on her neck."

"That wasn't me!"

"Buttons!" I could not manage, *Yuki's*. *Mine*.

Saito Sensei tapped her desk. "Perhaps we never know truth of this afternoon. However, we do know what, if something else happens. You will be fired."

Brian leapt up. The pencil flew from behind his ear and bounced into Saito Sensei's lap. She placed it across the desk calendar as he all but shouted, "Any little chit takes it into her head to tattle, and I get the sack?"

Saito said, "Perhaps you refrain from dating Office Ladies."

That was a slap for Brian. He treated me to a lizard-look to rival Ted's at the cabin.

"Do not blame Carlie Sensei. Everyone could see." Saito placed both hands flat on her desk, tilting her head marginally. "In Japan, we do not mention. Now, I regret I did not do."

Brian did not return the bow, let alone a lower one. He didn't even sit. "I want to speak to Carlie."

"Please, speak," said Saito Sensei.

"Alone."

I would do anything to avoid what was coming, but it would happen sooner or later. After I said in Japanese, "It's okay," Saito Sensei left cautiously.

Brian snatched his pencil from where it lay on the calendar to point it at me. "Do not tell me who I can and cannot—"

"These women are not here—"

"They all want gaijin boyfriends—"

"Don't you interrupt me."

The furrows that appeared above Brian's eyes showed he hadn't thought me capable of such authority. He recovered quickly, jabbing the pencil into Saito's desk so forcefully that the point broke.

"When's the last time you had it, Carlie? From a bloke, ey? A real bonk'd do you no end of good."

I came to my feet. "If I ever want it from you, Brian, I will let you know. Until then, keep your distance."

"Fuck off!"

"You're fired."

"I quit!"

"Good."

Saito's office was behind the reception desk. Before I went to the teachers' lounge, I waited 15 minutes for Brian to get his shit together and get out of my face. I entered to find the full company of teachers, was flabbergasted when I learned they knew Brian had been canned and why, but backed him in spite of it. Mona Lisa quit, loudly, Yvette at her side—though, tragically, not inclined to leave herself. Remembering tremors in slight shoulders and a voice repeating "kitanai," I blocked Mona Lisa with, "You've always made a more committed bar hostess than you did a conversation teacher. Sayonara."

Only my block didn't do the trick. Distaste spiked in the faces of the teachers, adding a glint of victory to Yvette's eyes. The bitch passed it to Ava, who leaned against the open door of her office, saying nothing, doing nothing, looking extra-slim in her lilac-colored sheath. Taking sides against Yuki.

I faced the teachers. "If anyone else wants out, please wait until Monday. I'm leaving for the weekend. Oh," I turned a final time to Mona Lisa. "Tell Brian that we assistants to co-heads have a cabal. I've already put the word out. He might as well leave for Taiwan now."

I grabbed my stuff and passed Ava, who said, "A moment?"

I stopped with a muted, "Did you plan to apologize?"

"For what?"

"Then, no, I have no moments."

Ava's lips pulled back slightly from her teeth, a Yvette expression if ever there was one. The implied intimacy hit me as painfully as her abandonment of Yuki. I managed to keep myself from storming out, simply left for my usual pay phone, my path to Margot. Except I wanted to speak with Doug.

"Hey, man," I said when he picked up. "Wanna practice?"

We met at the street-corner park near his house. As we stretched, I boiled it down for him, the part about Ava at the meeting, so painful, but not half what it was to feel Ava's betrayal of a fellow survivor.

"Doug, I don't think I can even look at her anymore. We can't live together. I can't block her."

"Blocking isn't always the most effective way to respond. You might have to stop fighting."

"Don't give me one of your I'm-so-emotionally-hip—"

"You know first-hand I'm not emotionally hip—I just come at it from . . ." Doug dropped into a crouch " . . . caring about . . . both of you and seeing, you know. Patterns. Bigger patterns."

I squatted next to him. "Tell me more."

"Instead of fighting her, Push Hands."

"I don't Push Hands," I whined, afraid of the two-person pattern that looked like bears on hind legs, trying to propel each other off balance.

"You already did. She tried to get you into her office, and you didn't lose your equilibrium. On your feet. Distribute your weight fifty-fifty, between both legs."

I did. Doug impelled my right shoulder, not even that hard. I almost fell over.

He walked in a circle around me. "If your weight had been seventy percent on the back leg and thirty percent on the front, you could have absorbed that attack. Move your left leg forward and right leg back. Knees bent. Shift weight so you are seventy percent on the front leg. Now shift seventy percent to the back. Now forward. Now back. Stop."

Doug stepped so that he stood opposite me, an arm's length away. He placed his legs so that ours created a rectangle: left legs forward, right legs back. He said, "Go." He transferred his weight to his forward leg as I transferred mine to my back leg.

"Go," he said again.

We switched, him bringing his weight back as I brought mine forward. "Go," he said, "And, go." And then we were switching front and back. It was a bit like dancing and a bit like having sex standing up. I blushed and giggled. He blushed and said, "Arm."

Our right arms met exactly between us, bent at the elbows, wrists touching. Totally hot. Doug's eyes drilled me as he went into a remarkable brogue falsetto. "Come into my office, Carlie." He brought his weight seventy percent to back, causing me to bring mine thirty percent forward.

"Screw you, you skinny bitch."

Doug barely moved his wrist, yet I tottered.

"Anger," he said. "Easiest way in the world to flip someone. Step into my office."

We took the position. This time, I moved forward not quite thirty percent. I didn't trust going too far.

"That's what I mean by listening," Doug said. "Say what you said to her."

I drew my weight seventy percent back. "Are you going to apologize?"

"For what?" he said as Ava. Fury roared down my arm in a punch. With a different turn of the same wrist, Doug again off-balanced me. We re-established ourselves. He said, "Come into my office," as we moved toward him.

Toward me: "Are you going to apologize?"

Toward him. "For what?"

When I said, "I believe you know," Doug said, "Dang! Dang!

Dang!" as he faked wiggling like he was on a tightrope. Then he jumped back into position. "If you'd gone into her office, you'd just have gone back and forth. But you pulled your weight away. Leaving her wide open."

"Why is it called Push Hands?"

"Arm."

Hot.

"Focus, Carlie. Imagine that I've drawn a circle around us. My goal is to push you out of this circle. Yours is to push me out. Go."

We shifted, but not forward-back. Instead, I let Doug maneuver me along the circumference of our imaginary circle. He said, "Come into my office," so suddenly that he was able to eject me from the circle without a problem. We tried again, then again, circling forward and backward, forward and backward along the perimeter, Doug correcting me. "Do absolutely nothing but respond to my movement until . . . you sense . . . a weakness." He sent me out of the circle.

We Pushed Hands in silence, except for the occasional correction from Doug. I never launched him, but a few times, I was able to absorb his attack. Push, circle, yield; push, circle, yield. I really felt like a bear: soft and round, pushing without exertion. Impossible, when you thought about it; yet so was the idea, two hours ago, of dancing in a park with Doug, of him saying, "Let's get noodles," and taking me to a famous ramen shop that I'd never heard of on Ameyoko Street near Ueno Station, a real working man's place on a Friday night, the prices of dishes listed on slips of paper push-pinned to the wall. Once again, Doug became the Rhinestone Cowboy he had been in Bangkok. The owner knew him; the cooks knew him, and the waiters knew him, as did a bunch of customers, Japanese men of Chinese descent. I spoke Japanese with them, as did Doug, purely terrible Japanese—I'd never seen Doug be bad at anything—but his Mandarin was good. Everyone asked if I was his girlfriend. He reddened. He asked me if it was okay if he had a couple of beers, and it was, it really, really was. When it became clear that he wanted to have another couple, I said I could get myself home, happy to avoid how we would handle goodnight at the turnstiles. When I got home around midnight, as high as I'd ever been on plain existence, the house was dark with the exception of Ava's light left pointedly on, or so it seemed to me. My clean and clear rage at her abandonment of Yuki told me to leave it fifty-fifty between us and get some sleep.

The next morning, there was a note from Ava on the kitchen table . . . *so much to be done at work with these changes . . . will be there most of the day."* I planned a Sunday hike with Margot to a glistening lake with a formidable view of Mt. Fuji. We did a lot of breathing and so I felt calm and connected the first time I saw Ava, Monday morning at tai chi. Doug started the session by saying, "Carlie and I were Pushing Hands over the weekend." During the philosophizing which ensued, at least half of the women gave me a subtle thumbs-up. Yep, I blushed.

Doug told us all to pair off for some Push Hands. Elise and I got to work. Next to us, Cho took on Johnny. The limby Australian was half again Cho's height. Nevertheless. she sent him stumbling. "Help me, Carlie, help me," he yowled—Johnny's great gift was to make everyone within fifteen feet laugh—and so we four agreed to switch it up. I was saying, "I'm not sure why you think I will be any easier on you than Cho was," when Mickey inserted himself.

"Hel-lo. I want to Push Hands with Carlie."

"Nah. I'm Johnny's karma for the morning."

Johnny said, "All hail, my causality"—which was adorable and kind of hot but which not the reason I asked him to walk with me to the station. His eyes gleamed, highlighting their hazel flecks. Hadn't noticed those since—when? Anyway, I was sad to detect the glow dim when I asked, "Hey, man. Would you consider a job with an annual completion bonus of a hundred-thousand yen? There are a couple issues."

Before Johnny started at Achieve English, we agreed that I wouldn't drag him between me and Ava and he wouldn't relay any office gossip. In the staff room, he mingled easily with the other teachers—"Bangkok's good fun, but I prefer the islands, Phangan and like that"—until Ava stage-whispered, "Carlie's recruiting!" loudly enough to be heard by everyone in the room. They hushed.

Johnny looked as alarmed as I'm sure I did. He said, "Ava?"

The bell rang. Teachers dashed for their classrooms. Johnny went right up to Ava. "There was no need for that."

She touched his shoulder. "You're right, mate."

And that was that. I'd have pushed back so fast—

As if she could tell, Ava turned toward me. "Oh, assistant to the co-head, I buggered up the photocopier."

Johnny didn't say, "Ava?" again, but his face sure did. He offered to take care of the copy machine. Ava made her noise and I flared at Johnny, "Are you kidding? I'll handle it"—and proceeded to sacrifice fifteen minutes of my lunch break to unjam it, opening and closing drawers and pulling out trays and pushing them in. The back and forth brought the realization, "She flipped me." Ava proceeded to disable the photocopier three minutes before the bell rang for three days in a row. The fourth day, Wednesday, I stretched alone in the humid practice area, cataloging resentments. At ten past ten, I started the form. At twenty-goddamn-'til, Mickey padded like his panther self around the red-gilded shrine. Fuckin' light a fire, man.

Taking in me by myself, Mick rubbed his five o'clock shadow. "Others have left, have they?"

"What others?"

It came out with the same control with which I told Brian not to interrupt me, and Mickey reacted with Brian's disbelief. A hardening of jade eyes indicated that Mick would be a more adept opponent. I envisioned me, opposite him, on a windy hillside, both of us ready in white fighting silks.

"You said you wanted to Push Hands."

Mick considered me the way he might an obstreperous puppy. When our wrists connected, the zing was far stickier than it had been with Doug. Mick could probably use it to flip me right then. And he knew it.

A bear wouldn't care about Mick. I imagined being a bear. Five, six times in a row, he ejected me. I found myself closing my eyes, focused on accepting his movement. We picked up speed. I felt a *chink* in his energy and went with it.

My eyes flew open. His "Thaaat's better," told me he let me have that one.

We resumed. As we circled, the sun more condemning than ever, his gaze held mine. He will take me in his arms. That fantasy was the enemy. Mick was only the opponent. Instead of resisting, I went into him. I went farther into him than I allowed him into me. Then, I absorbed him. And Mick was outside the circle. From the way he wiped his forehead, I knew I'd earned that one. I said, "I've got to get to work. We should do this next week if no one shows."

He leveled a glare at me, ejected from a very real circle. "Why does no one show?"

Another fantasy: I read him the riot act; he changed.

He erupted, "Because of Akiko?"

"You really thought you'd get away with that?" Oops.

"What right have any of you to judge me?"

My voice came out calmly. "Who operates in a vacuum?"

He waited. I did, too.

"Carlie, do you ever wish you could be a better person?"

Good thing I'd been watching Mick so obsessively and for so long. I could see that move for what it was: the part in Snake Creeps Down where he pulled me into his chi and turned mine against me.

"I'm gonna be late. Good talking with you, Mi—Michael."

Snake Creeps Down occurs twice in the form. The first time

is shortly into the second section. The other comes at the end. The second time, I am invariably better prepared.

I hit the staff room bear-sweaty. Ava jammed the copier. Lost in the marvel of flipping Mick, I said, "You have three minutes."

From his desk, Johnny actually laughed. As Ava crash-bang-boomed the copier into submission, I leaned a hip against Johnny's chair. "You're making me look good."

"You've always looked good to me."

I couldn't breathe. It took me all the way until Sunday morning, in our kitchen, boiling water for tea, to acknowledge that I didn't know how to handle the response I'd so obviously angled for, and Johnny spent Thursday and Friday chatting with Joan. Just like—oh, man, I'd done it again—Doug made that statement about "Carlie and me over the weekend," and the first thing I did, the first thing, was leave for the station with Johnny. To top it off, Sunday morning giggles wafted from behind Cho and Ava's closed shoji. Couldn't call Margot; she was going to be with Horst. The way Johnny would soon be with Joan.

I heaved open the refrigerator. A carton of eggs. Clutching it as if it held rubies, I charged to a deserted park around the corner and positioned myself about ten feet from a barrel-thick tree. The first egg hitting the trunk made not a smash, not a shatter, yet golden yolk oozed down the rough bark like a plea. Too soon, the eggs were gone. I hauled ass to a convenience store, marched past the ice cream, bought two dozen. In the park, eggs, tree. Yuki, trembling. Ava, abandoning her. Abandoning me. There was an awareness I could almost—

The eggs were gone again.

Being bulimic finally paid off: I knew the location of every convenience store in the neighborhood. I came back with a stack of six more cartons and slammed away.

There weren't enough eggs in the world.

I phoned the only other person in Tokyo I could be sure was not getting laid this fine Sunday morning. "You once said 'if I ever needed you.' I need you."

Doug said, "I'm there."

I marked time in the park, one big Angry Fist: feet two shoulders' width apart, knees bent, hands balled at the hips. Slow punch, right arm straight front, looking with a warrior's eyes to the angry fist at its end. Then, as challenging as it would be, you had to let everything go. Body had to soften as you returned the right fist to your hip. Body grew taut as you slowly stretched into the left punch. Taut, soft, taut, soft; right then left, right, left. I punched faster. Far off, the drone of traffic. A similar discordance hovered on the edges of my consciousness. The awareness became evident. It became my mother. My fists flew.

"You cunt! You fucking cunt! They played pool to see who'd get me first! And you were drunk! You were drunk!"

I lunged toward a tree, craving the relief of injury and so pushed against it instead, against the irregular, lumpy bark. Pushed and pushed, grunted and grunted, until a power I didn't possess coursed through me, bashing a hole in the anger, thrusting me through. I felt as if I were merging with my mother, a mother I remembered from photographs of her college days. What was she wearing? Sweater sets? She met my father. Broad-shouldered and handsome, I thought as if I were her. He would make a good income. How did I know, but did: part of her sensed he would do it to their children. How did the same part of me understood that her father did it to her?

I screamed and dripped to the foot of the tree, immobilized by the insight.

"Carlie!" Doug was less than twenty feet away and closing in fast. I called his name, raised weak-strong arms. He held me. I couldn't tell him because I couldn't prove anything, would never prove it. But I would know.

I said only, "My mother let my father rape me. For years."

"Oh, Carlie." Barely audible. He held me, if possible, closer.

"It's not news to me, it's just . . . this rage . . . I hated her for not saving me. She should have. But she wasn't able to."

Doug said, "Yeah."

Once it started, I couldn't stop it. I babbled like Ava, explaining everything as we scooped egg mess into empty cartons. Punctured yolk, glutinous white, tree bark, dirt. Kitanai. No.

I had a pure, pink cervix. I was the albino child of my dream. Any filth was theirs.

We dropped the last of the muck into the trash. Doug brushed my hair off my face with the clean back of his hand. "Sometimes, we'll be cutting up before practice and I'll see right through this tunnel to the kind of kid you must have been. My sister used to play like that. You have Angel's light, you know? She was the only one Pop wouldn't hit. 'Til she got older and so pretty. She cleared out. Word around the neighborhood was, Angel was hooking."

I took his eggy hands. He squeezed mine.

"She brought me over. A ticket to Tokyo showed up in a letter one day. I guessed she was hooking here, too, but, dang, a ticket to Tokyo. She took me to Bali. The first time I ever went traveling. I haven't been back since . . ."

"You can say it."

"Since she died." Doug took the kind of breath you are supposed to take after the Angry Fist punch. We listened to each other until Doug said, "Me n' Johnny are going to Bali, for August. He'll be good to travel with, but I want someone along that I really trust. Will you come, too?"

On my way home, the fantasies were so good they hurt—being with Doug for four weeks, knowing precisely when he was in the shower, watching him sleep.

There I was, looking for love in the Friend File. Meanwhile, I blew off Johnny. Come to think of it, I'd blown off Doug, too. And there we'd all be in Bali, the most sensual island in the hemisphere. I slumped into the kitchen to discover Ava at the table. She was ashen.

"Oh, Carlie, Ma's got—!" She snatched up a thin, blue Aerogramme. "Here. 'The pain got bad enough that I went up to see Old Doc. It seems I'm ailing as Gran did.' My gran died of uterine cancer, Carlie. I should have—" She choked.

My arms circled her. "Ava, you couldn't have done anything."

"I'm going for a visit. I called, when I got the letter."

"Ava! What if your father had answered?"

"Sis picked up."

My spine didn't ping. It buzzed.

"Why was your sister at their house?"

"She's never moved out. Listen, Carlie. Ma was too far gone by the time she finally went to have everything looked at. The best they can do is make her comfortable. I must go. I must."

"Ava, your sister is still sleeping with your father."

"My mother has six months to live, Carlie! I've got one holiday! If it was your ma, you'd go."

"I can't remember the sound of my mother's voice."

"Because you don't want to. Then you'd have to—"

Ava stopped herself. We pushed at each other without touching, neither seeming to blink, until I realized that this was one round it wasn't my job to win.

Flower Attracts Male Bumblebee

Landing in Bali. Even as Doug, Johnny, and I grabbed backpacks off the outdoor rotate-y thing, I was distracted by the idea of Ava in Scotland, what she must be going through. Soon, however, the excitement over being where I was and with who supplanted all other thought. Our first stop was the town of Ubud. The express bus was five bucks, U.S., per person. Doug said, "The local bus is less than fifty cents each."

Johnny said, "Local'll take ages."

"And no air-con." I employed my used ticket as a fan.

Doug said, "You both agreed to travel my way."

"Right-o, buck-o." Johnny gave Doug a funky salute. For the first time I'd ever been witness to, Doug had no response to Johnny's humor.

The local took two transfers and three hours to deposit us in Ubud's famous travelers' area, a curving road leading to the monkey-run of a temple that gave the street the name Monkey Forest Road. Doug—man, it was like a space alien had eaten our sensitive, nineties guy. He was no less than cantankerous in his refusal to fork over the fifty dollars a night required by the high-end hotels that I didn't remember as having choked Monkey Forest Road.

Split by three, I reminded Doug, whose mood baffled Johnny, who knew nothing—now I understood—about Doug's sister.

Johnny waved over a boy selling Cokes. He had the thing open and half of it down his throat before he moved to pay the worried kid. Poking around his pockets, Johnny tossed him a loose coin he found. The little guy caught it. He stared at the hole drilled through the center.

"That's Japanese money," Doug said, kneeling so that his solid shoulders were on level with the little guy's skinny ones. "Fifty yen."

"Why it broke?"

"They just make 'em that way."

"You Japanese?"

Finally, a smile from Doug. "Chinese American."

"You buy one more Coke?"

"Just his is fine." Doug traded the kid some Indonesian coins for the 50-yen piece, which he lobbed to Johnny as the kid skipped away. Then he stood. "The currency here is the *rupiah*, in case you hadn't noticed that we changed countries." Doug waited for Johnny to make some funny comment before he continued, "What you threw a child is what each of us should be paying, per person, per night. And that is what I will pay."

Doug hauled his pack over his shoulders, weight dead even, setting his focus beyond the touristy shops and restaurants. We sweated farther down Monkey Forest Road. Restaurants thinned out, and shops were fewer and sold only one thing each, like silver jewelry. Doug found us a losmen like I remembered from my first time in Bali: a walled-in compound filled with barrel-sized succulents and flowering bushes, all interspersed with bamboo-roofed bungalows. Large goldfish in the ponds, kissy-kissy lips. Priced just as Doug had called it, breakfast included.

"Beauty," said Johnny.

The guys took one bungalow. I had my own. Outside my window and over the high stone wall, unseen people chattered on the street, the choir of birds I also remembered from last time.

My arms reached overhead, and my back arched luxuriously. I was a song.

A noise behind me turned out to be Johnny. He was on my terracotta porch, taking me in through the doorway. Then he moved to me. Faster than Johnny ever moved. A fishing wire of terror tightened around my lungs.

Doug was on my porch. At the same time, the young daughter of the family who owned the losmen scooted up the steps. She tugged Doug's shorts. "You Japanese?"

Big Brother crouched low, explaining that he was Chinese American. She giggled in confusion. Doug noticed Johnny in my room, his shoulder nearly touching mine, and Doug's fraternal smile tapered into the unusual, barbed mood from earlier. That night, I was unable to sleep. Geckos darted across the bamboo ceiling. Dogs howled in the streets. Maybe Doug's mood wasn't only because of his sister. I replayed the conversation we'd had on a bench near Shinobazu Pond after Mickey came to practice with Akiko. Doug admitted that his reaction to me and Mick was to get mad. If Doug was interested now, and Johnny was, too, that put me in the same position I'd been in all through my Lonely Planet months: one guy too many and not enough courage. By the time crowing roosters supplanted the caterwauling hounds and the earliest motorbikes caroused Ubud's wakening streets, I'd resolved that, this time, if Doug wanted me, he could come and get me. And if Johnny got there first, well.

I surprised myself by starting a head-letter to Ava: *Well, I don't know what.*

Of course, at breakfast on the guys' sunny, terracotta patio, Doug treated me as if he'd spent the dark hours deciding I could do the same. Johnny handled most of the conversation until the gent who owned the place breezed by. "Hello, all Americans."

A long, flat grunt from our resident Aussie.

"Cremation today. Eleven o'clock."

Electricity passed between me and Doug.

Sliding into the hammock, Johnny stretched his legs as if he were never planning to leave it, let alone the losmen. "Why go to the funeral of someone we don't know?"

Doug clapped him on the back. "My friend, you are in for something special."

Quietly, I asked Doug, "You sure you want to go?" but Doug— regular Doug, traveler Doug—hustled us to the Temple of the Dead that rested on the outskirts of every Balinese village, town, and city. Hundreds of people milled about the sidewalks, tourists and Balinese. Hawkers worked the growing crowd. *Dear Ava, As soon as we settled into a place in the crowd, Doug's head tilted downward. As if all of a sudden he remembered the only reason for a cremation.*

Johnny elbowed me. "Big something coming, ey?"

The crash of cymbals, drums, and gongs eclipsed the noise of the crowd. A hundred yards down the street, the huge figure of a white bull sailed toward us atop a sea of people. In front of it paraded a cortege of women in gold-edged sarong and vibrant yellow sashes, each balancing on her head a pyramid of fruit and brightly colored cakes.

"How do they do that, with no hands?" Johnny marveled. Loudly. Doug remained silent.

I shouted, "Those will burn, too."

"What? The women?" Johnny feigned horror as Doug flinched. The papier-mâché bovine passed on a bamboo platform borne by men in black sarong with white prayer scarves around their heads. Johnny indicated the tail end of the bull.

"That's where the body is, then?" Johnny asked.

"The body goes in there once we get to the temple. That's where the body is." I gestured to the next papier-mâché creation, a vanilla-colored tower trimmed in gold and decorated with vibrant blossoms, also carried by men in black and white. They surged to the right and left, hollering as they zigzagged their way toward the temple.

"They're going in!" Johnny screeched. He charged with the rest of the crowd through the temple gates. I stayed with Doug.

"Do you still wanna do this?" I asked him.

He took my hand and walked beside me into the tree-lined courtyard. The bull was settled at one end, the tower across from it. The band took its place with a final flourish. The well-wrapped corpse was paraded around, then inserted into the bull. Across the yard, mourners lined up to add their offerings to the bull that would burn. More than an hour passed before someone struck the match. It took fifteen minutes until a sweet, meaty smell I did not want to identify drove me toward Doug, who was hanging back from the pyrotechnics. Johnny followed. He nudged me.

"Fancy something along these lines when it's your turn?"

"What's it matter, anyway?" Doug said.

Johnny and I turned. Doug continued the only way you could in a crowd this size and still be heard: quietly. "Once you're gone? The big display is for us left behind."

Johnny said, "Mate, I can't believe it's you saying that."

At the end of the week, we headed north, to the beaches of Lovina, then dawdled east through the volcanic lake regions of Bratan and Batur. I head-lettered to Ava: *Half the time, Doug seems into me, half the time he doesn't. And the other half— because there is more time on this trip than two halves will hold—he is more concerned with the ocean-blue or rice-field-green horizon.* Most Balinese we met asked if Doug was Japanese and if I was Johnny's wife—perhaps because Johnny's eyes stayed on me, flecked with hazel and patience as the three of us hiked mountains and took in dance performances in quaint towns, so different from the slick professionalism of the troupes in Ubud. Here, a skeleton stage, a homemade batik backdrop. There weren't always mats for the *gamelan* musicians and their pulsating tingy, plingy, melodies. From the last time I was here,

I remembered *Oleg Tamulilingan,* "Flower Attracts Male Bumblebee," but had clean forgotten how sexy it was. The dancers moved with imperial grace, their calm walk more like skating, their precise hand movements and facial expressions sexual without an ounce of vulgarity. The balance was embodied by a red hibiscus behind the ear, Balinese for "smitten."

When the duet ended, Johnny shifted closer to me on the uneven wood bench. I waited for the fishing wire. This time, nothing tightened. *Ava, part of me wished it would; at least I would know how I felt.* To my right, Doug stood smiling like a brother with a birthday gift he was afraid I wouldn't want.

A boy tried to sell him a Coke. "You Japanese?"

Johnny said, "If I hear that one more time ..."

Doug said, "It's about me, not you. What do you care?"

Johnny let out a languid whistle. I'd seen that face. That was the Johnny who was never cowed by a new guy at tai chi, not even when the new guy outweighed him by thirty pounds of muscle.

Doug said, "Okey-doke, meet you guys back at the losmen."

Johnny and I ambled the dirt roads. Smoke from the streetlamps filled the humid night air, and for the first time, he took my hand.

Nothing.

Must be the way Doug felt about me.

Johnny squeezed my hand. I stopped us by using my free hand to cover the hand of his that was curved over mine: power and the correct use of power.

I said, "Here is the deal. I didn't grow up trusting men. I'm not sure what to do with a good one."

"Any idea when you might?"

When someone as cool as Johnny asked, "Any idea when you might?" and the real answer was, "My mom let my father rape me for years," well then, the only way to respond was as kindly as I knew how. I said, "I'm sorry, no."

Another sleepless night, this time spent as one big, angry fist.

Ava, a flower knows how to do this.

With less than a week remaining, we traveled toward Besakih, the Mother Temple. All twenty thousand temples on Bali faced Besakih—three holy complexes a third of the way up Agung, the island's largest volcano. At the main complex of stone, history, and a surprising number of large spiders, Johnny attracted the attention of two Japanese women. Two thin, Akiko-adorable Japanese women. Since Johnny's Japanese was worse than Doug's, guess who was drafted as translator? His Australian accent, low and flat; their Japanese, hilly and silly.

For three of the temple's six levels, Ava, I reminded myself who said no, but resentment was burning more fiercely than the afternoon. When I could no longer stomach myself, I charged to the last wide staircase and mounted it, alone except for the dragons carved into thick, sun-hot railings. Below me, rice terraces and then green fields reached into the denim-colored blur of nearby mountains. Breathing hard and so sweaty that I was almost woozy, I watched the progression of what looked like ants trooping up the side of Agung, people with lives as important to them as mine was to me. Without warning, I was the Emerald Buddha, peering from the pinnacle of golden statuary. I saw myself down there with the rest of the hard-working bugs, yet I was also me last summer, on Phangan, begging for guidance. Then I went out and for the longest time, did exactly what I felt like doing about Mick, about food. About Ava. We chuckled, the Buddha and I, at our precious children. *Maybe one day, our mothers will discover this freedom.*

"Carlie?"

How long had Doug been standing there? How long had I? Returning to the lush spread of life before me, I brought my hands together to give thanks in a Balinese dancer's gesture of supplication.

As the sun set, we descended all six levels, slender Yoko and enchanting Waka right with us. Johnny whispered to Doug that

Waka had asked him for a stroll.

"The thing is, mate, do you have a condom?"

Given the way I'd just let go, I didn't expect anything could hurt as much as that did. Doug mumbled something, "at the losmen." Striving for the serenity with which I had greeted Doug earlier, on the pinnacle, I reached into my fanny pack and slipped one to Johnny.

Moments later, I had to say, "Close those mouths, young gentlemen. You never know what's going to happen."

The taller young gentleman hurried to catch up with Waka. Doug continued to stare.

I was planted at the head of my bed, eavesdropping on the cicadas outside my window, when there was a tap on the arched wooden door. I'd been waiting for it. A hesitant Doug entered wearing his nervous-brother look and a red hibiscus in the dark hair behind his ear. His face was a slightly lighter red.

I thought I was ready. Then why did my laugh sound wobbly?

Doug stayed standing. "So, Johnny and Waka, huh?"

"U-huh."

"Wish it was you?"

"Not with Johnny."

The smoke between us was like incense from Besakih. Still, he did not move to touch me. Instead, he took the flower from behind his ear and rolled it into pulp between his fingers. I folded my hopes back in my heart.

He said, "You know, you come in here thinking you're ready, when what I really want is to tell you about Angel. I've never told anyone. Not even my mom. About identifying her body."

Startled, I tucked my legs. He sat next to me on the bed.

"One morning, she didn't come home. As dumb as that. She was missing four days before the cops found her. Crammed into a garbage can in a back alley in Shinjuku."

"Did they catch who did it?"

"They didn't even try. She was a gaijin hooker, Carlie. Half Chinese. She was still beautiful, you know? I couldn't believe it, when they opened that drawer she was in. A God I didn't even know existed let me remember the Angel I loved even though rats had left . . . bites. Taken bites. She'd been raped."

I was not sure who enveloped who. Heat came off his body as his sobs rocked us. As they gradually lessened, I wiped his face with the soft edge of my sarong. The dragon-strength of the Mother supported me in saying, "The hardest part about being God must be having the power to save everyone and choosing instead to offer comfort."

Doug twirled my hair around his finger, as if it only now occurred to him that we were on my bed, similarly wound around each other. He didn't smile when he said, "If I were any less a paragon of mental health, I'd get you naked this minute and use you as the substitute for self that I'd know you to be."

"And I'd let you."

Gradually, we uncoiled. Pulling to one side of the mattress, he asked, "Can I sleep here anyway?"

He slipped under the blanket, fully clothed. Lying next to him, the terrible ache of the flower finally blossoming only to die on the counter for lack of water became something else. It became a pirate's map. With many X's.

The Eighth Treasure

As I sat between Doug and Johnny on the train from Narita Airport to Ueno Station, it sank in that I would no longer be spending all day every day with Doug. At Ueno, big hugs. Johnny headed toward the Yamanote line, Doug and I, the subway. At the point in the tunnel where the stairs to my train led up and his down, I was ready to suggest a workingman's noodle dinner. Before I could, he asked when Cho and Ava were expected back.

"Next week." X-X-X-X-X.

Doug twirled my hair. "See you at practice."

In our genkan, the surprising number of shoes and a heavy feeling in the house denoted their early return. I heard Cho: "Kitchen!" Her embrace was all Cho.

Ava didn't seem to bear me any of the animosity of our parting fight, but she wrapped her arms around herself instead of me, beyond anything I'd ever seen from her, even over Mickey or work. She barely got out, "I purged. We arrived August third, I purged the fifth. We left the sixth."

"You've been home all month? Did you see your family at all?"

"The fifth."

Cho took a firm hold of her shoulder. "You go back to Achieve English in two days.

"Achieve ... ?"

"It will be the best thing—"

"Cho. I can't. My ma."

Cho held Ava's face in her hands. "You can. You will."

They kissed. Ava squeezed Cho, infinitesimally more herself. "What would I do without you?"

Cho waved her hand by her ear before saying, "Tell us about Bali, Carlie. Oh! I don't want to forget."

Cho passed me my mail. Sorting through the few missives, I described Balinese dances and Besakih climbs, keeping all mention of Doug and Johnny strictly friendly. Cho shocked me by snatching up my opened statement from Liu. When I said, "Cho!" she hastily returned it.

"Sorry. I saw that return and—which stock is that?"

"Microsoft. Liu convinced me to put five thousand into it two years ago."

"Goddamn it, I went with Apple. I'm calling Liu!" Cho dashed off, leaving me with Ava.

"You appear to have plenty of money now, Carlie."

"It's my money, Ava. They are my parents. Stay out of it."

Ava jumped to her feet and slapped the table. "You're trying to punish them! It doesn't work! Nothing works. I thought I was healing, away from them." She slouched into her seat. "I wasn't near him five minutes before I felt the same, exactly the same, the bloody weird daughter of the man the whole town loves. Her doctors, the neighbors, everyone. They'll never believe me." She hit her own thighs.

I stopped her hands. Ava used a wrist twist to free herself. Then she grasped my forearms—surprisingly strong. "Return that money! Keeping it is you saying, 'I've won.' We never win."

"Cho!" I yelled down the hall.

"Embrace what they have done!"

Cho came running. Ava threw my arms away from her. I never got from Ava what that meant, embrace what they have done, and I was afraid to bring it up again. Ava did not return to Achieve English in two days. She took a leave for fall quarter.

"The nightmares," she said to Cho, who shot back, "Which will only get worse if you do nothing but mope around the house."

I told Doug, "It feels like listening to your parents fight," as we walked to the station after our first practice back from summer. Doug said he would treat Ava for free, but, when he phoned with the offer, she hung up on him and gave me the evil eye. "Stay out of it."

She refused to come to breakfast the next Saturday. Surprised to feel lonely in the booth with only Margot, I said, "She tried to kill herself, before."

"I know, eh? Honestly, I don' think we need worry unless she stops coming to tai chi."

I didn't tell Margot, but I had an actual date to meet Doug. He'd called to formally ask me out. We met at the practice shrine for a stroll. Not until we had settled onto a bench behind a large bush did he touch my arm the way I had yearned for in that hotel room at Besakih. His lips brushed mine. I almost peeked, to see if he really meant it.

Fuck it. I kissed Doug the way you kiss someone you've wanted for more than three years. His earlobe, an apricot. His hands slid under the light wool of my coat, grasping the outside of my thighs, bringing to mind the word "haunches."

"Real estate," he murmured. The whole tableau was refreshingly carnal. When the sun dipped behind the shrine, I said, "We should be getting home."

"Whenever you're ready."

That goddamned Balinese fishing wire.

Doug ran his nose along my neck. "We're not gonna rush this, Carlie. I want this to work."

On Saturday, Margot beat the tabletop of our booth gently yet rapidly with her fists. "Knew it, knew it, I just knew it. The instant I saw you two back from Bali."

227

"Last night, I stayed over. You know that show, Beatlemania? Doug goes, 'All the stimulation without the real thing.'"

Margot yowled. The waiter appeared. She shooed him away. "That beats, 'Half an inch, no thrusting.'"

My turn to holler.

She said, "I thought you went to Catholic school, too?"

At last, I managed, "It took me a long time, though."

"It is a clitoris, eh? Not a light switch."

Over the next month, I told Margot everything. That I didn't freak out when he wanted to get sexual, that he didn't walk out when I was not ready to have intercourse. We talked. And sexy. So sexy. I expected a new memory, some calamity to destroy every first—the first time he ran his thumb down my cheek in front of the tai chi crew, the first time I took him in my hand. Instead, it was, man—exploring him without feeling like I owed him anything, even initiating, a long-held fantasy involving the treatment table. He was afraid that both of us on it would break it. Instead, he massaged me, saying, "Let's make like it's really a treatment." Totally worked: I had to squelch moan after moan until I had to let one rip, at which point he scooped me off to his futon. I continued to feel comfortable saying, "Not yet." And he still didn't walk out.

Oh, Doug Doug Doug.

One night, I was nuzzling across his pecs when I felt him slide up. I made sure to move with him. He asked, "Don't you wanna stay down there?"

Doug's face was smooth and brown and so sweet. I couldn't say a thing.

He contemplated the Tibetan *thangka* on the wall, an azure Buddha painted in the center of sky-blue cloth edged with subdued yellow silk. "Don't get me wrong. It's good, our, ah, alternative activities. But it's kinda like high school, in the back seat. I don't get how we're supposed to move to the next level."

"I sucked off too many guys, Doug. Just to get it over with."

I was sure he would leave. Doug surprised me by taking my hands. "Then we won't. I love you, Carlie."

When I didn't reply, he said, "But you're not ready to love me the way you're not ready to make love with me."

"I feel more now than I ever hoped to feel for anyone."

His kiss was a concession. It morphed. When I squealed, he said, "Well, I'm a guy."

"Can I interest you in an assortment of alternative activities?" Oh, man.

I loved finding the soft spots—behind his knee, the luscious fold covering his elbow—and, weirdly, watching him read the sports' page. How was that hot? He was a Mets fan. He called the Yankees bastards and slapped the paper against the table.

"I didn't even know you liked football."

"Baseball." His shock was freakishly delectable. Some nights, as we rolled around his futon, I was able to tell him how lucky I felt. The first time I said it, he grasped me by the arms. "Do you mean that?" After he fell asleep, I watched him. Almost every night, I watched the fragility that strong Doug exuded and wanted to absorb all his pain so he never had to feel it. We were two of the wounded trying together to make sense of things. Which, as far as I could tell, made us about even with every other couple out there. At home, Ava was throwing up. Cho told Margot, Doug, and me at the end of the first practice that Ava would not attend. Cho said, "Yesterday, I found empty ice cream cartons in the trash. I went looking for them."

Then she sobbed. A lost sound, terrifying from the person we all expected to be in control. Through her tears, she said, "Boy, you think you know someone. Or yourself. I suggested in-patient treatment at a place in the States called The Meadows, but she screamed that I was breaking up with her. In January, I have a two-week business trip. The thought of leaving her is killing me."

I took Cho's hand. "We're gonna work this out." To Doug: "Do you know someone who could help?"

Doug and Cho took the long path to the station. Margot and I remained silent for longer than we ever had. I broke into the quiet with, "For the longest time, I thought that, once you felt loved, the eighth and most precious treasure, that everything else took care of itself."

My eyes could not let go of Doug, his arm around Cho's shoulder. His arms were often taut around my bare torso as he'd slipped me out of layer after layer of clothing and fear. Over the next couple of weeks, he used his hands on me. I liked doing that for him, but when it came my turn, I wasn't around anymore. And then, an orgasm just happened. Nights, I spent more time watching him. One night, he spread out to read on his futon, propped on one tender elbow. I laid my cheek against his smooth, bare back. "This is a stupid 'if,' but, if we got married, would you want me to change my name?"

"Are you asking me to marry you, Carlie?"

Thank God he was smiling. "I am asking, if we got married, would you want me to take your name?"

"Up to you." Doug returned to his book. "I always thought it was kinda weird, though. Like, I don't know, branding cattle?"

I reached to place my hand in the middle of the page.

"I love you, Doug."

He rested his book deliberately on the tatami. When we got to the part where he entered me, I thought, Well. This is pretty normal.

Folded Cranes

One dry, frosty morning, Cho placed on the kitchen counter a list of what needed to be done while she was out of the country inspecting affiliate stores. At the table, Ava began to shake. "Why didn't ya tell me you were going?"

"I did. Over a month ago. And again, two weeks ago, before I finalized my reservations." Cho tightened the lapels of her red silk robe across her chest.

Ava wore limp gray terrycloth. "You can't leave me!"

"Then meet me in Singapore! Or Hong Kong. Or Malaysia. You loved Malay—meet me there. Meet me halfway, Ava. It's been six months. You need a job. A shower."

I said, "Achieve English will take you back in a second."

Ava raised her head, her eyes like the dinosaur seeking prey that I'd hated yet now was overjoyed to see. She said, "A conversation school. I worked for a college."

I said, "Call them. Say you want your job back."

Ava lapsed into a vacant stare. Cho pulled her loose hair into a ponytail that fell apart as she said, "Ava, I love you, I want to help. But I cannot do it for you." An hour later, she stuck her head into the kitchen to say she was leaving for the airport. Ava seemed to have disappeared into herself.

I accompanied Cho to the front door. "I'll do my best."

"I love her," Cho said softly. "Please . . ."

When the door closed behind her, I braced myself and returned to the kitchen. Ava hadn't stirred. I said, "When we first met on Phangan, you said there was only one me. It meant a lot."

"Five minutes, Carlie. That's all it took. He didn't have to do a thing. At least you've something to do about it. You can return their money. I want this torture to end."

Our landlady came into the room, a flat package tucked into the sash of her navy-blue wraps. First, the tiny woman bowed considerately. Then, in fastidious, old-fashioned Japanese, she apologized for intruding. "Yet in winter's darkest months, I cannot always fight my sadness."

A strangled gasp escaped Ava. Kashiwabara-san opened the brown parcel to spread dainty sheets of origami paper—blues, greens, yellows, and magentas; some solid while others were patterned with diamonds, stars, or flowers. Over Ava's sobs, Kashiwabara-san said, "In those times, I fold paper cranes. Japanese people believe that to fold one thousand cranes brings immortality. Perhaps in folding, we capture the part of ourselves that flies up."

Kashiwabara-san reached up. For a moment, she flashed as the Goddess, the woman who survived by eating only onions though her baby could not.

Then, the gentle old soul I thought I knew was back. "Ava-san, we will make *orizuru* together. *Ne*?"

Start with a square piece of origami paper. Fold it in half on the diagonal, into a triangle, then fold that triangle into a smaller triangle. After that, I struggled. I set my first endeavor, wrinkled and pathetic, on the table. It promptly keeled over.

Ava said in English, "I'm to rely on that to save my life?" She was focused so intently on copying Kashiwabara-san's open-fold-reverse-refold, that I was almost certain she'd made a joke.

Kashiwabara-san gingerly unfolded my *kamikaze* crane. "Here is the problem. You only folded this one halfway. Fold it all the way. Up to its behind." She used the very polite *o-shiri* for "behind." I couldn't repress a giggle. Neither could Ava. With a semblance of her former verve, Ava searched out a favorite James Taylor album. By the time "Something in the Way She Moves" played for the second time, we had a veritable orizuru production line going. Kashiwabara-san instructed us to note early on which corner would become the bird's back, its *senaka*. "Keep your eye on it, to retain your orientation."

For the rest of the week, I discovered folded cranes on the kitchen table, at the bathroom sink. Ava answered an ad for a conversation position. The day she was supposed to interview, I returned from work to a completely dark house. In the kitchen, a half-finished crane lay on its side near an abandoned teacup. I went to Ava's room, barely made out the bump of her long body across the unmade futon.

"You didn't go, did you?" I asked.

"My life in five minutes, Carlie. How do you keep on?"

"It has nothing to do with me, Ava. You can't give up."

Looking straight at me, Ava tore a pile of origami paper in half. In the sound, I heard, saw, felt myself in the first few months after Ted, Lyle, and my father took me to the cabin, the first months after my father started coming into my room at night. I wanted to scream at Ava to stop feeling sorry for herself, to pray the way she'd taught me to. But that would be like yelling at a twelve-year-old to get it together.

I snatched the remaining whole sheets of origami paper from Ava's reach. "You are the first person I ever heard use the words 'incest' and 'survivor' in a single sentence. Right now, we will make more orizuru."

I practiced on the train to work and in between classes. Without Kashiwabara-san over my shoulder, I had trouble keeping the sequence clear. Whenever the process broke down, however, a Japanese woman materialized to help me. A grandmother on the train, Marcie from reception. A massive network of female strength folded into this society by the girl-games of their youth. Into each crease, I pressed a prayer, as if that were the secret to Ava rediscovering her backbone. As if Ava weren't the only person with the power to save Ava.

Sex with Doug was not working.

"Ever since we moved past the nice rubbing phase into intercourse," I told Margot the Saturday before Cho's return, "we've been having problems." I was vaguely pleased that I had no appetite.

"You need a vibrator."

"I have a Doug. That is not the problem. You know, I used to envy anorexics. So you've got to learn to eat. Big whoop. Well, here I am, an anorexic at the table of sex."

"With Doug."

"Tell me about it. We'll be going along, totally grooving, then it's time to get the condom on, and I find myself in a warm cocoon where I have no sexual needs. A lot of times, I would rather stay there."

"Then what?" Margot asked.

Down a tunnel, a trainload of shame.

The following morning, I woke up at four-thirty, then fell back into Doug's futon to dream of a garnet yam. I took a kitchen knife—black handle, wicked blade—and made little chops and nicks. The yam became a puppy, so small that it fit in my palm. And blood. I'd made so many chops and nicks that the puppy was going to die. I was going to have to eat it. A kitten wound around my ankles. In my throat, my stomach, the feeling of already having eaten the puppy.

The kitten leapt for the puppy's throat.

"No!" I shrieked, waking myself and Doug.

"Hey, Carlie, hey. C'mere. Another bad dream?"

His penis brushed my leg, not innocent. The yam-puppy.

"Cut it out."

He let go, saying, "I'm sorry."

"Would you have some feelings? I was just awful to you!"

"Okey-doke. Quit insisting your turn-off isn't my fault."

"It isn't."

"I haven't noticed anyone else in bed with you."

The phone jangled. Doug grabbed it, reverting immediately to Mr. Sensitive. "No, it's not too early. I'm glad you called. Sure, I can come to your place. Eleven's fine."

He hung up. "That was Ava. She wants acupuncture."

All morning at work, I waited for his call. I had a summer session proposal to prepare for a noon meeting with Saito Sensei and a report to finish before Cho returned at four. Just after eleven, I asked Johnny to look over the proposal. As he was reading, reception buzzed him with a call.

Johnny had never gotten a call, here.

I would not hear it. I would not.

Johnny came toward me, his mouth moving, *Carlie, Carlie.* Someone shrieked *No!* I scrambled across a desk, ripping my skirt up the seam. Johnny pulled me back, *Carlie, Carlie.*

I shrieked, *No!* one last time before I smacked him full in the face, shocking myself into stillness.

Johnny straightened. "Doug's already rung the police. They'll try to have her cleaned up before Cho returns."

Someone, wailing.

Me.

Dear Dougie, read the neatly printed letter. *I am so sorry to do this to you, truly I am. I suppose they will all be wanting to know why. Isn't it terrible, but there is no more reason today than there was last week or there would be next month. I wish I could say I thought I would go to a better place, but that's not it, I know. The cycle will begin again with me on a lower rung for what I am about to do. Don't pity me. I am not thinking one thought of any of you from the moment I put down this pen until it is finished. I won't bring you into this.*

Cho, I love you so very much. I wish I could have been better at this life.

Be well and go with God.

Ava had slit her wrists. Her bloodied body laid across the bathroom tiles for Doug to discover. Next to what used to be Ava, he found a bottle of whiskey, half full. She drank herself into a place where she could do it, and then suffered until she bled out. I knew she took special care to avoid the bedroom futon because the blood would have ruined them, and she understood how Cho loved those homemade gifts from her grandmother.

Blue-suited Japanese policemen strode purposefully through our house in their stockinged feet. They bowed formally each time they encountered one of the pitiful-faced members of the tai chi crew, who showed up throughout the afternoon. Soon, the police were outnumbered three to one. They bobbed continually. The chief inspector told me, "You have a large family."

Doug and I answered most of his questions, once the chief finally started asking us instead of Kashiwabara-san, who came home from her tea ceremony an hour after Doug found Ava. My landlady knelt on the tatami, inaccessible, as Doug arranged with the police to ship Ava's body to Scotland. He said to me, "If I hadn't told you about Angel, I'd be shattered."

The Japanese word for "bulimia" was *Kashoku-sho. Kinshin-sokan* meant "incest." The inspector closed his notebook with a hurried scribble. At four o'clock, we heard Cho in the genkan. "*Todaima*—hey! Ava? There are about a thousand shoes . . ." A laugh. "Boy, what a great trip! Singapore is—"

She burst into the living room, took in the circle of gathered friends, the police. We'd all agreed that I would be the one to speak, but I was incapable of it. I opened my arms.

Cho was hysterical, demanding that Ava be buried in Japan. The upright officers shifted uncomfortably, even though they didn't understand English.

Doug said, "She's a British subject. She has to be sent home."

"This is her home! I am her family!"

The chief inspector ordered the police doctor to give Cho a sedative. As she began to fade, he announced that someone must telephone Ava's family in Scotland.

"Me," Cho spat from the couch. Margot held her. Doug and I closed ourselves into their bedroom to make the call. Looking through Ava's desk for the number, I came across a photo, Ava and Cho on the beach in Thailand. I had taken that shot.

"McDowell's," sang a voice so like Ava's that I felt punched in the stomach.

"Is this . . ." I didn't know their names. "Ava's mom? I'm her housemate in Tokyo. I have some bad news I don't know how to say, so I'm just going to say it. Ava killed herself."

"Oh." A diminutive sound, then a hush. "She'll come 'round, won't she, then?"

"She is dead, Mrs. McDowell." I hated this woman.

"Oh, oh."

I hated the pity I felt for her.

And then her voice changed, "What're goin' on about," as ringing and mean as any time Ava took my head off. Doug could hear fine without leaning in. "You've no call, saying nonsense!"

I said, "Look, the police will ship . . . the body. There'll be a report you can have translated." Kashoku-sho. Kinshin-sokan.

Ava's mom was calling to someone, hand-almost-over-the-receiver. A masculine voice came on the line, soft but full of pomp. He was saying, "Perfectly happy little girls do not kill themselves," and in the background, Ava's mom, "She was a perfectly happy little girl, do ya hear?" Meanwhile, Ava was dead. They would use every means they had used all along to deny everything they had always denied, and I would live my life surrounded by those I loved. The only revenge God would grant.

The day I used the Angry Fist to punch through the wall separating me from my understanding of my mother's story, I truly went into the relaxation that followed each enraged punch. When I told Ava's father, "I need to hang up," I felt myself completely in the post-Angry Fist release.

"We call ya later, then. To—talk?" Ava's father's last word was as wary as it was piteous.

"I promise you, Mr. McDowell, you do not want to talk to me."

I replaced the receiver. Doug and I embraced for a long time.

As the police took away Ava's body, Kashiwabara-san motioned me aside. "You must care for Cho-san. She lost her wife."

In more than three years of living in her house, I have touched Kashiwabara-san only once: the morning I bawled unreservedly into her lacy handkerchief. Now, I ran a quiet hand down her bent back. On Sunday morning, we sat on either side of a silent Cho in the front pew of a Unitarian church, all in black dresses so new they crinkled. Over a hundred people filed into the very church-like church. A full half of the seats were taken by students and teachers from Achieve English. Of course, Marcie, Lisa, and Satsuki. Next to Johnny, I spotted Joan and Yvette and even Mona Lisa. Yvette nodded kindly then gestured to the next row, where Saito Sensei waved a gloved hand.

I had a very large family.

Afterward, standing in the sunshine, Margot declared it a fine service, if patriarchal. The word went out: tomorrow, after tai chi. People came who hadn't been to practice for months. Doug stood before thirty of us, made a fist with his right hand and covered it with his left. "This one is going out for my friend, Ava."

Margot was the first to sob. Then I started. Then Johnny, and then we were all weeping. "Keep going," Doug encouraged us. We finished the kata and gathered in a circle. One by one, people recounted memories: the time she called just when they needed to hear a friendly voice, those goofball, extended *rrrrr*'s. There was a lot of talk about her radiance. All I could think was, If she was so great, why did she commit suicide? When it was my turn, I said, "Ava didn't want to kill herself. She wanted them to die."

I cried into the silence in a way that made my throat hurt, afraid I would be told to go home.

"One thing that I love about you, Carlie," Doug said, right in front of everyone, "is you'll say what a lot of us think but don't want to admit."

Horst tugged his beard. "Suicide over psychological pain never made sense to me. I don't blame Ava. I'll say it: incest. I hurt for her. But I cannot truly understand this choice."

"What about her spiritual beliefs, then?" Johnny's voice was high, unsure. "If there was one thing I knew about Ava, she had those. Why couldn't she go there?"

Everyone looked to Cho, our former social worker. After her initial eruption, Cho had said barely a word. Like, not for days. She gazed at us as if we should have the answer. Just when I thought she was going to refuse to speak, she laughed jaggedly.

"Ava loved enough and gave enough in her life to cause almost a hundred and fifty people to mourn her at two different services. Yet suicide is the ultimate statement of aloneness. The numbers aren't adding up."

Returning to work lent the days a modicum of normalcy, but there were still the evenings I returned to an empty house, the foggy weekend mornings that no one hummed as she bustled about the kitchen, preparing our first pot of tea. There was the afternoon I came across a faded, half-folded origami crane. I shredded it and then went out intending to binge. Instead, I bought a can of soda and pounded it against a cement wall in the park until it burst open. That night, I found Cho smoking. She hollered, "No!" when I twisted the pack, ripping it in half, but she didn't buy another. We were well into March before I decided that there was no way around it. We had to pack away Ava's stuff. No one had been in their room since the call to her parents.

"I don't want to let her go," Cho said.

"She's already gone." I led Cho by the hand to the middle of their tatami. We stood for a time before I began by placing into a box the photograph I took of them in Thailand.

From Cho, an asphyxiated noise. She held a purple rug woven with yellow, green, and blue. "We got this in Manila. We'd been up to Sagada, where they weave them, so she knew the real price. The guy in Manila wanted triple. Ava kept saying it was 'bloody extortion,' and he kept telling her to go back to Sagada."

As if haggling over a few dollars with a street vendor clarified this chaos, Cho lay face up on the tatami and rammed the purple into her face. She keened as if the earth had opened up to mourn. We sludged toward spring, surviving by not blaming each other. I did not blame God. I blamed Ava. I kept hearing Johnny's strangely high voice, asking: "What about her spiritual beliefs? Why couldn't she go there, then?"

Because she gave up.

She fucking quit.

The next Saturday morning, Margot insisted that Ava's suicide did not negate all the good that she'd done and was. I hissed, "I am no earthly good at bullshit," and stormed away from our regular booth. Another session of can-pounding left me only an aching hand's breadth closer to acceptance. Sinking into Doug and my favorite bench near Shinobazu Pond, I wished I had the emotional wherewithal to buy me some eggs.

The sun glinted off the water. Spring was coming. Brown chaff would become flat green leaves growing slowly, slowly, across the surface. They would blossom, white flowers with yellow centers, and it would matter, even though right now, there was nothing but brown chaff and the cold, gray pond. When Doug showed up, I greeted him with, "I keep wanting to know 'Why.' She gave up. That's why."

Doug sat. There was something unformed in the way he took his seat that made up my mind. I said, "Ava was always after me to return the money I stole."

"Carlie, are you kidding? People like them don't deserve it."

"Agreed. Why, then, when I open to the idea, do I feel peace?"

Doug took my face between his hands. "This is survivor guilt."

"Of all the things I've had the opportunity to feel guilty about, being a survivor is not one."

"I mean about Ava."

"Seems like it might be most effective, big picture-wise, for me to deliver the money personally."

Doug yanked his hands from my cheeks as if they were on fire. Then he pulled me roughly into his chest. "Look what happened when she went home."

"I am not Ava."

"This is unhinged. Do it by check."

"All the bank people said that, the day I stole the money."

Doug began to weep, which terrified me. It took him a while before he could say, "But—" and then "but—" and finally, "People like them don't deserve shit." I let him cry. When he stopped, he said, "You're not even gonna let me come with you, are you?"

"I love you, Doug. But I want to know that I can stand up to my parents without you."

"I'm not the only one who's not gonna like this."

"No!" Cho slammed out of the living room.

I followed her to the back porch. "It's not that you can't control this, Cho. It's that you don't have to."

Cho shoved the heels of her palms into her eye sockets. "I wish to goddamn fuck motherfucking fuck that I had a cigarette."

I mimed lighting up, inhaling, passing. My dear Cho mocked a very long drag. Then, "It's understandable to want to confront the perpetrator, to demonstrate growth and personal power."

"I have grown. I have personal—"

"These are your parents, Carlie. They will always be able to hurt you."

"Embrace what they have done."

Cho fired off a look I imagined was similar to the one I shot Ava when she first told me that. Cho followed up with, "Sometimes Ava had her head up her ass."

"You wanted me to, also. Only you said it differently."

"Too bad I'm such a genius." Cho yanked her hair into its usual, falling-apart ponytail. She did it second time. "My presence is non-negotiable."

"Thank you."

"Thank me when we get you back."

Embrace Tiger, Return to Mountain

"There's your fuck fuck motherfucking money." I balled up the check and threw it in their faces.

Felt great. Too bad I only imagined it to the snowy slopes of Mount Rainier out my window. An announcement asked all passengers to return tray tables to upright and locked positions in preparation for landing at Seattle-Tacoma International Airport. I said to Cho. "What if, when I return the money, they have me arrested?"

"Girlfriend. The statistical likelihood is that they won't want to have anything to do with you."

"You don't know that!"

Cho's sleep-deprived face was stretched tight. "Just stick to the plan, Carlie. Cash out your stocks, deposit the money in my account, and I write a check."

Tersely, I recited, "And they never have to know about my name change." I saw myself laying the check calmly before them. Mom would say, "Jenny-Jen-Jen. I've felt awful all these years. I'll stop drinking. We'll get your father some therapy." I would say, "We could use the ten thousand for family sessions." And then, yes, she would hug me.

Did that woman once hug me? I shoved my tray table into its upright and locked position. Cho's eyes looked like newly-laid tar. We collected our luggage and took a taxi to the hotel. The cab turned off the highway, mounted a steep incline, and cruised Capitol Hill, a neighborhood everyone in high school whispered about because it was supposed to be gay and druggy. I shot glances up and down the street, afraid, for the first time in almost four years, that I would spot my father or Lyle. Fat chance. Too many Pride banners for them. But a lot of shops sold sex toys. They could surely emerge from one of those. Instead, anorexic vampires smooched women dressed as if they'd just stepped out of a rehearsal for a high-school production of *A Midsummer Night's Dream*. While Cho paid off the taxi, a homeless woman offered to sing me a song for five bucks.

A gang of teens descended on the bus stop in front of our hotel. I felt more like them than the exterior they undoubtedly saw in me, some lady leaning toward them, trying not to look overly interested in their *Nu-uhs, No ways,* and *Ways!* Sounds of high school, lunch hour after lunch hour spent reading my Lonely Planet, only vaguely aware of the pretty girls with their popular boyfriends and their Proms and Homecomings.

From the bus stop, a boy told a girl to go to hell.

"Been there. I'm back."

She was normal-skinny, jeans about three sizes too big riding low on her hips. She batted overly-made-up eyes, but he couldn't tell that she was flirting. He called her a cunt.

"My cunt is not an insult!"

Another flash fantasy: I raged into my father's office in her baggy hip-huggers. In front of every secretary I used to work with, I pounded the living shit out of him.

That night, before bed, I wrote a well-known address on an envelope. I fell asleep convinced that in the morning I would tell Cho, "Screw this," and mail them the check. But when I woke, Cho was a jet-lagged lump of sleep. She muttered at me to go practice and went unconscious.

Near a graveyard, I found a large park. I began slowly, feeling all sixes and sevens, as Ava might have said. Instead of starting by sinking down, I faced north, arms loose but with shape at my sides—an upside-down horseshoe, yet soft. Without my guiding it, my body took the posture that had me sinking into my left leg and stepping to the right back corner. I brought my left arm overhead as my right arm came from under to meet like jaws coming together. A great stretch through the arms. Doug taught the posture as Carry Tiger to the Mountain, but I preferred the dreamy term Mr. Tan used during our lengthy practice sessions in Hong Kong: Embrace Tiger, Return to Mountain.

When I finished practicing, I drifted through Capitol Hill as Seattle roused, eventually following Pike Street downtown. I found myself at a bank, the secret bank where Shelly almost didn't give me the money. After a time, I crossed to the King County Courthouse and learned all I needed to know about a legal name change. Only then did I phone Cho.

"Do you want me with you?" she asked.

"You know, I think I'm good."

At the start of the morning session of District Court, I paid the thirty-five-dollar filing fee and waited with forty-some odd people in a commissioner's courtroom. He processed several dozen name changes before calling out, "Jennifer Brewer?"

It was surreal to hear that name—my name—spoken. Aloud. I feared I would be thrown into jail. Regardless, I stood. The commissioner was an older man with salt-and-pepper hair. He asked if there was a reason that I would like to record along with my request to change my name.

"I am an incest survivor. I no longer wish to be associated with my family."

Nothing in the courtroom changed, not the heat, not the chatter. The commissioner gave me an encouraging nod and asked *de rigueur* if I was fleeing creditors or otherwise changing my name to avoid a legal something-or-other. I shook my head—*not for much longer, anyway*—and by him signing a bunch of papers, I was Carlie Adams.

In the chalk-yellow hallway of the King County Courthouse, I sat. That should have felt more empowering than it did.

Later, I curled into my hotel bed so that Doug could comfort me long-distance. He said, "I mean, you've been Carlie Adams for a while. Hey, how'd you work the legal stuff in Japan? Your passport said—"

"I got a visa in my real name and—"

"—Cho made her magic with the personnel office."

If a smile had noise, it would sound like Doug, breathing on the other end of the line. For the first time in months, I wanted to make love with him. When I shared the second part of that thought, I heard a rich sigh.

The next silence was very peaceful.

When we'd listened enough, I said, "When I hang up, I'm going to call Liu. Cash out. But I can't figure out what to do with the capital gains. After taxes—you are not going to believe this. After taxes, I'll have twenty thousand dollars."

"And you're giving them ten."

"Giving back. Pretty freaky, huh?"

"Look, some things just have to be. So that everything before it happens and everything after falls into place. Even deaths. You're right, about giving back the money."

Then he said, "Do me a favor, though? Don't give them the extra ten. You made the smart investment."

"I don't want it."

"Do you need it?"

Doug sounded tentative. We didn't discuss finances. I said, "I have savings. Money I earned, not stole.

When the money cleared, I had only one name for the two checks Cho wrote. The first was for my father in the amount of ten thousand dollars. The "Pay to the Order Of" on the other remained blank.

I told Cho, "Maybe I'll lose it on Broadway and a homeless fellow will have the time of his life."

"Do you want me to come with you?" she asked. This time, I

said, "Yes."

It had to happen at their house. I needed to be Carlie Adams in that house. I chose Sunday morning. They always had brunch on Sunday mornings. At least, they always used to. I'd never known less about my own parents.

"My mom is going to blow a gasket," I told Cho as she drove us up roads that used to be my bus route home from ballet.

"Don't expect too much from this, girlfriend. It could only take a minute."

"Five. I know. Hey, that's my street! Turn down there. Mother of God, here we go."

Taking in the ample spread, the Colonial front, Cho whistled. "Looks like these motherfuckers really need another ten grand."

We crossed the manicured grass. At the front door, I peered through the living room window. My grandmother's portrait still hung over the grand piano. No one ever played that stupid thing.

"Should I knock or go right in? Is that polite?"

Cho patted my arm with soft knowing. "We're not here for a tea party, girlfriend."

I stared at Grandmother. This was not my home. "Let's go around back."

They were on the porch. It was as if they were seated at the end of a long tunnel, my mother and father. I had to squint, they were quaffing Mimosas as Mom gazed across the misty Sound. My father was reading the paper. He appeared slightly older, but he was still broad-shouldered with dark, movie-star hair. You would buy anything from that man. Not a surprise, my mother had kept her figure. Her hair was now a soft amber, cut in a neat line at her shoulders. Buttering my father's toast, she exuded efficiency. Already buzzed, I suspected.

Little.

Matt had been a boy when I left. Now he was a young man,

and good-looking, with our father's height and our mother's small bones. None of her ambition. His baseball cap worn backward, he enjoyed his Mimosa with mellow, satirical sips, looking like every druggy white guy I ever slept with.

He saw me before either of them did. His eyes sharpened as if he, too, was hearing the tunnel collapse.

He rasped, "Jenny-Jen-Jen."

My mother dropped her knife. I blessed the clatter.

My father lowered his paper.

Mom retrieved the cutlery, to place it by her plate. Only with it exactly where she wanted it did she lick thicker lips than I remembered. She asked, "Where have you been?" as if I were home late from ballet.

A phone call from Patrice. A glass shattered; wine spilled. And cleaned. She would throw herself between my father and a great white shark to protect everything that kept her together. I felt Cho's firm presence behind me—this time, a firm knowing—and remembered to yield.

"I stole ten thousand dollars from you."

I looked directly into my father's eyes. He did nothing.

Mom stood. Matt shoved himself backward in his chair, scraping it along the cement of the patio.

This point was where Ava got sucked back in. To fling myself into screaming battle would give my father, give both my parents, every excuse they needed. Though I was clearly on the patio I grew up on, I was on a beach in Thailand, Gemma in my ear with the basics. Wave Hands Like Clouds.

"I'm here to return your money. And to say I'm sorry."

The last slipped out on its own.

An actual reaction from my father. He looked uncertain.

Freedom.

I laid the check on the table. Warily, Mom placed it by her recovered knife. She would never cash that check.

"You've gained weight," Mom said. My father's momentary

fumble stiffened back into blankness.

Margot's babysitter composure infused me; water became tea. "I'm leaving now." And I did, as graceful as the ballet girl I used to be. The simplicity lasted until I felt my palm against the door handle of the rental car and my forehead pressed into its warm, green roof. I got nothing I wanted.

Cho was right behind me. I couldn't look at her when I told her, "For a second there, I thought I understood something."

Then, there was no way I was not going to look.

Cho's eyes were the same wide as Doug's had been, in Bangkok that time, when he realized I wasn't some kid, anymore. She said, "I wish Ava could have gone home and only felt let down."

"Jen?"

I turned. "Little."

"Nobody calls me that anymore."

Cho stepped discreetly into the car as Matt said, "Where in the hell did you go?" His face was totally blank.

"Japan."

Matt slid his hands into the pockets of his over-sized jeans. "Nuh uh."

"It's, like, as far as you can go. Before you have to come back."

"You apologized." Face still blank, Matt turned his baseball cap sideways, an accusation.

"I didn't plan to. It—" I started over. "Look, I'm not sorry I took the money. What an idiotic thing to say. I sure am sorry I had to, though."

If I expected another "Nuh uh," I got the sub in enemy waters. Without thinking, I simply had to ask. "Did you guys ever talk about it?"

"Talk?"

"Yeah. Like, when you came down for breakfast and I wasn't there. Or when it was my birthday and I still wasn't there."

"Patrice ran away, too."

"Did they notice I left?"

Matt's eyebrows all but said, *Duh*. "The mail pile was fuckin' Mount Rainier."

Aaaaaaaaaaaaa. The one thing I didn't think of.

They must have known instantly.

"So what happened?"

"Mom pro'lly cleaned it up."

Five words. Matt was back to blank.

All the energy I put into getting out. The control I felt when I thought I'd outsmarted them. I could have just left. Patrice did.

"I did not believe they could still hurt me," I said to Matt, and wiped away tears—thankful for them. "What about Patrice? Do you know where she is?"

"Last time she called she was living with some dude. Near Vegas. Trailer park."

"What about . . . Matt, do we have, like, a niece?"

"She lost—how'd you know it was—she's lost a couple. One at seven months."

Leaden sadness stunned me. I was powerless to protect her, to protect my blank-faced brother, all his anger right beneath the surface, from smashing into a similar emotional existence.

I embraced him.

After we let each other go, he said, "I killed your fish."

"Matt, I am so, so sorry I ran out on you."

Meanness stabbed through the void of his face. "Flushed it. Still alive."

"I doubt I can ever make it up to you. But I can give you—" I pulled out my wallet, envisioning his eyes going round as I wrote his name on the check for ten grand. And paused. My family was the tiger. I did not have to embrace what they had done, only to accept that they had done it. To do that and remember that they were the tiger, that was freedom.

That's why God had me say, "I'm sorry." So Matt and I could come to this moment.

I left the check where it was. Instead, I pulled out my business card. "This is my contact information in Japan. Call me anytime. Call collect."

Then I said, "Do you have Patrice's phone number?"

Like a little boy with the answer, Matt rattled it off. I nailed the string of numbers to the inside of my forehead. I knew what I was going to do with the ten thousand dollars.

Matt's thumbnail underscored my name on the card. I wished I could touch his shoulder, or at least brush it, so I said, "I changed my name legally."

"Carlie Adams?"

"I'm out for real, Matt. Do you and Patrice talk?"

"Um, not really."

"Well, maybe we can."

Matt was pure stillness as I kissed his cheek and climbed into the car. He remained rooted in his too-big jeans as Cho drove us away. I could never be the one to call. One of them might pick up.

No. I would call Matt.

I watched him through the rear window until he receded from sight. Speeding along a bluff high above the rough and ready Puget Sound, Cho patted my knee. Ever the Cho, she said, "How you doing, girlfriend?"

Standing

I had no answer for Cho until our stopover in Hawaii on the way back to Japan. In Honolulu, we hopped a small plane to Maui, retiring to someone's convincing idea of paradise. We headed to the secluded beach for a late-afternoon swim. There was chitchat, but I gave her no response to the previous day's question until I said, "Let's practice."

We went through the form. I said, "Let's keep going." We did. After the third time, I slipped off my bikini top. I breathed. Then I stepped out of the bottoms. I went back to standing. I stood, simply stood, with an empty mind and a heart open to whatever made me. I sailed across the sea into the reddening sky, past my grief over Ava and my hopes for Matt and Patrice, past the residue of a bump that used to be a number of feelings about my parents, and yes, past my love for Doug. I came to rest where the horizon met the water, and thought, "This."

This new. This safe. This ready. This was the way I was meant to be.

Acknowledgments

When a book takes thirty years from conception to publication, you can bet there are a great many people to thank. To the Wednesday night group at Dick's house then the Thursday night group at Marylin's; to Martha and Molly Dee; and, finally, to Bill, Carolyn, Criky, Debby, Kim, and Sandy—poets, every one of you.

To my beta readers: Laura, Suzanne, Peggy, Risa, Eve, Amanda, and Joe; your willingness to commit to what was, at the time, a purely terrible draft still affirms me deeply. A cherry on top goes to Laura. That you trust my work leaves me speechless.

The Team! You guys were my rocks: you read, you cheerled. Your faith propelled me through those final, formidable months. I appreciate each one of you and every task you undertook.

To Carole L. Glickfeld: as you graciously stewarded me through draft after draft, your gifts as an editor and your fearless eye truly shaped this work. You are a gem.

To Laura S. King: this book would not exist as it does without your influence. You came along at exactly the right time for the drafts that needed precisely your breadth of knowledge. You are amazing.

Finally, to Reagan, David, Christopher, Justin, Minna, and everyone at Black Rose Writing with a hand in *As Far as You Can Go Before You Have to Come Back*: thank you for giving me the opportunity that literally hundreds did not. I don't know how I will ever truly thank you.

About the Author

Alle C. Hall's short fiction appears in journals including Dale Peck's *Evergreen Review, Tupelo Quarterly, New World Writing,* and *Litro*; and her essays in *Creative Nonfiction Magazine, Hobart,* and *Another Chicago Magazine,* among other places. An adaptation of a chapter from *As Far as You Can Go Before You Have to Come Back* placed as a finalist for The 2020 Lascaux Prize. Hall has also won the Richard Hugo House New Works Competition and been a Best Small Fictions and Best of the Net nominee. She is the former senior nonfiction editor at *jmww journal,* and the former associate editor of *Vestal Review.* She lives in Seattle with her family. *As Far as You Can Go Before You Have to Come Back* is her first book.

Note from the Author

Word-of-mouth is crucial for any author to succeed. If you enjoyed *As Far As You Can Go Before You Have to Come Back*, please leave a review online—anywhere you are able. Even if it's just a sentence or two. It would make all the difference and would be very much appreciated.

Thanks!
Alle C. Hall

A Guide for Book Groups

1. With whom in this book do you relate most strongly, NOT including the protagonist? What insight does that offer you about your own journey from adolescence to adulthood?

2. In your group, explore the use of tai chi as a vehicle for knitting Carlie back together. Is tai chi a metaphor? Or is this novel partially about the integrative effects of that practice? Share your experiences with other practices—physical, emotional, mundane—that served this function in your own life.

3. At the end of the novel, does Carlie forgive her parents? Is there a verb or phrase other than "forgive" that makes sense to you?

4. In the latter half of the book, Carlie comes to terms with the actions of at least three other characters. Which three characters? What was required of her, internally, to bring herself to that point?

5. Do you yourself believe that insightful forgiveness is one of the hallmarks of adulthood? If you can, share a story of your own on this theme.

6. To whom would you recommend this book? Is it only applicable to women who've had similar experiences? Or do you feel that Carlie's struggles are more universal? Try to explain your thinking to the others in your group.

7. Would you offer trigger warnings as you recommended this book? Why or why not?

8. At the start of the novel, Carlie is a child then an adolescent, albeit a very resourceful one. By the end, she is a healthy, adult woman. Does she do it alone? Who helped and how, specifically, did they help? Is this a passage anyone makes alone? Who helped you?

9. Share a story with your group.

We hope you enjoyed reading this title from:

www.blackrosewriting.com

Subscribe to our mailing list – *The Rosevine* – and receive **FREE** books, daily deals, and stay current with news about upcoming releases and our hottest authors.
Scan the QR code below to sign up.

Already a subscriber? Please accept a sincere thank you for being a fan of Black Rose Writing authors.

View other Black Rose Writing titles at
www.blackrosewriting.com/books and use promo code
PRINT to receive a **20% discount** when purchasing.